A Chronicles of Fate novel
Book One

MARKED BY FATE

by K.B. RILEY

K.B. RILEY BOOKS

Published by K.B. Riley Books, an imprint of Riley Publishing Studios
Marion, Ohio, United States

First Edition: May 2025
Printed in the United States of America

ISBN (Paperback): 979-8-9929983-1-3

Playlist

Set the mood for your reading enjoyment.

Somewhere I Belong - Linkin Park
The Only Exception - Paramore
Break - Three Days Grace
Sparks - Coldplay
Safe and Sound - Capital Cities
The Middle - Jimmy Eat World
The Unforgiven - Metallica
The Pretender - Foo Fighters
Behind Blue Eyes - The Who
High Hopes - Panic! At the Disco
Going Under - Evanescence
Dancing Queen - ABBA
Resistance - Muse
Bittersweet Symphony - The Verve
Rise Up - Imagine Dragons
Dog Days Are Over - Florence + The Machine
Run - Snow Patrol
The Sound of Silence - Disturbed
Rebellion (Lies) - Arcade Fire
Centuries - Fall Out Boy

You can find the complete playlist on Spotify.

This book is dedicated to my rock, with whom I've built my life. His unwavering support and love have been my greatest inspiration.

Chronicles

Prologue

The storm tore through the night, an unrelenting force that howled against the glass like a living thing. Lightning split the sky in jagged, merciless streaks, illuminating the world in violent flashes before surrendering to the darkness again. Thunder followed, a bone-deep tremor that rattled the windows and sent a shudder through the earth. Rain lashed the building, an angry drumbeat against the thin barrier separating the chaos outside from the tension within.

Inside the provisional operating room, the air was thick—heavy with the sterile bite of antiseptic and the raw metallic tang of blood. Fluorescent lights buzzed overhead, cold and unforgiving, casting sharp shadows across the faces of the doctors and nurses. The rhythmic beeping of machines warred with the storm's rage, their mechanical precision a stark contrast to the frantic energy simmering beneath the surface.

They moved with methodical urgency, hands steady, minds racing. The C-section was underway, every movement precise, almost detached. The mother lay still beneath the harsh glow of the lights, her face pale, her body limp under the haze of anesthesia. Sweat clung to the brows of the doctors, catching in the artificial light. The air crackled—not only with the storm's static, but with something else. Something unseen, pressing down on the room like an unseen force waiting to unfold. Then, a breathless moment. A single, fleeting pause in the chaos. The first baby of the new millennium entered the world.

For an instant, the world held its breath. The storm seemed to hush, as if bearing witness to the moment. The wail of the newborn shattered the silence, thin and raw, yet powerful enough to rival the thunder outside. Relief rippled through the room, a brief exhale before duty took hold again. A nurse moved forward, ready to clean and swaddle the child. She froze.

Her breath hitched, eyes locked on the child's forearm. The room constricted, the air pressing inward as every gaze followed hers. There, pulsing against the infant's delicate skin, was a mark—a digital clock, its numbers ticking downward in eerie precision. The glow of it bathed the child's skin in an otherworldly blue, casting ghostly light across the sterile room. It wasn't ink. It wasn't a trick of the light. It was embedded in the flesh, alive, counting down.

A figure stirred in the corner. Until now, he had been a shadow, a presence unnoticed in the frantic rhythm of the birth. But now, as he stepped forward, the light caught his face—sharp angles, a stillness that unnerved. His eyes, impossibly bright, locked onto the child's mark with an unsettling focus. The same blue eyes that stared back from the newborn's fragile face.

"This is... unexpected." The lead doctor's voice barely rose above a whisper, the weight of the moment pressing into his chest.

The man moved, swift and soundless, until he stood over the

child. He reached down, his fingers brushing the infant's soft skin, his touch both reverent and possessive. The baby's cries stilled for a brief second, as if sensing something beyond comprehension.

"What you've seen here tonight is not your concern." The words cut through the charged silence, cold and absolute. "You've been paid well for your silence. Remember that."

The staff exchanged uneasy glances, some shifting their weight, others gripping instruments they wouldn't dare use. But none spoke. The room had changed; the very air carried something heavier than fear. The man's presence swallowed every unspoken protest before it could form. A monitor shrieked, shattering the uneasy stillness.

"Doctor, her blood pressure is crashing—she's hemorrhaging," a nurse gasped, hands already moving, voice tight with urgency. The fragile line between life and death wavered, tilting dangerously toward the latter.

The man didn't turn. His silhouette loomed in the doorway, framed by the erratic strobe of lightning. "Do everything you can to save her," he ordered. "I need her for my research."

And then he was gone, the storm swallowing him whole.

Chaos erupted behind him, voices sharp with desperation as they fought to keep the mother tethered to this world. The scent of blood thickened, spreading across the floor like spilled ink. Machines blared, commands snapped into the suffocating air, hands moved with frantic precision. Life and death waged war on the operating table.

Down the hall, the man walked with purpose, the child nestled against his chest. The baby's tiny fingers twitched, their luminous mark still pulsing its ominous countdown. Outside, the storm surged, wind shrieking like some ancient thing awakened. He glanced down at the infant, his expression unreadable.

"You are special," the man whispered, a flicker of a smile ghosting across his lips. "And I will make sure you fulfill your purpose."

The man slipped into the waiting vehicle, the doors sealing shut with a metallic finality. The engine rumbled to life, headlights slicing through sheets of relentless rain as the car pulled away, leaving behind a room drowning in urgency and blood.

Inside the operating room, the battle for life waged on. The mother's body trembled on the edge, her vital signs swinging wildly between survival and surrender. Blood slicked the floor in an ever-growing tide, staining gloves, dripping from trembling hands. Commands snapped through the air, frantic and sharp, but outside, the world remained indifferent. The car disappeared into the storm, its presence fading like a ghost, detaching itself from the chaos it left in its wake.

The storm swallowed it whole. The child, small and fragile in the man's arms, was carried deeper into the unknown. His luminous mark pulsed steadily in the dim interior of the car, casting eerie shadows, an unspoken weight settling in the space between them.

Fate had already turned its wheels. The countdown had begun.

CHAPTER ONE

Somewhere I Belong

Christopher

I woke to the hum of my alarm clock, its numbers glaring 6:00 AM. The room around me was mine, or as close to mine as anything could be in the Countdown Control Agency's Headquarters. Unlike the sterile uniformity of the rest of the facility, this space was a quiet rebellion—an armchair worn soft with time, the scent of old books curling at the edges of the air, a corkboard above my desk cluttered with postcards, magazine clippings, and photographs of places I had never been. A world I could only touch in fragments.

Stretching, I ran a hand through my hair and let my gaze settle on the scattered pages across my desk—thoughts that weren't really mine, not with the Agency breathing down my neck. Every word felt like it belonged to them first, like I was borrowing my own brain. Even my notebooks weren't safe—every page skimmed, every stray thought inspected. Sometimes I hesitated before writing, knowing whatever I put down would never really belong to me. Privacy was a joke, a concept that didn't exist here.

A slim wall screen above my desk blinked faintly—standard Agency-issued, capable of projecting schedules, orders, or sudden messages from anyone from my handlers to the top floor. When inactive, it displayed the CCA emblem with the words 'The

Agency is Always Watching' hovering beneath it. My daily schedule was always there too, down to the minute, as if the screen itself was reminding me that choice wasn't part of the equation. Cameras lurked in every corner, their tiny red lights like unblinking eyes. The Agency saw everything, owned everything. Pretending otherwise was a waste of energy.

My fingers instinctively traced the Countdown Mark on my left forearm, its dark blue glow steady, pulsing beneath the web of scars. A roadmap of every test, every procedure, every supposed advancement in understanding the Marks. The Agency called it progress. I called it endurance.

But today was different. Today, I would step outside, if only for a few hours. The Agency had orchestrated a school visit—an outreach program meant to instill trust, to justify the laws that governed people like me.

I shoved the thought aside, focusing on the day ahead, but the past never really stayed buried. It had been drilled into me, worn into my bones by repetition. Dr. Ezekiel Foster, the Agency's lead scientist, had made sure of that.

He had told me the story so many times, I could recite it like scripture. My parents were good people, he said. My mother had died bringing me into this world, my father in a car accident when I was too young to remember. Samuel and Judith Hawthorne. Names that felt more like echoes than truths. My father had been instrumental in founding the CCA, one of the first to study the phenomenon of Countdown Marks. And I? I was the first child born with one.

The way Foster told it, my life had been inevitable—like I'd been born into a script someone else had written, every page already decided before I had a say. And maybe that was the part that burned the most.

I pulled on jeans and a plain t-shirt, one of the few choices I was allowed. A weathered coin on my desk caught my eye—a relic from a childhood visit to a park, a brief taste of something beyond these walls. I slipped it into my pocket, a tether to a world that still existed, even if it had always been out of reach.

Stepping into the hallway, the air shifted, colder, stale. The walls were lined with propaganda posters, their slogans a quiet chant of control. The CCA Protects. The CCA Preserves. The CCA Prevents.

I had long since stopped seeing them.

Dr. Foster appeared ahead, his tall frame casting a long shadow in the fluorescent glow. Great. Exactly what I needed first thing in the morning—another round of Foster's mind games. If he had a heartbeat, I was convinced it ticked instead of thumped, like some kind of human metronome set to 'perpetual disappointment.' Instinct tightened in my gut—a reflex I barely controlled anymore. Every encounter with him felt like stepping into a well-laid trap, his presence a constant reminder that I was never more than a piece on his board. He studied me, his blue eyes—strangely so much like mine—assessing, searching. A man who never moved without purpose.

"Good morning, Christopher," he greeted, voice crisp, devoid of warmth.

"Good morning, sir," I replied, keeping my tone measured, obedient.

7

"Today is an important day." His gaze remained fixed on me, calculating. "Your presentation will be a success as long as you stay focused."

"I understand, sir."

"Good." He didn't linger. "Eat. Be ready to leave soon."

Then he was gone, his lab coat flaring slightly as he turned the corner, his presence lingering like the aftertaste of something bitter.

The dining hall was alive with muted conversation and the mechanical clatter of trays and utensils. I found myself slipping into my usual mental game—counting the exact number of steps it took to get from the entrance to my seat. Twenty-four. Always twenty-four. One more thing in this place that never changed. The illusion of normalcy. I took my usual seat alone, staring at the plate before me—a perfectly squared piece of toast, eggs that looked engineered rather than cooked. Breakfast was another exercise in control.

"Mind if I join you?"

I looked up. Agent David Harris stood there, tray in hand, his expression open, familiar. He was in his early thirties, tall, sharp-featured, with brown eyes that held something rare in this place—warmth. The small scar on his cheek hinted at a life before the Agency, though he never spoke of it.

"Sure, Harris," I said, a grin threatening to surface.

"How's our game looking?" he asked as he slid into the seat across from me.

I took a bite before answering. "I'm two moves from checkmate."

He sighed, shaking his head. "Guess I'll need to rethink my strategy."

I smirked. "Guess so."

"Nervous about today?"

"A bit," I admitted. "It's not every day I get to leave this place."

"You'll do great," he assured me, taking a bite of his food. "Stick to the script so you don't piss off the higher-ups. But try to relax and be yourself. You've got this."

My stomach tightened, a reflex I caught before it settled into something heavier. His confidence in me was steady, unwavering—a quiet reassurance woven into the moment, but I wasn't sure I trusted it. I glanced down at my plate, suddenly finding the perfect symmetry of the toast annoying. Trust wasn't exactly my thing. No one ever gave anything for free, and if they did, it usually meant they were about to take something bigger. Harris was different... maybe. Or maybe I didn't want to waste the energy convincing myself otherwise. Trust was exhausting, and doubt was easier. There was always a cost, always a consequence, and with Harris, I wasn't sure which one I'd end up paying. At least in his presence, the tension in my shoulders eased.

I finished my meal and headed back to my room, gathering my notes for the presentation. My eyes lingered on my surroundings, memorizing the details, drawing strength from the small rebellions that made this space mine. Today, I would be Christopher Hawthorne, the Countdown Control Agency's carefully crafted spokesperson.

Taking a deep breath, I stepped into the hallway, letting the air wrap around me like a second skin. The elevator ride from the third floor to the first was silent, the faint ding of arrival signaling the official start of my day.

The doors slid open, revealing the heart of the Agency—orderly, efficient, devoid of warmth. A machine built to control, to dictate. As I stepped forward, the doors whispered shut behind me, and I braced myself for whatever lay beyond them.

I climbed into the dark SUV, the door shutting with a hollow thud that reverberated through my ribs. A sense of entrapment washed over me. The air inside the SUV felt thick, heavy with recycled breath, pressing in like invisible walls. The space was too small, the presence of the agents too close—suffocating in its quiet restraint.

Today wasn't only a presentation on Countdown Marks—it was a performance, a spectacle for the masses, with researchers practically salivating at the thought of watching my mark tick down to zero. My existence was reduced to a countdown they couldn't wait to see hit zero.

For a fleeting second, I wished Harris were here—a thought that felt more like a plea than an idle wish. I clenched my jaw, hating the way the idea lingered. I didn't need him. I didn't need anyone. Relying on people meant giving them the power to disappoint you. No thanks. But still, the thought refused to let go. His presence had a warmth that made me feel human, which would be far better than the chill radiating off the agents flanking me now. They were detached, their faces as unreadable as stone, dark glasses hiding eyes that were probably as void of feeling.

The SUV rumbled to life and pulled away from Headquarters. I watched as the monolithic building receded. Washington, D.C. unfurled around us, the cityscape blurring by. The hum of traffic merged with the sharp outlines of neoclassical buildings. The Washington Monument pierced the sky like an alabaster needle, and the dome of the Capitol building stood resolute against the backdrop, a reminder of the forces that shaped and controlled everything in this world—including me.

Through the tinted windows, I saw life continuing as if nothing extraordinary was happening only feet away. Tourists snapped photos, locals hurried to work, laughter rippled from street performers—another ordinary day for them. Meanwhile, I was locked in a moving cage, my life dissected under a microscope. Must be nice, not knowing what it feels like to be a walking experiment. The world was so close, yet it might as well have been on the other side of an ocean. I pressed my fingers against the glass, the cold seeping into my skin—a tangible reminder of the barrier between me and them.

Propaganda billboards, polished to the same soulless perfection as everything the Agency controlled, lined the streets like silent sentinels. My own face stared back at me from some of them, frozen in a carefully curated expression, framed by slogans like 'Protecting Our Future' and 'Securing Our Tomorrow.' My stomach turned. It wasn't me they saw—it was the version of me the Agency had created, a puppet stitched together by their agenda.

As we left the heart of the city, towering buildings gave way to brick townhouses and tree-lined streets. The noise of urban life softened, replaced by the steady hum of tires on snow-laced roads. The pristine blanket of white glistened in the winter sun, casting a rare brightness across the cold.

I cracked the window, letting the crisp air cut through the staleness inside the SUV. It was sharp, real—nothing like the recycled, artificial air of Headquarters. For a second, it almost felt like freedom, fleeting and distant, but there nonetheless. The crunch of snow under the tires was almost soothing, a sound that belonged to a simpler world. For a heartbeat, I let myself imagine what life might be like without the Countdown Mark, without the suffocating hold of the CCA.

As we passed a park, the sight of children hurling snowballs at their parents made my chest tighten. Their laughter rang out, clear and carefree, a sound I hadn't heard in longer than I could remember. The ache of longing pressed against my ribs, an uninvited weight that made my breath hitch. My fingers tightened around the fabric of my jeans, grounding myself against the pull of something I had no right to want. I shifted in my seat, forcing my focus onto the snow-covered road ahead. Better to think about the cold, the dull monotony of the drive—anything but the life that would never be mine. My fingers curled into a fist against my leg. It was useless, dangerous, to want something I could never have.

We crossed the Anacostia River, the city shrinking behind us as rural Maryland sprawled ahead. Fields stretched out, blanketed in white, and patches of dense forest loomed, their silent presence a contrast to the urban chaos left behind. The roads twisted and wound like ribbons through the countryside, the isolation both beautiful and suffocating.

I stared out at the landscape, at the fields that seemed to go on forever. There was a stillness here that made me feel exposed, which pointed out how vast the world was and how narrow my path had become. The numbers on my arm glowed faintly under my sleeve, a silent countdown ticking ever closer to zero. My fingers twitched toward it before I caught myself. As if touching it would change anything. As if I had any control over what was coming.

The air inside the SUV was thick with unspoken tension. One agent adjusted his cuff, the only movement in the otherwise rigid stillness. Another tapped a slow rhythm against his thigh, each beat stretching the silence thinner. We were all waiting, every breath stretched tight with the weight of the presentation ahead, the mark on my arm, and the unknown that loomed beyond it. My stomach twisted, an uneasy churn I couldn't quite shake. What if today changed everything? What if it didn't? My fate was only a few hours away.

We pulled up to Annapolis High School, a sprawling brick building that stood as a blend of invitation and intimidation. Outside, students were scattered across the grounds, their laughter and chatter filling the crisp February air. They moved through the morning, unaware of any worries greater than their own teenage dramas. With Valentine's Day around the corner, an electric anticipation hummed through the crowd, a kind of excitement only they could summon.

I watched them, my fingers curling slightly as a tightness settled in my chest, my breath catching for a second before I forced it steady. It felt like a weight pressing down—heavy, lingering—but I shoved it aside, unwilling to let it root itself any deeper. They had no idea how lucky they were, how easily they could laugh and move through life without a second thought. Despite their Countdown Marks, they still embraced high school rituals—flirtations, plans, and moments of giddy uncertainty. At nineteen, I was barely past their age, yet worlds apart. Shaking off the bitter thoughts, I tried to refocus on the task at hand.

As we stepped out of the SUV, the eyes of curious students fell on me, whispers traveling like static through the air. One of the operatives, a tall woman with sharp features and an expression carved from stone, leaned toward me. "Stick to the script," she said, her voice clipped. "We need to maintain control of the narrative."

"I understand," I replied, letting my nerves settle into the familiar rhythm of discipline.

The principal, Mr. Thompson, approached with a smile that almost reached his eyes. He was middle-aged, with hair thinning at the temples and a kind demeanor marked by a hint of apprehension. As I rolled up my sleeves for comfort, his gaze flickered to my Countdown Mark. I saw his eyes widen as he realized how close I was to zero. He quickly masked his surprise, clearly having been kept out of the loop. It still surprised me how much unease Marks inspired after nineteen years.

"Welcome, Christopher. We're honored to have you here," he said, shaking my hand firmly.

"Thank you, Mr. Thompson. I'm looking forward to speaking with your students," I replied, managing a polite smile. Anxiety simmered beneath the surface, but I tried my best to hide it.

He led us down the hallway, past rows of lockers painted a dull gray, each marked with stickers and scrawled notes, personal touches in an otherwise uniform world. The air was thick with a mix of bleach, perfumes, and the sharp bite of body sprays. It was sensory overload, chaotic in a way that felt almost freeing.

As we moved, I observed the students. They leaned against lockers, sharing laughs and secrets, couples stealing moments and whispers. It was the kind of everyday scene that felt foreign to me, a glimpse into a life I'd only imagined. Some noticed me, their eyes flicking with curiosity before drifting back to their conversations.

The gymnasium was eerily empty when we arrived, the echo of our footsteps swallowed by the vast, open space. It reminded me of Headquarters late at night—quiet, sterile, holding the weight of everything that had happened within its walls. But this place, despite its emptiness, still held the ghost of life, the promise of voices soon to come. Rows of wooden bleachers climbed the walls, worn smooth by years of use. Banners draped from the rafters proclaimed school victories, a large one above the stage featuring the school's mascot, a panther, its painted eyes glowering with fierce pride.

A few staff members moved about, adjusting the placement of chairs and testing the microphone. The CCA operatives oversaw everything, their presence a silent force ensuring nothing was left to chance. Spotlights flickered as they were tested, casting brief bursts of light before settling into an even glow. I exhaled slowly, rolling my shoulders as I took in the setup. It was a strange sight—so much effort for an assembly that would last less than an hour. I knew better, though.

This wasn't about the students. It was about control. About the Agency shaping their narrative, making sure I stood under these lights like a carefully staged exhibit. My jaw tightened, the artificial glow of the spotlights burning against my skin, casting me in a role I never agreed to play. The gym smelled of polished wood and stale sweat, a scent that mixed with the faint hum of an overhead vent. I checked the time—still hours to go. We would wait in an adjacent classroom until the students were brought in, giving the press time to set up their cameras and the operatives a chance to remind me, yet again, to stick to the script.

Dr. Bennett, the head of the CCA, had orchestrated every detail of this spectacle, ensuring not a single moment would go undocumented. Nothing was left to chance—not when my existence served as their prized experiment, a walking testament to their so-called progress.

The distant rumble of voices grew louder as students filed into the gym, their footsteps echoing off the polished floor. The quiet, empty space from earlier transformed into a restless sea of teenagers, their conversations bouncing off the high ceilings, mixing with the occasional burst of laughter or the sharp call of a teacher herding them into place.

I sat off to the side of the stage, hands curled into my lap, forcing myself to breathe through the rising tension in my chest. I could feel the weight of the moment pressing in from all sides—the operatives stationed near the exits, the press setting up their cameras, the CCA personnel murmuring among themselves. My Mark pulsed beneath my sleeve, a constant reminder of why I was here.

Mr. Thompson adjusted the microphone, tapping it twice before clearing his throat. The static crackled through the speakers, pulling the room into focus. Conversations died down as the principal stepped forward, his voice carrying through the gym.

'Good afternoon, students,' Mr. Thompson began, his voice carrying through the gymnasium. 'Since February 2006, schools across the country have held these assemblies in the week leading up to Valentine's Day as a reminder of the importance of your Countdown Marks and the responsibilities they bring. The Countdown Control Agency has sent representatives to reinforce these messages and help guide you. Today, we have a special opportunity. Please join me in welcoming Christopher Hawthorne from the Countdown Control Agency.'

Applause rippled through the room, polite but lacking real enthusiasm. A few students clapped with the obligation of someone trying to avoid eye contact with their teacher, while others hardly lifted their hands. Well, at least they weren't booing. I forced myself to stand, my legs stiff as I crossed the stage toward the podium. The lights overhead were blinding, turning the faces before me into a blurred mass of shadows and movement. My pulse thrummed in my ears.

'Good afternoon, everyone,' I began, my voice steady despite the nerves crawling beneath my skin. 'You probably already know who I am, but for those who don't, my name is Christopher Hawthorne. I'm here to talk to you about the Countdown Marks and the work done at the Countdown Control Agency.'

A ripple of interest, tinged with boredom, moved through the crowd. Some students glanced at me, their attention fleeting, while others whispered to friends. I caught a sharp look from one of the agents nearby, warning me not to stray too far from the prepared script. My gaze swept over the crowd and landed on a girl in the front row. She had jet-black hair and striking hazel eyes that caught me off guard.

"From the moment I was born, my life became part of a story bigger than myself," I said, the practiced words flowing smoothly despite the bitterness I felt. "The Countdown Mark appeared on my arm with my very first breath, starting a clock that none of us truly understand." I paused, letting the weight of that statement hang in the air. "For nineteen years, the Countdown Control Agency has dedicated itself to researching this phenomenon. They've poked, prodded, and studied every moment of my life, determined to unravel its secrets."

My eyes moved over the crowd, their faces a blend of curiosity and vague interest. I steadied my voice, choosing my next words carefully.

"Being the first person marked has been both challenging

and rewarding," I continued, meeting their eyes to anchor myself. "From the moment my Countdown Mark appeared, I became part of something much larger than myself."

I paused briefly, allowing the statement to settle. "Growing up, I've always been aware that the Countdown Control Agency's mission began because of me. That carries its own weight—a responsibility I've always taken seriously." My voice softened slightly, carefully skirting the line without ever breaking protocol. "I've spent my life surrounded by researchers dedicated to understanding these Marks—why they appeared, what they mean, and how they'll shape our future. Knowing that my experiences directly contribute to answers for everyone marked after me has made every sacrifice worth it."

I glanced down at my Countdown Mark, its glow a stark reminder of the minutes slipping away.

As I spoke, the time allocated for the presentation dwindled, my mark counting down with it. I knew I needed to address why today mattered, but the words caught in my throat. The researchers watched me, their eyes calculating, eager to record the exact moment when my mark hit zero. I wasn't the first to reach this point, but to them, I was the most valuable.

Scanning the room for a lifeline, my eyes found hers again—the girl with the hazel eyes, her expression steady and attentive. Instinct told me to look away, to break whatever this was before it started. But I didn't. Something about her held me there, unsettling and impossible to ignore. Why her? The thought flickered before I shoved it aside, forcing myself to focus. The connection unsettled and grounded me at once.

"Each of us with the Countdown Mark has a unique journey," I said, letting my gaze hold hers for a heartbeat. "They are more than just a trait; they're a sign of something greater, something we're all trying to understand."

The operatives moved to select students for questions, sensing my distraction. Hands shot up across the room, and I nodded to the first chosen student.

"How do you feel about living at the Countdown Control Agency?" they asked.

"It's challenging," I admitted, carefully choosing my words. "But it's also an opportunity to be part of something bigger. We're working to unlock the mysteries of the marks—why they appeared, why they matter—and that makes it worth it."

More questions came, each one met with answers that balanced the script with my own touch.

"Do you ever wish you had a normal life?" another student asked, their voice hesitant.

I hesitated, images of the snowball fight I'd seen earlier flashing in my mind. It was stupid to dwell on it—another fleeting moment that had nothing to do with me. Still, the thought lingered, unwanted but stubborn, before I forced it away. "Sometimes," I said, truth pushing at the edges of my voice. "But I've learned that normal is relative. This is my normal, and I've come to embrace it."

The final bell rang, a sharp, jarring sound that cut through the last murmurs of conversation. It felt too loud, too final, echoing sharply as students began shifting, their movements suddenly chaotic. I stood frozen in place, still grappling with everything left unsaid. Relief and regret tangled in my chest—I never mentioned why today was different. Would they notice? Would they care? Or would they see it as yet another reminder that I was more a subject than a person? I hoped that the significance of my mark reaching zero would be enough to distract the higher-ups from my oversight.

Students began gathering their things, but the girl with the hazel eyes stayed behind, her gaze fixed on me as the room emptied. The researchers watched her, their attention sharpening.

She approached the stage as I collected my notes, the air felt charged between us. Her jeans and cozy sweater hinted at comfort, but her expression was anything but relaxed. "Hi, I'm Noa Mitchell," she said, extending her hand.

"Nice to meet you, Noa," I replied, shaking her hand. My fingers trembled slightly, an unfamiliar rush of nerves sparking through me. I immediately tightened my grip on my notes, pressing my palm firmly against the podium to suppress the sensation, determined not to show any sign of weakness. I flexed them subtly, pressing my palm against my thigh to steady myself before anyone could notice. Now was not the time for this—whatever this was. Her presence felt significant, like a memory I couldn't quite reach. I kept my composure, though her steady eyes made it difficult.

Then, a strange sensation rippled across my left forearm. My Countdown Mark heated up, the numbers whirring faster. I glanced down and saw it ticking down—seconds, milliseconds—until it hit zero, and the glow dimmed to nothing.

I looked up, finding Noa staring at her own mark, realization dawning in her wide eyes. When our gazes met, the world seemed to stop. The connection between us was instant, electric, defying logic. A strange pull tightened in my chest, my feet shifting slightly forward before I realized I had moved. My breath hitched, caught between instinct and understanding, as if something deep inside me recognized her before my mind could catch up.

As the researchers swarmed, cameras snapping and pens scribbling, I understood that this was the beginning. In that instant, I knew our lives were about to change forever. In front of me stood my soulmate.

CHAPTER TWO

The Only Exception

Noa

The alarm clock buzzed, a relentless drone slicing through the warmth of my bed. I groaned, rolling onto my side and tugging the blanket over my head, as if that might muffle the sound and buy me a few more seconds of peace. No such luck. The red numbers glowed harshly in the dim room: 6:00 AM. Outside, snow blanketed the world in icy stillness, the February air seeping through the cracks in my window frame.

"Time to get up, Noa!" my mom called from downstairs, her voice laced with fatigue.

"I'm up!" I lied, pulling the covers over my head, savoring the last moments of warmth. Today wasn't just any day. My Countdown Mark was close to zero. That little glowing clock on my arm had been counting down my entire life, and now it was almost done. A restless energy twisted through me—part excitement, part unease. My stomach clenched, my fingers twitching against the sheets. What if this moment that had been building for seventeen years turned out to be nothing?

On top of that, Christopher Hawthorne—the face of the Countdown Control Agency—was coming to give a presentation at school today. Normally, some researcher or agent handled these things, but this time, it was him. The thought sent a strange mix of nerves and curiosity through me, a feeling I couldn't quite place. I tried to brush it off—it was only another assembly, another scripted speech. Maybe I was restless because everything about today felt too significant all at once. But still, seeing him in person—someone who had been paraded around in carefully curated soundbites and propaganda—felt strangely surreal. The CCA controlled everything about his image. What was he actually like beneath it all?

With a sigh, I kicked off the covers and let myself lay there for a second, pretending I had the luxury of staying in bed. But reality wasn't that generous. I sat up, wincing as my feet hit the ice-cold floor—a sharp reminder that the day wasn't waiting for me. My room was its usual mess. The dark forest green walls were plastered with posters of bands I adored, with Panic! At The Disco and Paramore claiming prime spots. Clothes lay scattered across the floor, remnants of last night's frantic search for the perfect outfit. I settled on a pair of jeans and my favorite sweater, then ran a brush through my tangled hair.

I dragged myself to the full-length mirror and ran a hand over my hair. Same hazel eyes, same frame that never quite felt right—too slight in some places, too rounded in others—same tired expression. My jet-black hair fell in loose waves around my shoulders, framing eyes I always thought lacked something, though I could never pinpoint what. Against my fair skin, they were my most striking feature, though I never felt remarkable. Slender but not fragile, I was caught in that awkward space—too young in some ways, too old in others.

I glanced down at my Countdown Mark, its soft green glow a

reminder that time was slipping away, bringing me closer to a fate I couldn't fully understand. Today was the day. The number was so low it felt unreal. I wondered what it would be like when it hit zero, hoping, deep down, that I wouldn't be disappointed.

"Breakfast is ready!" Mom's voice cut through my thoughts. I could smell the faint scent of slightly burnt pancakes waft into my room, laced with the rich bitterness of coffee. I grabbed my backpack and headed downstairs, the smells of breakfast growing stronger with each step. My younger brothers, Ethan and Lucas, were already at the table, shoveling food into their mouths as if it were their last meal.

The twins were practically mirror images, light brown hair and bright blue eyes that sparkled with the same mischievous energy. Lucas had a small birthmark on his left shoulder, and Ethan had a slight gap between his front teeth, differences that were not very noticeable. Even their Countdown Marks mirrored each other, glowing bright red—Lucas's on his right arm and Ethan's on his left. At twelve, they still found excitement in everything, but it wasn't only wide-eyed wonder anymore—it was curiosity, the kind that made them eager to uncover secrets, push boundaries, and figure out the world on their own terms.

Caroline Mitchell stood at the kitchen island, drizzling syrup over a plate of pancakes before setting them in front of me. Her long greying hair was pulled back in a claw clip, dark eyes peering over the edge of her glasses. Despite her stern posture, there was a flicker of something behind her exhaustion—hesitation, maybe, or the remnants of a thought she wouldn't say aloud. It was gone before I could place it.

"Morning, Noa," she said, her voice gruff as she set down my plate. I tried not to notice that my pancakes were burnt while the twins' were perfect. It was a small thing, really, but it fit the pattern—the little ways I was always a step behind, an afterthought in a house where responsibility weighed more than fairness.

"Excited about today?"

I shrugged, aiming for nonchalance. "I guess. It's just another CCA presentation. We have these every year."

Ethan and Lucas exchanged a knowing glance, mischief flickering in their eyes. Lucas elbowed Ethan, his grin widening. "Bet he thinks he's too important to talk to regular people," he said. "Probably just stares past everyone like he's above it all."

Ethan smirked but shook his head. "Nah, I think he's a CCA experiment. Like, what if he doesn't have real thoughts? Just programmed responses they upload straight into his brain."

Lucas snorted. "Yeah, but it's Christopher Hawthorne," he said, drawing out the name like it was something out of a legend. "The guy the CCA treats like their personal golden boy. You'd really think he would have all the answers? He's just a poster boy."

Ethan leaned back in his chair, grinning. "Yeah, and by tomorrow, everyone's gonna think Noa and the poster boy are, like, best friends or something," he joked. "Maybe even secretly dating."

Mom shot him a sharp look as she set down a plate. "That's not something to joke about," she said, her tone flat. "The law is the law, whether people like it or not."

I rolled my eyes and jabbed at my pancakes, forcing indifference and ignoring them all. Because it wasn't a big deal. Just another CCA presentation, another overhyped public figure. Except my stomach twisted at the thought, and I hated that it did. "Whatever," I muttered, keeping my focus on my plate. "It's not like he's going to notice me."

"Enough talk—eat before you're late," Mom said, clearing their plates with slow, deliberate movements. She leaned against the counter, her shoulders curved inward like the weight of the world was folding her in half. I braced myself, half-expecting a sharp remark about hurrying up or wasting time, but it didn't come. Instead, she stood there, lost in her own exhaustion.

I opened my mouth to remind her about my Mark hitting zero, to share the excitement of the day with her—but the words caught in my throat. She looked tired, worn down by the weight of everything she carried. I swallowed the urge, pressing my nails into my palm instead. She had enough to deal with already. Her health was fragile, and I took on what I could to keep the household running. Adding to her worries felt selfish—except, deep down, it also felt unfair. I always held back, always made sure I wasn't another burden. But did she ever stop to notice?

"Sure, Mom," I muttered, tossing most of my burnt pancakes into the trash and rinsing my plate. The flutter of anticipation for the day warred with the familiar sting of her dismissiveness.

As I reached for the door, a memory surfaced—a rare moment from years ago when she held me close after a tough day at school, whispering that things would get better. That was before her health declined, before the distance between us became an unspoken wall neither of us tried to tear down. Responsibility pressed heavier on my shoulders each year, but my Mark's countdown buzzed beneath it—an unknown waiting to unfold, something entirely its own.

I wanted to ask if she had ever wondered what it would be like to have a Countdown Mark—if she would have been scared or hopeful, if it would have changed anything. But I already knew the answer. She never talked about it, and maybe that silence was an answer in itself. It had shaped me in ways I wasn't sure I understood—teaching me that some questions weren't worth asking, that some things were better left buried. Maybe that's why I stopped expecting answers from her a long time ago.

The cold hit me the second I stepped outside—sharp and biting, slipping under my clothes before I could brace for it. I yanked my jacket tighter, rubbing my hands together as my breath curled into the air in soft, misty puffs. It was the kind of cold that burrowed deep, stiffening my fingers and biting at my face, making me wish—for a second—that I had an excuse to stay home. The school bus idled at the end of the driveway, exhaust twisting into the frigid air. I hurried toward it, pushing away the thought that I had to ride the bus while my mom drove my brothers to school. It was small. Stupid. But it gnawed at me anyway—one more reminder that their needs were priorities, while mine were obligations.

As the bus pulled away from my house, I watched the familiar suburban landscape slip by. Snow blanketed lawns and rooftops, transforming the neighborhood into a winter wonderland. Bare trees stood stark against the white. Digital displays mounted on lampposts flickered with the time and the ever-present reminders of Countdown Mark protocols—flashing warnings that felt more like surveillance than guidance. It was as if the CCA was watching us through every glowing digit. No dating before your mark hits zero. Physical relationships are banned for those whose marks are still moving. Two of many mandates CCA looms over our lives, a constant shadow.

The ride to school was uneventful for the most part, but excitement simmered beneath the surface. The rumble of the bus engine vibrated through the floor under my feet, mingling with the chatter of students swapping weekend plans and wild rumors. The air was thick with the damp scent of wet clothes and overstuffed school bags, clinging to the heavy winter coats draped across seats.

Valentine's Day loomed around the corner, and the bus felt like a shaken soda can—a little chaotic, ready to burst with energy. It was ridiculous, really. Everyone pretending they weren't waiting on fate. I sat in the quiet eye of it, pretending I didn't care either, even though my stomach had been fluttering since I woke up. We all knew exactly when we would meet our soulmates, and dating was essentially off-limits until your Mark hit zero.

Yet somehow, high school dating drama seemed to never end. I shifted my gaze to my own Countdown Mark, the numbers ticking steadily toward zero. The certainty of meeting my soulmate today was both thrilling and terrifying. What would change? Would it be everything I'd hoped for, or would reality fall short of my imagination?

As we passed an elementary school, the low hum of conversation behind me caught my attention.

"Did you hear about Jessica Simmons? She just stopped coming to school," one girl whispered, her tone laced with intrigue.

"Yeah, I heard she got pregnant," another voice chimed in, scandal dripping from her words. "And because her boyfriend wasn't her soulmate, the CCA found out and she got in serious trouble."

"Trouble? Maybe. But I heard she didn't make it when the CCA made her have some sort of procedure," someone else added, their voice low, fearful.

A third voice cut in, trying for authority. "Well I heard she ran away before the CCA could arrest her. She's probably hiding out somewhere."

The first girl scoffed. "You know all of that's exactly the kind of stuff parents and teachers say to scare us. I doubt any of that is true."

I rolled my eyes at the absurdity of their gossip, but part of me couldn't help wondering if there was a grain of truth buried beneath the drama. I didn't know Jessica well, but the thought of her vanishing made my stomach twist. The real story was probably mundane—Jessica's family might have moved, or she transferred schools. But in a town so close to Washington, D.C., the smallest absence sparked a wildfire of rumors. Conspiracy theorists thrived here.

The bus trundled on, and the view shifted as we entered the commercial part of town. I tuned out the buzz of voices around me and watched frost-laced shop windows blur past—cafes with handwritten chalkboard signs, boutiques with red hearts taped to glass, everything screaming romance. Couples walked hand in hand, sharing warm drinks and whispered conversations, their breath visible in the cold. It was a scene plucked straight from a romance movie, and a tight coil of excitement and anxiety pulled in my gut. Would that be me soon? Walking with someone, my soulmate, feeling that warmth? Or would it feel awkward and disappointing?

The bus finally approached Annapolis High, and the scenery changed to the sprawling campus of red brick and large windows, its front lawn blanketed in snow. Students stood outside, their breath visible as they laughed and talked. The crunch of snow and the crisp bite of the air enveloped me as I stepped off the bus.

Inside, decorations splashed pinks and reds across the usually neutral hallways. Students clustered around lockers, their conversations a buzzing hum. Posters for the upcoming dance were tacked up on bulletin boards, a reminder of the night set aside for those whose Marks had already hit zero.

"Noa!" a familiar voice called out. I turned to see my best friend, Amelia Collins, weaving through the crowd to catch up with me. Ami was striking as ever—dark brown hair dyed a deep burgundy, piled into a messy bun that somehow looked intentional. She always had that put-together look without trying, and while part of me envied it, I was mostly grateful to have her in my corner. Next to her, I always felt like the understudy stumbling through rehearsal, hoping no one noticed the lines I forgot. Her skin had a warm glow, and her almond-shaped green eyes sparkled with mischief. She wore a fitted jacket over a simple dress, balancing confidence and kindness with that sharp wit always tucked in her back pocket.

"Hey, Ami," I said with a smile.

"You ready for the big presentation?" she asked, her eyes gleaming with curiosity.

"I guess," I shrugged. "It's just another school assembly, right?"

"Maybe, but it's not every day *Christopher Hawthorne* comes to speak. He's practically a legend," Ami said, her excitement palpable.

I tried not to laugh. She sounded like my brothers. "Legend or not, it's still just some guy from a government agency giving a speech—nothing earth-shattering, right?" I said with a shrug, though the flutter in my chest betrayed how not-casual I really felt about it. I teased, hoping to downplay my own curiosity. "Let's get to class."

Ami stepped in front of me, stopping me mid-stride. "Not so fast. We're not going anywhere until we talk about the other big thing happening today. Aren't you nervous?" she pressed, trailing after me as I walked around her. I didn't answer, instead pretending not to hear her. I tugged at my sleeve and picked up my pace, guilt prickling at the edge of my thoughts. Ami didn't deserve the cold shoulder, but talking about it made everything too real. I'd gotten good at keeping things locked up, smiling through the silence. It was easier than facing the flood of what I really felt.

The usual cadence of school life faded to the background as my thoughts drifted to the assembly, the weight of what would happen making my heart pound. I tried to act indifferent, like my Countdown Mark didn't consume me. But deep down, I knew that today would change everything.

By the time Algebra II rolled around, the whole day had already blurred together—half-heard lectures and restless energy building toward the assembly like pressure behind my temples. My thoughts were scattered, ricocheting between quadratic equations and the impending assembly like my brain couldn't decide which stressor it hated more. The rhythmic sound of pencils scratching on paper filled the room, punctuated by the chill of winter air seeping through the old window frames. I pulled my sweater tighter, like it could shield me from the cold seeping in and the quiet panic curling low in my gut.

At the front of the classroom, Mr. Matthews explained a complex problem with practiced patience. Tall and greying, he was known for making the driest math seem engaging. But today, his voice floated in and out of my consciousness as my gaze slipped to the Countdown Mark on my arm, the numbers steadily ticking away. My breath caught for half a second, and I clenched my fists beneath the desk, pressing my palms against my knees to stop the trembling. The closer I got to zero, the harder it became to fake indifference—to pretend this was yet another ordinary day when my whole world might be shifting beneath me.

The room buzzed with a subtle energy—whispers and quiet laughter mingled with Mr. Matthews' lecture. The walls were plastered with posters of mathematical formulas and motivational quotes, and his desk was a mess of papers. To my right, a group of students leaned in, their voices low as they discussed the assembly. I caught a few words—speculation about Christopher Hawthorne, curiosity about what he might reveal. To my left, Rosalyn Williams, a petite junior with auburn hair braided neatly to the side, sat with her eyes locked on Mr. Matthews, ever the diligent student.

"Remember, everyone," Mr. Matthews said, snapping me back to the present, "the assembly after class is mandatory. I don't want to call any parents about someone ditching again." He cast a stern look at the boys in the back, known for skipping anything that wasn't graded. "If anyone has questions about the assembly, now's the time to ask."

Rosalyn raised her hand, her voice tentative. "Why is Christopher Hawthorne doing the presentation today? It's usually a random agent or scientist every year. What's different now?"

Mr. Matthews paused, a thoughtful expression crossing his face. "Good question, Rosalyn. I'm not entirely sure. Maybe that's something you can ask during the assembly, if there's a Q&A."

Annoyed glances flickered across the room, and a low pulse sparked beneath my skin—like my Mark was tuning in to the tension, a hum sharp enough to make me straighten in my seat. Rosalyn's question stuck with me, hit harder than it should have. Why was he here? My Mark would hit zero at the end of the assembly—was that a coincidence? The thought made my stomach flutter and tighten all at once, like my body knew something I hadn't let myself consider. The idea was almost laughable, a stretch too far. But still, the thought itched at the back of my mind.

One of the guys in the back—the ones Mr. Matthews had quietly warned—let out a scoff. "Do you really think Christopher's gonna answer that?" he said, rolling his eyes. "Isn't it obvious? The pretty poster boy is all grown up, so now the government has to shove him down our throats in person. Pictures aren't enough anymore."

Despite myself, I almost smirked—a flicker, a twitch at the corner of my mouth—before I bit the inside of my cheek and forced it away. A reflex. No one needed to see that crack in the armor. It was ridiculous—and yet, the tiniest part of me kind of agreed. The stoner had a reputation for conspiracy theories, always rambling about government cover-ups and hidden agendas. Most of the time, I dismissed his rants, but today, there was a ring of logic to what he said that I couldn't completely ignore.

Mr. Matthews gave a small shrug. "I suppose there's only one way to find out. Pay attention during the assembly; maybe you'll learn something new this year."

The bell rang, jolting the class to life. I gathered my things, my fingers brushing over my Countdown Mark. The skin beneath it tingled faintly—warm, alive—like it knew what I didn't. The contact sent a jolt through me, not painful but sharp enough to make me pause. For a second, I let my palm rest there, grounding myself in the steady pulse of the glow. A shiver ran down my spine, and I felt a tightening around my chest. Today felt like a line drawn in the sand—or maybe I was imagining it that way, reading too much into things because I didn't want to admit how much this all meant to me.

Ami was waiting for me outside the classroom, her eyes bright with excitement. "Come on, let's get to the gym. I want a good seat."

We wove through the crowded halls, the air buzzing with overheard whispers and half-baked rumors. Two girls near a locker argued over whether Christopher Hawthorne had ever actually left the CCA building before. Someone else speculated he was here to announce a new soulmate law. I didn't chime in—I listened, absorbing it all like background static. I was detached but keenly aware of how everyone seemed to know exactly what he was supposed to be, even if none of them had a clue. Voices swirled around us, full of guesses and theories about Christopher Hawthorne and what he might say. My heart continued to thud against my ribs.

We stepped into the current of students flowing toward the gym, the low thrum of overlapping voices was echoing down the hallway, growing louder with each step. The air shifted with every step—tension buzzing beneath the chatter, the scent of floor polish and recycled heat rising around us. I tried to shake off the weight creeping down my spine. My eyes darted around, catching sight of researchers in white coats scattered throughout the space, their presence unsettling. What should have been a routine school assembly felt different, almost charged. More unnerving was the number of press members mingling along the edges.

I glanced at my arm, the soft green glow of my Mark pulsing faintly as it inched closer to zero—a quiet countdown threaded with too many questions and not enough answers. The thought of meeting my soulmate sent a jolt through me. What would this mean for me? How much would my life change after today? Ami stood beside me, her energy almost infectious, but I kept my turmoil to myself, unsure how to voice it.

For us seniors, these presentations were old news, something we sat through every year. But Christopher Hawthorne's presence changed everything. Conversations swirled around us, students speculating about what he might say. I took a seat near the front, twirling a strand of hair between my fingers. Ami dropped on the bleacher next to me, practically bouncing. I wasn't sure if she was more worked up about seeing Christopher or me hitting zero.

I didn't ask, afraid it would invite questions I wasn't ready to answer.

The lights dimmed. The principal, Mr. Thompson, stepped onto the stage and cleared his throat into the microphone. "Good afternoon, students," Mr. Thompson began, his voice carrying through the gymnasium. "Since February 2006, schools across the country have held these assemblies in the week leading up to Valentine's Day as a reminder of the importance of your Countdown Marks and the responsibilities they bring. The Countdown Control Agency has sent representatives to reinforce these messages and help guide you. Today, we have a special opportunity. Please join me in welcoming Christopher Hawthorne from the Countdown Control Agency."

The room filled in polite applause as Christopher stepped up to the podium. He was taller than I'd imagined, standing with a practiced composure that gave the impression of effortless confidence. But there was a glint in his eyes, something restrained and unreadable. The way he commanded the space was magnetic, and as he began to speak, it felt like the air shifted.

"Good afternoon, everyone," he said, his voice steady, with an undertone that made it impossible not to listen. "You probably already know who I am, but for those who don't, I'm Christopher Hawthorne."

I leaned forward as he spoke, absorbing every word. He explained the basics of the Countdown Marks and the CCA's ongoing research, the same information we'd heard time and time again. But hearing it from him made it feel different, more personal. He shared snippets of his life—what it was like growing up as the first with a Countdown Mark, and how the Agency had shaped its image around him. He didn't talk about how that made him feel, but there was something in his tone, a pause here and there, that hinted at the strain beneath the surface. It wasn't what he said—it was what he didn't—that made it feel like more than a speech.

"Each of us with the Countdown Mark has a unique journey," he said, his eyes sweeping the room and landing, for a fleeting moment, on mine. "They are more than just a trait—they're a sign of something greater, something we're all trying to understand."

As he continued, a strange sense of connection stirred inside me, pulling me closer to something I couldn't quite name. I had been so focused on him that I forgot about my Mark ticking ever closer to zero. The room around me faded; all I could hear was the cadence of his voice, all I could see were his blue eyes, intense and searching.

Christopher was everything the rumors made him out to be—confident, composed, and almost untouchably polished. But the longer I watched, the more I started to question whether he saw himself that way, too. His posture was steady, his voice smooth, but there was a hesitation tucked into the silence between sentences—like he was weighing each word a little too carefully, trying not to give too much away. It didn't feel like nerves. It felt like pressure—the kind that settles into your bones after years of carrying too much.

The posters, the headlines, the whispers—they'd all painted him as some unreachable symbol. And on the surface, he fit the part: athletic build, tousled dark brown hair, piercing blue eyes. But up close, there was more. I couldn't tell if it was vulnerability or control—but whatever it was, it pulled me in.

Ami leaned over to say something, but her voice blurred into background noise. The crowd, the lights, the press—they all melted away. All I could see was him. Something about the way he stood, the way his gaze locked momentarily with mine, made my pulse trip over itself. It felt like a shift in gravity—the kind that changes everything without warning.

When he opened the floor for questions, hands shot up across the gymnasium. I noticed Rosalyn's go up first—of course. Christopher answered each question with patience, never losing that steady composure. As the Q&A wrapped up, the bell rang, signaling the end of the school day. I caught sight of Rosalyn hurrying out, visibly annoyed that she hadn't been called on. Students began gathering their things, heading for the exits. I stayed put, a gnawing feeling that I needed to talk to Christopher pulling at me. Ami squeezed my hand, giving me a look I couldn't decipher before leaving.

I approached the stage, trying to ignore the cluster of researchers hovering around him. They parted slightly as I walked up, their eyes darting between us like they were watching something important unfold.

"Hi, I'm Noa Mitchell," I said, my voice surprisingly steady as I extended my hand. Boldness like this was not in my nature, but something compelled me forward. Maybe it was adrenaline.

Christopher turned toward me, his eyes locking onto mine with that same quiet intensity I'd seen from afar—steady, searching. "Nice to meet you, Noa," he said, taking my hand. His grip was firm but gentle, and the warmth of his palm sent a pulse of awareness up my arm. His eyes held mine, and for a second, it felt like everything else dropped away—like he could see through the noise and nerves and land directly on whatever this moment was. Does he feel this, too? The thought struck hard, making my breath catch and my heart pound.

"Your presentation was interesting," I said, my voice dropping as I nodded toward the researchers circling us. "It must be tough, living under constant surveillance."

A hint of a wry smile tugged at his lips. "It has its moments," he replied.

"I can only imagine," I said, my tone softening. "Thanks for sharing your story."

"Thank you for listening," he said, the warmth in his voice feeling almost private.

The space around us seemed to shrink, the noise of the gym fading to a dull hum. Christopher's eyes softened when he smiled, and something in that look made my breath catch. I didn't notice the researchers inching closer, didn't register the flash of cameras or the scratch of pens. The press hovered along the edges, their lenses trained on us, the air thick with anticipation. I should have felt exposed. Instead, with his eyes holding mine, the rest of the world faded away. All that mattered was him.

A jolt of heat surged across my left forearm, sharp and electric, jerking me back into my body before I realized I'd drifted. My Countdown Mark glowed, the numbers racing down—seconds, milliseconds—until it hit zero. The soft green light dimmed, fading to nothing but a faint scar.

I looked up and saw Christopher staring at his own mark, realization dawning in his eyes. Our gazes met, and the world blurred around us. My heart thudded once, hard, before seeming to pause entirely. There was this connection that didn't make sense but demanded to be felt. It was as if everything in my life had led to this moment. A tremor ran through my fingers, and my breath caught in my throat. In that split second, I knew that everything was about to change—but a quieter part of me bristled with doubt, whispering that maybe I was imagining it, that this couldn't possibly be real. *Not him.* But in the end, there was no doubt. Here, in front of me, stood my soulmate.

CHAPTER THREE

Break

Christopher

Reporters hovered like vultures, their shouted questions echoing off the walls, cameras flashing as they jostled for the best angle. Researchers and agents flanked me on either side, closing in. But somehow, through the chaos, it still felt like Noa and I were the only two people in the room. The shouting felt like a low murmur as it bounced off the walls, distant and muffled compared to the electricity coursing through me. My heart thundered. My breath turned uneven. A rush of heat climbed up my arm and bloomed in my chest. Noa's hazel eyes reflected the same shock and wonder that I felt.

Her presence was like a live wire beneath my skin—my fingers twitched, breath caught. She was petite, but the strength in her gaze belied her small frame. Soft waves of black hair framed her face, catching the light with each subtle movement.

"You said your name was Noa, right?" I managed, my voice unsteady. My eyes flicked toward the agents and press nearby, and my words felt too vulnerable beneath their judgment. I wanted to take her hand and run, to escape the eyes watching us and explore this connection unfettered—then instantly scolded myself for the thought. It was reckless. Selfish. But the longing pulsed anyway, raw and unrelenting.

She nodded. "Yes, and you're Christopher." Her voice was soft but sure, with an undertone of curiosity and something else that stirred something deep inside me.

Before I could say more, Dr. Lang stepped between us, his presence a cold wall. His eyes were unreadable, and his authority filled the space, snapping me back to reality. The cameras clicked faster, and the loud buzz of questions from the press pricked at the edges of my awareness.

"We need to take you back, Christopher. We have tests to run," he said, his voice smooth but laced with command.

Frustration coiled inside me, not sharp but familiar—a tightness in my jaw and a flicker in my hands, the instinctive way my body braced for disappointment before my thoughts could catch up. Too many moments like this, stolen by obligation, buried under the Agency's grip. "Can't it wait?" I pushed back, though I already knew the answer.

Dr. Lang's dark eyes met mine, unflinching, and something in his stare twisted in my chest—a silent warning, or maybe a reminder that I wasn't in control here, not really. "It's imperative we get you hooked up to monitors and do a blood draw immediately." His tone was as final as the lock on a cell door.

Noa's expression softened, understanding flickering in her eyes. "It's okay, Christopher. We'll talk later," she said, carrying the promise that this was only a temporary separation.

I sighed, the weight of defeat settling over me. My shoulders slumped under the familiar pressure of surrendering to the Agency's demands. Some part of me hated how easily I gave in—but the last time I resisted, I spent three days in isolation while a camera watched me sleep. "Okay, I'll see you soon, Noa." The words felt inadequate, but they were all I had to give.

Lang's voice carried to the press as he informed them that Dr. Bennett would address their questions at a scheduled press conference. Two agents gripped my arms from either side as they led me away. I glanced back at Noa one last time, and she stood there in the wide expanse of the gym, arms folded loosely across her chest, watching me with a mixture of resolve and quiet sadness. It clung to me, heavy and persistent, long after the agents pulled me away.

The view melted from snow-covered suburban quiet into the towering steel and frantic pulse of Washington, D.C.—a blur of motion I didn't really notice. All I could think about was Noa—her presence lingering. What we shared in that moment was unlike anything I'd ever known—a magnetic pull that coiled through my chest like a second heartbeat.

The SUV wove through the city, past towering monuments and steel-framed government buildings that rose like indifferent giants. I caught their reflections in the window, but they didn't ground me—instead, they made me feel smaller, more displaced. My thoughts looped back to Noa, again and again, her face surfacing no matter how I tried to bury it. The city, with all its noise and movement, couldn't compete with the pull she'd left behind.

Headquarters rose before us, an imposing fortress of glass and steel. Stepping out of the vehicle, I made my way through the grand entrance and into the lobby, its sterile blend of glass and marble bustling with staff moving purposefully. The echoes of voices and footsteps bounced off the polished surfaces. I couldn't help but notice all the glances towards me as we bypassed the front desk and headed for the elevators.

The ride up to the fourth floor was quiet. The doors slid open, revealing a stark corridor lined with glass walls, offering glimpses into labs filled with white coats and the low thrum of machinery. The fluorescent lights overhead cast a harsh, clinical glare, making everything feel cold and impersonal.

Dr. Lang stood waiting in the lab. Every step closer to him felt like walking toward judgment, flanked by instruments that looked more like tools of dissection than diagnostics. The sterile light bounced off metal surfaces, draining the room of any trace of warmth or life. Tall and imposing, Lang's sharp features were framed by meticulously styled jet-black hair. The overhead lights glinted off his glasses, hiding his eyes. Every movement he made was precise, calculated.

"Christopher, sit here," Lang commanded, gesturing to a chair that looked unnervingly like it belonged in a dentist's office. I sat, a familiar sense of dread settling over me. The white coat assistants moved around with detached efficiency. One tied a tourniquet around my arm, the rubber biting into my skin. I watched the needle slide in, felt the familiar sting as vials of blood were filled one after the other.

After applying multiple electrodes around my body, monitors

began to beep steadily, their rhythm punctuating the mechanical hiss of a scanner passing over my now dormant Countdown Mark. The once vibrant dark blue glow was gone, replaced by a lifeless series of zeroes—like a brand burned into my skin.

"How's it look?" I ventured, breaking the silence.

Dr. Lang barely glanced at me, his eyes fixed on the data displayed on the screen. "Nothing for you to be concerned about. The mark is dormant, as expected. We need to monitor your vitals and brainwaves," Dr. Lang continued, his tone devoid of warmth. "So be quiet. Any fluctuations could be significant."

Time blurred—first minutes, then hours—as wires pressed against my skin and monitors hummed in rhythm and questions I couldn't answer stacked higher than the monitors tracking me. My muscles ached from staying still, and my thoughts frayed at the edges, drifting back to Noa despite my best attempts to stay grounded. Blood pressure readings, more blood draws, brain scans—the prodding made me feel like a specimen on display. But through it all, my thoughts refused to leave Noa. Her presence, the way she looked at me, the pull that still lingered.

"Christopher, focus," Dr. Lang's voice snapped, his hand waving in front of my face. "We need accurate readings, and you can't be shaking—"

I was shaking? "I'm fine. Just finish this already," I interrupted, forcing myself to comply. But my mind continued to wander. Was Noa thinking about me too? Did she feel the same pull I did?

"You're distracted," Dr. Lang noted, irritation seeping through his usual composure. "This isn't like you. You're normally more cooperative."

My jaw tightened. "I'm fine. Just get it over with."

He sighed, frustration sharpening his gaze. "We need to run a few more tests. This might sting." He held up a syringe filled with a clear liquid, another unwelcome intrusion. I hardly flinched as it pierced my skin.

After a moment, he clicked his pen and noted something on his clipboard. "Everything appears the same as always," he said, his tone edged with disappointment. "You're free to go for now—but you'll be monitored as tightly as ever. Stay in your room and report anything unusual immediately. We can't afford for you to withhold any data. We'll send out a message if we require more blood samples or tests."

"Understood," I said absently, already planning my next move. No matter what they claimed they needed, I couldn't shake the need to see Noa again—not only a desire, but a tight, aching pull behind my ribs. Something irrational and raw refused to let go.

The impersonal walls of the lab loomed as I walked out, their lifelessness, as always, suffocating. The elevator doors at the end of the hall slid open with a cold mechanical click, and welcomed a brief moment of solitude before returning to my confines. I pressed the button for the third floor and waited.

The elevator opened onto a hallway identical to the one I'd left—same sterile walls, same hum of overhead fluorescents. Cameras blinked from every corner, their quiet, mechanical focus a constant reminder that I was never truly alone. My footsteps echoed, the silence stretching around me like a wire. The corridor seemed endless.

Outside my room, Agent Harris stood waiting. His usual easygoing expression was tinged with concern. "Hey, Christopher," he said, his scarred cheek twitching slightly. "How'd it go?"

I shrugged, masking my frustration. "The usual tests. You'd think something would be different now—some shift in protocol, some change in how they looked at me—but apparently not."

He studied me for a moment, his blue eyes thoughtful. "You seem different, though."

I hesitated, then admitted, "I feel different. I met her. My Mark hit zero."

A knowing look passed over his face. "I know. It's all anyone's talking about 'round here. How do you feel?"

"Overwhelmed," I said honestly. "I barely got to say two words to her before Lang had me hauled away. I need to see her again."

Harris nodded slowly. "I get it. Or at least, I can try to. Never had a Mark, so I don't know exactly what that's like, but I can imagine it's intense. If you need anything, you know where to find me."

"Thanks, Harris," I said, my voice quieter. "I appreciate it."

As I lay in bed, my eyes kept drifting back to my now still and branded Countdown Mark. I wondered if Noa's mark looked the same, if she was staring at it as I was. Maybe her thoughts were as tangled in this strange, exhilarating bond between us. The faint glow of the city filtered through the curtains, casting shadows that stretched and shifted across the shelves. The glow-in-the-dark stars on the ceiling—remnants of childhood nights spent tracing constellations and naming imaginary galaxies—seemed dimmer now, stripped of the wonder and comfort they once held. The silence pressed down on me, heavy and suffocating.

The connection I felt with Noa was undeniable. It tugged at something deep in my chest, urgent and relentless, making it impossible to sit still. I couldn't let the Agency's suffocating grip dictate my life any longer. My heart beat faster at the thought of seeing her again, breaking free from these walls, for a moment.

A soft knock on the door broke the silence. "Come in," I called, pushing myself up. No one ever came to my room. Why bother when they could summon me to them? Agent Harris stepped in, closing the door quietly behind him. A small, knowing smile tugged at the corners of his mouth. His eyes darted to the hallway before he turned back to me.

"Got a minute?" he asked, his voice low, a whisper that almost didn't reach me.

"Sure, what's up?" I replied, curiosity weaving through my tension.

Harris pulled the chair by the window closer to the bed and sat, leaning in until his face was inches from mine. "I have a plan," he said, voice hushed. "If you want to see Noa without the Agency breathing down your neck."

Hope flared in my chest. A sudden light cutting through the fog of doubt and frustration. The possibility of seeing Noa, of stepping outside the Agency's watchful eyes, even for a brief moment, was like oxygen to a flame. "I'm listening," I said, my voice almost unable to conceal my excitement.

Harris's eyes shifted to the door, vigilant. "We'll need to be careful. If you're caught, you're on your own. But if you play your cards right, you can slip out for a few hours. You in?"

"Absolutely," I said, without a heartbeat of hesitation.

His gaze sharpened. "Good. Timing is everything. We can't leave room for mistakes."

I nodded, the reality of the risk sinking in. My heart raced, a mix of fear and exhilaration coursing through my veins. "Tell me what I need to do."

The room seemed to tighten around us, as if the walls themselves understood the gravity of the move I was about to make. Harris outlined a plan in quick, precise details—a series of diversions and timed moves that would let me slip past the CCA's night watch. It was bold, risky, but it was my only shot at seeing Noa without a sea of onlookers taking notes and analyzing every blink and breath.

"You'll need to move fast," Harris said, his voice carrying urgency. "Stick to the plan, stay focused, and don't give them a reason to suspect anything."

"I can do it," I said, the words more for myself than him.

Harris's expression softened as he stood. "You've got this, Christopher. Just be smart."

"Thanks, Harris," I nodded, a grin breaking through the tension in my voice.

He slipped out of the room, the door closing softly behind him.

I lay back, staring at the ceiling as the adrenaline coursed through me, my pulse thrumming in my ears. I pictured Noa's face, the warmth in her eyes, and let the thought fuel me. This was it—the first step toward breaking the chains of the Agency and finding a piece of freedom.

CHAPTER FOUR

Sparks

Noa

Ami had insisted on driving me home, too excited to wait for details. But the chaos that met us wasn't what either of us expected. As soon as we turned onto my street, reporters crowded the sidewalk, cameras flashing, voices shouting questions I couldn't hear over the blood rushing in my ears. Ami practically elbowed a path for us through the swarm, shielding me with fierce determination as we reached the door. Inside, the phone rang shrilly—again and again. Ami didn't hesitate. She stormed over and yanked the cord from the wall, silencing it with a muttered curse under her breath.

Once we made it upstairs, she practically yanked me down the hall, her questions tumbling out in a rapid-fire stream before I had the chance to close the door behind us. "What happened? What was it like? Is *Christopher freaking Hawthorne* really your soulmate?! Why didn't he stay?" She almost didn't pause for breath. "Tell me everything!"

We settled onto my bed, the familiar quilt beneath us adding a touch of comfort. I felt almost dizzy from the emotional storm inside me. "It was... intense," I said, the word falling short as my fingers fidgeted with the edge of the quilt, trying to find the right words. "Christopher is... different than I expected."

Ami raised an eyebrow, leaning forward. "Different how? Dreamy different or creepy different?"

I laughed, shaking my head. "Dreamy different, I guess. He's... I don't know." I paused, trying to capture the sensation. "There's just something about him."

She smirked, giving me a playful nudge. "Sounds like someone's got a crush."

I blushed, nudging her back. "It's not that. It's more than that. When our marks hit zero," I stopped, reliving the moment. "It was like everything else just disappeared. He looked at me like he really saw me, you know?"

Ami's eyes widened, and she let out a small gasp. "Wow, that does sound intense. I can't wait for my mark to hit zero. I can't believe I have to wait six more months!" She glanced down at the purple glowing Mark on her wrist. Her thumb hovered near the numbers, then dropped as she glanced back at me, a fleeting vulnerability flashing in her expression. She sighed. "Sometimes I wonder if it'll feel that strong for me too. What if it's not like that?"

I tilted my head, surprised by the shift in her tone. "I think it's different for everyone. But I don't think you have to worry, Ami. You're going to feel it. I just... know it."

She smiled, softer now. "Thanks." For a heartbeat, that hint of vulnerability lingered in her eyes—then vanished, replaced with something sharper. Determination. That was more like her. She sat up straighter, eyes gleaming with purpose. "Okay, so what did you guys talk about?"

"Not much," I admitted, a sigh escaping me. "One of the CCA

researchers interrupted us before we could really say anything. It was frustrating. I wanted to talk to him, get to know him."

She groaned, leaning back against the wall. "That sucks. But you'll see him again, right? I mean, he's your soulmate. You're meant to be together. It's fate!"

"I hope so," I murmured, the uncertainty lacing my voice. "It's just... overwhelming. I've imagined this day for so long, but now that it's here, I don't know what I'm supposed to do."

Ami's reassuring smile eased some of the tension in my chest. "You'll figure it out. One step at a time. But I have to know—do you think he's as hot as everyone else does? Because honestly, I think his voice alone could melt steel."

I laughed, the sound breaking through the tightness in my throat. My shoulders sagged a bit, tension momentarily slipping from my muscles. "Yeah, I do. Plus, he has this quiet sort of confidence, but underneath it, I feel like there's something vulnerable—like he's spent a long time learning how to hide it and still hasn't quite figured it out. It's hard to explain."

She nudged me again, her eyes sparkling with excitement. "Ugh, I'm both happy for you and insanely jealous. You better tell me every single detail along the way so I can live vicariously through you."

I smiled, warmth blooming in my chest—not only because of Christopher, but because Ami was here, rooting for me without hesitation. "Promise."

"Well, I can't wait to hear more, but I've got to go home and help my dad grade papers." She rolled her eyes dramatically. "It's the weekend, so we have plenty of time to hang out later. Let's grab coffee tomorrow morning, and we can gush some more."

"Deal," I nodded. After she left, I lay back on my bed, my fingers tracing idle patterns over the quilt. Thoughts of Christopher, my Mark, and what the future might hold swirled through my mind in relentless waves, refusing to still no matter how hard I tried to breathe through them. The continued quiet of the house pressed in on me—too loud, too still. I closed my eyes, replaying the encounter in vivid detail, the memory searing and sweet, unsure where this new path would lead but unable to stop walking toward it.

I woke with a start, heart pounding, breath shallow. The dream was already slipping away—smoke through my fingers, taking its meaning with it. The room was still, shadows curling along the walls, moonlight casting a soft, silvery glow through the curtains.

Hunger nudged me, dull but insistent, curling low in my stomach like a quiet ache I hadn't noticed until now. My legs felt heavy, like they were still half-asleep, and the weight of the day clung to my skin. I pushed off the covers and crept into the hallway, the floor cool beneath my feet. At the base of the stairs, the scent of something warm and familiar wrapped around me—rosemary, garlic, maybe onions. It should've been comforting. Instead, it made my stomach tighten.

Mom stood at the stove, posture tight, every movement too precise. The quiet sizzle of the pan filled the space between us.

When she glanced over her shoulder, her eyes were unreadable. Distant. Hard.

"Why am I cooking dinner when you're supposed to be?" she asked, not quite harsh—drained, like the words themselves cost her something. Like she'd already written me off for the night.

"Sorry, Mom. Something happened today, and—"

"I don't care what happened," she cut in, and something in me flinched. I didn't realize I'd stepped back until my heel touched the cabinet behind me. "You're supposed to make dinner. You know this."

She handed me the spatula without looking at me, her eyes fixed somewhere past my shoulder. She let out a quiet sigh, barely audible over the hiss of the pan. "I don't have the energy for this. Just finish it."

Then she was gone, her figure sinking into the couch while the sound of sitcom laughter spilled through the room. It felt jarring, out of place. I stood there for a moment, spatula in hand, throat tight. The kitchen felt smaller all of a sudden, the air thick with steam and the faint, bitter smell of something beginning to burn. My shoulders tensed without meaning to, chest tightening like I couldn't quite catch a full breath. Cramped. Like the walls had moved in without warning.

I stepped up to the stove and picked up where she left off—stirring sauce, checking the oven, chopping vegetables. My hands moved like they always did. On autopilot. But they trembled, enough to betray me.

The tension in the house never shouted. It hovered—low and steady. I found myself walking slower, softer, always listening for the shift. A tone change. A drawer shut too hard. A pause in her footsteps. Every day felt like walking a tightrope. One wrong word. One missed step. One breath too loud. And everything shattered. It wasn't the anger that hurt the most. Or maybe it was. It was hard to tell sometimes—everything blurred together when you lived like this. What was worse, though, was the silence. The way she focused on the television, her eyes skimming past me. Like I didn't exist unless I messed something up.

Down the hall, I heard my brothers laughing—loud and carefree. A faint smile tugged at the corner of my mouth, something soft threading through the heaviness. I wanted to keep it that way for them, to protect that laughter for as long as I could. They didn't know. Not really. They hadn't learned how to read the air yet, how to sense the shift before the storm broke. They still believed the quiet meant peace.

I stirred, I chopped, I breathed like everything was fine. My grip on the knife was too tight, knuckles pale, and I stirred the sauce faster than necessary, splashes flecking the stove. In my head, I imagined slipping out the back door and walking until I didn't feel like this anymore—until the air didn't feel so heavy and the silence didn't hurt so much. And somewhere in that mess of half-thoughts and what-ifs, he drifted in again. Christopher. Thinking his name made my chest tighten in a way I didn't want to unpack. I wondered where he was now. Was he thinking about me, too?

A memory slipped in, soft around the edges. I was ten. The house had smelled like cinnamon and pine, the sound of laughter bouncing through the rooms. Christmas, maybe. One of the good ones. But then, her voice could cut through everything. Like ice cracking across a frozen pond. Even back then, I think it was there—beneath the surface. Or maybe I'm only seeing it now, looking back with older eyes. Distant. Exhausted. Carrying weight she never talks about.

The clink of plates pulled me back. I set the table—forks, knives, napkins. Motions that felt almost safe in how familiar they were. "Dinner's ready," I called, my voice quiet.

She returned and sat down, eyes staying locked on the glow of the TV. I hesitated, waiting for a glance, a nod, anything—but she didn't turn her head. Just kept watching, like I hadn't said a word. No thank you. No acknowledgment. Only more silence.

I watched her for a beat longer, hoping—again—for something soft in her face. Something kind. But all I saw was the same mask. The same distance. The same empty space between us.

After I got the leftovers put away, I made my way back to my room, determined to tackle my homework. But before I could reach the stairs, the sound of my brothers' voices pulled me back. Ethan and Lucas were huddled over their textbooks at the kitchen island, their laughter softening the edges of the night.

"Hey, Noa!" Ethan called, looking up from his science book, his eyes wide with curiosity. "Did you meet Christopher Hawthorne today? What was he like?"

I rolled my eyes, hoping it disguised how my stomach flipped. I shifted my weight from one foot to the other, suddenly aware of how jittery I felt. I hoped they couldn't see through it, couldn't tell how off-balance I still felt. "The presentation was good, I guess," I said, steering the spotlight away from me. "How was school?"

Lucas lit up before Ethan could answer. "We learned about volcanoes in science today! We made our own mini eruptions with baking soda and vinegar!"

"Yeah, it was awesome!" Ethan added, practically glowing. "Mine had lava flowing all the way down the sides. We got to paint them and everything."

"Sounds like fun," I said, their excitement threading warmth through my chest. I pulled out a chair and sat across from them, letting their chatter fill the empty spaces inside me—spaces I hadn't realized were aching until their voices started to patch them. "Actually, I have some news too."

Both of them looked up, eyes wide, waiting. I bit the inside of my cheek and fidgeted with the edge of my sleeve, stalling for a second longer.

"It's about Christopher Hawthorne—"

"Did you talk to him? Is he as cool as he looks? I wish he came to our school today instead of the boring scientist we had," Lucas interrupted, nearly bouncing out of his seat.

I couldn't help but smile. "Hold on, goober," I said, laughing. "Let me talk."

They settled. Lucas kept shifting in his seat, and Ethan tapped his pencil against the counter like his energy had nowhere to go.

"Yes, I met Christopher."

"I knew it!" Ethan cheered, throwing his fist in the air.

"I bet he's so awesome," Lucas added, his grin stretching ear to ear.

"Can I finish?" I asked, feigning annoyance, though the corners of my mouth betrayed me. They nodded, perfectly in sync.

I hesitated for a moment, picking my words with care, not entirely sure how much to say—or how real it might feel once I said it out loud. "I met him, and he's... well, my Mark hit zero today when I met him."

Their mouths dropped open. They turned to each other in perfect sync, eyebrows shooting up, like they needed visual confirmation that they'd both actually heard that right.

"Doesn't that mean he's your soulmate?" Lucas asked, his voice tinged with awe.

I nodded slowly, the mix of nerves and excitement settling into something almost fragile—like it might break if I let myself believe in it too much. "Yeah, it does. We didn't get to talk much, but I'm pretty sure we'll see each other again soon."

"That's so cool," Ethan said, eyes shining. "Maybe he'll come over sometime."

"Yeah! He can play video games with us!" Lucas added, now full-on bouncing.

"Maybe," I said, careful not to promise what I wasn't sure of. "We'll see."

"Bet you'll want to hog him all to yourself," Ethan teased, sticking out his tongue.

"Oh, totally," I said with mock seriousness. "But if he's nice, I might let him play with you guys too."

I reached out and ruffled their hair, a smile tugging at the corners of my mouth as their laughter rose. The simple contact grounded me, like touching something solid after drifting for too long. Their laughter followed me as I headed down the hall—light, familiar, and protective. I didn't realize how much I needed it until then.

My room was cluttered, but it was the kind of mess that felt like home—a quiet contrast to the emotional storm of the day. In here, nothing was expected of me. Nothing pressed in. It was the only space that didn't ask me to hold it all together. Books and papers lay scattered across my desk—remnants of an ongoing battle with schoolwork. Clothes were draped over the chair and on the floor, a reminder of a rushed morning that already felt like a lifetime ago. I gathered the stray clothes and tossed them into the hamper, stacking the books into a neater pile.

I sat at my desk, determined to focus on my homework. I picked up my pencil, tapping it against the page without writing a word. My eyes skimmed the same sentence over and over, but nothing stuck. My thoughts kept slipping away, pulled back to a pair of deep blue eyes and the memory of a smile that had no business living rent-free in my head. My brothers' laughter still echoed faintly down the hallway, comforting and grounding. But my thoughts drifted anyway.

To him.

I could still see the way Christopher looked at me—like he knew me. And that terrified me a little. How could someone feel so familiar after one day? Or more like one fleeting moment. A part of me wanted to lean into it, to believe in whatever this was. But another part whispered caution. I didn't know what came next, and that uncertainty made my pulse quicken in ways that had nothing to do with nerves. The connection had been instant, like something deep inside me had snapped awake. The memory of his smile sent a quiet thrill through my chest.

With a sigh, I flipped open my history textbook, trying to anchor myself to something ordinary. But before I could read a single sentence, a soft tapping broke the silence. I froze. Another tap. Then another.

I crossed the room and peeked out the window. There he was—Christopher—standing below, bathed in moonlight. The silvery glow caught the curve of his jaw, and for a second, the whole world narrowed to the sight of him. Seeing him there made something twist in my chest. A strange, aching hope I didn't know what to do with. Puffs of his breath curled into the air. His expression was a strange blend of nerves and excitement that mirrored the fluttering chaos inside me.

My fingers hovered at the latch for a second, a breath catching in my throat before I pushed the window open, leaning out enough to whisper, "Christopher? What are you doing here? How did you even find me?"

"I had to see you," he said, a sheepish grin spreading across his face, though it flickered like he wasn't sure if he'd made the right call. There was something guarded in his eyes, like he was waiting for me to push him away. "Movies say this is how you do that. Can I come up?"

"There's a tree next to the house," I whispered. "Climb up carefully."

I threw a nervous glance over my shoulder, half-expecting to hear footsteps in the hallway. My heart thudded in my ears as he grabbed the nearest branch and began to climb. The leaves rustled softly, the only sound in the quiet night.

"Be careful," I whispered, biting my lip.

He moved with a surprising ease, as the branches swayed beneath his weight. It was strange, how natural he looked climbing toward me. Within seconds, he was at my window. I reached out, and our hands brushed—a soft touch that sent a shiver racing through me. My breath caught, and for a split second, I almost pulled back—but I didn't.

"Hi, Noa," he said, voice low and steady.

"Hi, Christopher," I replied, my smile blooming before I could stop it.

We stood like that for a moment, eyes locked, and for a second, it felt like everything I'd been missing—like the quiet moments with my mom when I was younger, before everything became so complicated. But this was different. It was a connection I hadn't known I was longing for.

"Come in," I said, stepping aside.

He climbed through the window, pausing to take in my room. I could see the curiosity behind his eyes, and the nerves tucked beneath the surface. My heart beat faster. This felt like the beginning of something. Something big.

We sat at the edge of my bed, the silence between us electric. I fidgeted with the corner of my sleeve, and he traced the seam of the blanket with his thumb. The day still hung heavy in the air, but so did something else—hope. I met his gaze, those deep blue eyes already etched into my memory.

"I'm glad you came," I said quietly. "But how did you find out where I live?"

"Living in a big government building has a few perks," he said with a chuckle. "I'm glad I came, too. I couldn't stop thinking about you."

We talked until the night blurred around us—sharing bits and pieces of ourselves, filling in the empty spaces that had formed between that first glance and now. He told me about growing up inside the CCA, how it felt like living inside a snow globe someone else always shook. The image made my chest ache a little—so fragile, always on display, never in control. I wondered how long he'd felt that way, and what it meant that he chose to tell me. I told him about my brothers, about how sometimes it felt like I was raising them more than Mom was. Our words tumbled out with the kind of honesty that only happens when the world outside the room feels far away.

There was a moment where neither of us spoke, but it wasn't awkward. It felt like breathing the same quiet. The house creaked occasionally, but no footsteps came. No doors opened. The night was ours. Time passed gently, unnoticed. I didn't know how long we'd been talking until I glanced over, blinking at the clock like it couldn't be right. 4:00 AM? Christopher noticed it, too.

"I should go," he said, regret threading through every word.

"Yeah," I agreed, though I hated the word in that moment. I helped him to the window, hands brushing again.

He climbed down carefully, the tree shifting with each step. When he reached the ground, he looked up—his grin wide, unguarded. He was completely open. I wondered how often he let anyone see him this way, and what it meant that he was showing it to me.

"Goodnight, Noa."

"Goodnight, Christopher."

I closed the window and crawled back under the covers, the air still humming with his presence. The room felt warmer. Brighter. Full of something new.

CHAPTER FIVE

Safe and Sound

Christopher

Valentine's Day arrived with a thrill of anticipation I hadn't felt in years—and honestly, I didn't know what to do with it. The feeling was foreign. It buzzed beneath my skin, exciting and slightly unsettling, as if freedom and fear had gotten tangled up inside me. My reflection stared back at me from the mirror as I adjusted my shirt collar for what felt like the hundredth time.

After a week of monitored texts and calls, I finally got to see Noa again. It felt almost surreal. Like hope had wandered into the wrong room and decided to sit down anyway. I wasn't used to looking forward to something—not like this—and part of me kept waiting for it to be taken away. I shifted on my feet, rolling my shoulders like I could try and physically shake the feeling off.

Too much hope always came with a catch. Especially since I was still shocked I hadn't been seriously punished for trying to sneak back into the building that first night. I'd expected another stint in the isolation chamber. Lang let it slide. I knew I should probably question why—maybe even be suspicious—but I'd been too wrapped up in getting to know Noa to let myself spiral. Still, it unsettled me in the back of my mind.

My eyes drifted to the hallway, to the chessboard that sat eternally mid-game. Always thinking two moves ahead. Always playing defense. Even now, on the edge of something good, I could feel that same guarded instinct coiled tight inside me—a habit I didn't know how to break. This room, my cage for so long, now felt like the starting line.

A note on my desk caught my eye as I headed out my door. Crisp white paper, slightly slanted handwriting.

Good luck today. Enjoy your date.
– Harris

Agent Harris.

For a second, I stared at the name. Part of me wanted to trust it—trust him—but another part couldn't help wondering why he cared at all. Was it real concern or part of another strategy? And why was he in my room again? Even with my suspicions, the note made something loosen in my chest. Maybe kindness didn't always have to be earned. I picked it up, reading it twice before sliding it into my pocket. His easy tone always made the control around here feel a little less suffocating. I wasn't sure if his kindness was genuine, or something riskier.

With the small bouquet I'd pieced together from the Agency greenhouse in hand, I stepped into the hallway. Operatives moved past without a word, their eyes flicking over me, unreadable. Maybe they were told to give me space today. Or maybe they were tired of watching.

Outside, a black SUV waited. Sleek. Familiar. A chariot built for containment. But today, it felt like a door cracked open. Snow blanketed everything—soft, pale, untouched. Trees stretched bare against a washed-out sky, skeletal and solemn. My thoughts drifted.

To her.

To the moment our Marks hit zero.

To how fast everything had changed. I didn't understand how it had gotten this deep, this fast. We'd only met a week ago. Sure, we'd talked for hours that first night, and we'd texted each other more than I'd ever texted anyone in my life. But still. It didn't explain why I felt like this.

Would I feel this way if our Countdown Marks hadn't told us we should? Was this how it was for everyone, or did the years isolated at the Agency make me cling to her for an escape? Maybe I was desperate for something that wasn't cold floors, strict routine, and people watching me breathe.

When the car pulled up to Noa's house, my pulse surged. Seeing her made all my worries and doubts fade away. She was waiting on the porch wearing a soft blue dress under her fitted coat. She looked so different than the other night. Not just pretty—though she definitely was—but like she belonged somewhere better than this freezing front porch. Her hair curled around her face, loose and wind-kissed, and her cheeks were flushed with either cold or nerves—maybe both.

"Christopher," she said, her voice steady but quiet. Only my name. But it felt like something new when she said it.

I held out the bouquet, watching her eyes brighten as she

took it. Her fingers lingered a moment longer than necessary. She lifted the flowers to her nose, then tucked them close to her chest. "Thank you," she said, her voice soft, her smile shy.

"You look beautiful," I blurted, surprising myself. It wasn't smooth.

Her laugh was warm. "Thank you. You look pretty handsome yourself."

We walked to the park nearby, boots crunching through the snow. The silence pressed in, but not in a bad way. It settled in my chest—calm, yet unfamiliar. The kind of quiet that made me realize how loud my world usually was. Breath fogged between us, brief and visible.

"So, what's it like at the CCA?" she asked. Her voice was gentle. Not prying—curious.

I hesitated. "It's... difficult," I said. "Routines. Tests. Surveillance. It's like living in a glass cage. And there are these endless number of medical exams." I paused, shaking my head with a tired exhale, my fingers tightening slightly. "It's like they're always searching for something I don't understand, and after all this time, it makes me feel more like a lab experiment than a person. It's exhausting—not knowing what they're looking for, only that you're never enough for them to stop."

Her expression softened. But I thought I saw a semblance of understanding there—and something sharper. A flicker of anger, quiet but burning, like she wanted to fix it even if she couldn't. "That sounds really tough. I can't imagine having to go through that every day."

"It is," I said, meeting her eyes. "But being with you... I don't know. It makes everything feel a little less heavy. Since I met you... well, it's the first time I've felt any type of normal... almost ordinary."

Her fingers brushed mine. A spark. Real. Immediate. I inhaled sharply, every muscle stalling like my body couldn't quite keep up with what I was feeling. For a second, all I could do was hold still and hope she didn't pull away.

"I'm glad I can be that for you, Christopher." Her voice dipped slightly, like she was testing the words before fully meaning them.

We wandered deeper into the park. Wind creaked through the trees, the world muted and still. When we reached a small wooden bridge over a frozen pond, we stopped. The ice below shimmered faintly. For a second, I wondered if this was the first time I'd actually felt calm.

"I've always loved this park," she said, leaning on the railing. "It's like a little escape from everything."

"It's beautiful," I said, then instantly felt awkward. I wasn't sure if I meant the view or her—maybe both—but I hoped she didn't notice how weird my voice sounded. She blinked, a faint smile tugging at her lips. "Thank you for sharing it with me."

She turned toward me. Her eyes held something steady, searching. "Thank you for coming. I have a feeling it can't be easy for you to get away."

"It's not," I admitted. "But it's worth it."

The world faded. It was only us.

I took a breath, sharp and cold. "Noa, I..." The words caught, stuck somewhere between my chest and my throat. I second-guessed saying them as they formed. What if it was too

71

much? Too soon? What if saying it out loud made it real—and real meant it could be taken away?

And then she kissed me. Her lips were cool from the winter air, a soft contrast to the warmth blooming in my chest. Her coat brushed my arms as she leaned in, grounding me in the realness of the moment. It was soft. Hesitant. But real. The cold vanished. Time blurred. It was only her.

When we pulled apart, smiling and breathless, her cheeks were even redder.

"I've been wanting to do that all day," she whispered, her eyes darting away for a second before returning to mine, like saying it out loud made her feel both brave and a little exposed.

"Me too," I said, brushing a strand of hair from her face. "Me too."

As we left the park behind, our footprints carved a path into the snow, leading us into a nearby café. I shrugged off my coat and rubbed my hands together, the sudden heat making my fingers tingle. The place smelled like freshly brewed coffee and sugary pastries—comfort wrapped in sweetness. The soft hum of conversation blended with the clinking of mugs and a low acoustic guitar playing in the background. Dim lights cast a golden glow across the mismatched tables and chairs, adding to the laid-back, cozy vibe.

We picked a table by the window, the frost-rimmed glass

framing a postcard view of the snowy park. I ordered two hot chocolates—thick, rich, and exactly what we needed. The warmth sank into my bones, but honestly, it was Noa that made the most difference in the warmth I felt—and that realization made me shift in my seat. I wasn't used to this kind of closeness, and I didn't know what to do with how fast it was all sinking in.

She talked easily, painting little pieces of her world with every word. I didn't want to miss a single one.

"So, you and Ami seem pretty inseparable from the way you talk about her," I said, leaning back in my chair with a grin. "How long have you been friends?"

Noa laughed, light and free. "Since first grade. She threw sand in my eyes during recess, I cried, and she called me a crybaby," Noa said with a fond smile and a slight shake of her head. "We've been best friends ever since."

I raised an eyebrow, trying not to laugh. "That's an... unconventional start to a friendship."

"What can I say? We're not exactly normal," she said with a shrug and a glint in her eye. "And normal is overrated."

I smirked. "True. Do you two fight a lot?"

"Not really," she said, rolling her eyes like she was reliving some silly inside joke. "When we do, it's over dumb stuff—like who gets the last seat on the bus during band trips."

"Band trips?" I perked up. "Like marching band? You play an instrument?"

"Yeah, the flute," she said, her voice proud but casual. "I've been playing since I was ten. I want to keep playing after high school. Juilliard's kind of my dream."

Her eyes went a little distant, her posture straightening slightly. For a moment, I could see it, Spotlight in her face, music in the air, a quiet world waiting to listen.

I didn't know what to say. That kind of dream felt foreign to me—big, loud, untouchable. It made me wonder how different we really were. She could see a future so clearly, while mine always felt like a locked door I wasn't supposed to open.

"That's... wow," I finally said. "I envy that. I've never really let myself dream that big."

Her gaze came back to me, softer this time. Her eyes flicked away for a second before meeting mine again. "That's not surprising, given how you've grown up with the Agency. I imagine they don't leave much room for daydreams."

I sighed, the weight of it all settling over me. "They don't. No family. No normal. Everything planned. Watched... Controlled."

Her smile faltered, and she looked down, tracing the rim of her cup. For a second, it seemed like she might change the subject—but then she sighed, like she'd decided to say it anyway. "Sometimes, normal isn't all it's cracked up to be," she said, after a pause. Her eyes flicked toward the window like she was considering if she should say more. "My mom... she's complicated. Always seems like she's carrying something heavy. I love her, but it feels like I'm always walking on eggshells around her."

Something in me cracked a little at that. I hadn't expected her honesty to hit me so hard. I wasn't sure why it did—that hearing someone else admit to walking on eggshells felt way too familiar. And maybe it scared me how much I understood.

"That sounds tough," I said. "I wish I could fix it."

"You kind of are," she said, her voice warm, and her fingers brushing lightly against the side of her cup. "With you, I feel like I can just be. No pretending. No pressure. Just me."

Her words hit something I didn't expect. I didn't know I needed to hear them until I did. "Yeah. I know what you mean. With you, it feels like I can finally breathe."

We sat in silence, fingers brushing—close enough to touch, but not quite. My breath caught for a second, like my body wasn't sure how to handle the spark of contact. Then the conversation picked back up, easy again, full of laughter and little stories that filled in the blanks between us. For once, the Agency and all its shadows felt far away.

When it was time to leave, I walked her home. The air was crisp, the sky above us cold and clear. At her doorstep, the porch light cast a soft halo around her, catching in her hair and making her eyes shine. I tried to ignore the SUV already there, waiting to whisk me back to my cage.

Noa stopped and turned to me. "Thank you for today, Christopher," she said softly, her voice barely above a whisper.

"Thank you, Noa," I said back, my heart thudding like it didn't know what to do with itself. And then, without overthinking it, I leaned in and kissed her. My eyes fluttered shut too fast, my breath catching. It was soft. Tentative. A maybe kind of kiss, full of what ifs and quiet hope.

I settled into the backseat, catching a glimpse of the driver's eyes in the rearview mirror—cold, unreadable, and a little too focused. A flicker of unease tightened in my chest. Maybe it was paranoia, or maybe it was survival instinct—but either way, I didn't trust the silence between us. My freedom was an illusion carefully curated by the Agency.

Back at Headquarters, the weight of the environment hit me with suffocating force. I tried to shrug it off, to act like it didn't matter, but the tension in my shoulders said otherwise. The vibrancy of the day with Noa clashed against the monotony of my reality, suffusing me with a sharp longing. I ran a hand through my hair and glanced at the wall screen in my room, its cold glow a constant reminder of where I was—and who was still in control. "The Agency is always watching." I set the empty café cup down on my desk—a simple memento, but one that whispered of a world beyond these walls.

A soft chime broke the stillness, and I turned toward the screen. An alert blinked across it in bold letters.

Report to Dr. Lang's office.

I sighed. Of course. The Agency always knew how to bring you back to earth.

Dragging my feet, I left my room and made my way toward the elevators. Lang's lab and office were tucked away behind the research wing on the fourth floor—a place that always smelled faintly of antiseptic and metal. The moment the doors slid open, the air felt colder, more sterile. The hallway stretched long and clinical, lined with frosted windows and polished floors that reflected the overhead lights like they were trying too hard to appear spotless. Each step felt heavier than the last, my shoulders curling inward and my feet dragging slightly as if the weight of the entire Agency had settled on my back.

Lang didn't look up as I entered, but his voice cut through the silence. His desk was pristine—every item perfectly aligned, a clear display of his need for control. One hand rested on the surface, fingers tapping an even rhythm like a silent metronome of tension. "Christopher, we need to talk."

He didn't wait for me to settle in. His presence was commanding, filling the room with unease.

"What's wrong?" I asked, working to keep my voice neutral, though the pulse in my ears throbbed with unease.

Dr. Lang's gaze was sharp and assessing, his eyes glinting with an edge of authority. "You've been afforded significant freedom lately," he began, his tone steely—every word crisp and calculated. "But that comes with responsibilities. We need continuous data on your health and the potential effects of your Countdown Mark reaching zero."

The words struck like an old wound reopening, familiar and raw. I forced a nod, jaw tight. "I understand."

"Good," he responded without blinking. "Remember, this is about more than only you. You're critical to what we're trying to achieve—for humanity's sake."

I wanted to demand answers, make him tell me what it is they are trying to achieve. But part of me hesitated—did I really want to know? What if the truth was worse than not knowing? Easier to play along, to keep my head down and pretend I didn't care. I stood there letting a quiet "sure" slip out in practiced compliance, hollow and detached.

He handed me a sleek, palm-sized device, its surface cold against my skin and glinting beneath the lights. "This is a handheld monitor. Keep it with you at all times. It will gather data remotely for our records. Consider it a health tracker."

I took the device, a spark of resentment flaring in my chest. My grip tightened instinctively, fingers pressing into the smooth surface harder than necessary before I forced myself to ease up. In moments that felt like freedom, the Agency's grip tightened around me like a vice. "Understood," I muttered, placing the device in my pocket.

Dr. Lang's eyes lingered on me for a moment longer, searching for something I wasn't willing to show—compliance, weakness? Whatever it was, I didn't plan on giving it to him. Then, without another word, he dismissed me and I turned and left, heading back to my room.

I collapsed onto my bed. The cold glow of artificial light washed over me as I threw an arm over my face, exhaling hard. My limbs felt heavy, like they'd carried more than the weight of my body. I closed my eyes, but the ceiling stayed with me—flat, sterile, and inescapable. My thoughts spun—frustration simmering below the surface. I wanted to think about Noa, about the warmth of earlier, but it all felt too far away now. The contrast between that world and this one scraped against something raw inside me.

The disparity between the life I wanted with Noa and the life dictated by the Agency was a chasm I wasn't sure how to cross. With Noa, I felt untethered, like I could breathe and laugh and dream. Here, I was a specimen, scrutinized, monitored, and bound by an invisible cage.

The following weeks blurred into a dance of routines and stolen moments. A flash of her smile across a café table, the brush of our hands during quiet walks—little things that lingered long after I returned to the hum of Headquarters. I met Noa as often as they would let me, each visit an escape, a taste of freedom that fueled my resolve. We wandered through her town, laughter punctuating the air, and shared whispered secrets that made the world feel infinite. With her, I found pieces of myself I never knew existed. Noa became my reminder that life was more than cold corridors and rigid expectations. But admitting how much she meant to me—it scared me. And the looming shadow of the Agency was never far. The balance I was trying to maintain was as fragile as the snow beneath our feet.

We spent countless afternoons in the park near Noa's

house, watching winter surrender to spring in slow, reluctant increments. The snow retreated in patchy layers, revealing shy hints of green beneath—like the world itself was testing the idea of warmth again, as I was testing the idea that hope might not be a trap. The shift in seasons felt cautious. Hesitant. Familiar. The scent of thawing earth clung to the breeze, and the trees stretched with the kind of stillness that only comes before blooming. Something about it echoed the quiet shift happening inside me. As we walked hand-in-hand, the world didn't change—it invited us to believe in change.

"Do you ever think about the future?" Noa asked, her voice low but certain, like she already knew the answer. "What we'll do after I graduate?"

I hesitated, not because I didn't have an answer, but because saying any of them out loud made them real. Hope wasn't something I let myself touch for more than a second—not when the future had always been a script someone else wrote. Every time I tried to picture it, it unraveled into fear, into silence, into nothing.

"I do. More than I should, probably. But it's hard to imagine anything when I don't know what the Agency has planned for me."

Her fingers curled tighter around mine, steady and warm—but there was tension there too, a coiled energy beneath the calm, like she was already bracing for whatever fight might come next.

"You're not doing this alone anymore—not unless you want to. And I don't think you do."

We sank onto a weathered bench beneath an old oak tree, its limbs outstretched like they could shield us from something bigger than weather. Laughter from a nearby playground carried on the wind—bright, reckless, free. I watched the kids sprint in circles, cheeks pink from the cold, and something twisted in my chest—tight, breath-stealing. It wasn't only longing. It was the raw, unspoken ache for a life untouched by surveillance, untouched by scripts and cages.

Noa nudged me with her shoulder. "What's going on in that head of yours?"

I drew in a breath, let it sit heavy in my chest—like I needed a second to not freak out over what I was about to say. I had to convince myself I was allowed to want anything at all. Speaking the truth out loud felt reckless. Dangerous. Wanting something more for myself wasn't only foreign, it was essentially forbidden. But I said it anyway.

"I want a future with you. But I don't know how to make that happen when the Agency owns every part of me. You deserve more than being stuck with that. You have plans, dreams... college. I don't want to drag you into my mess."

She rested her head briefly on my shoulder, then pulled back, eyes locking on mine—but not before flicking away for a heartbeat, like the weight of her own words almost caught her off guard.

"I don't want a life that's handed to me, Christopher. Not from them, not from anyone. If we're going to have a future, it's going to be one we fight for—something real, something that's ours. Not scraps of fake freedom wrapped in fear."

Her words didn't only land—they hit like jumper cables to my chest, and it scared me how quickly something inside me responded. My fingers twitched in my lap, like my body didn't know what to do with the jolt of feeling. That part of me I always tried to bury—the one that still hoped, still dreamed, still believed in escape—stirred like it hadn't in years. I wanted to trust it, to lean into it. I didn't know if I could.

"I've thought about running for years. Maybe there's a way to get far enough, to start over. But if they find us..."

She straightened, her expression sharp, but there was a flicker of something else. "Then we don't run blindly. We make a plan. A real one. I'm not interested in being reckless—but I'm so tired of pretending I'm not already falling apart from the weight of staying careful."

"There's someone who might help," I said, the words out before I could stop them. It surprised me—how quickly I reached for hope, how easily it slipped through the cracks in my caution. I never spoke without thinking. But something about her made me want to believe out loud.

"One of the agents on my security detail—Agent Harris. He's... different. If anyone could help us pull this off, it's him."

Noa's grip tightened, urgency bleeding into her voice.

"Then he's our first move. We don't have to keep living like this, asking permission just to breathe."

Her defiance wasn't loud—but it was absolute. And it rooted something steady inside me.

"One step at a time," she continued. "We build something that's ours. I want that with you. A life that isn't shadowed by them."

She looked at me then—not with blind hope, but with clarity, her gaze steady and unwavering, like she'd already made the decision and was waiting for me to catch up.

"It's going to be hell. But if we don't try... we already lost."

The wind danced through the branches above us, loosening its grip after holding tension for far too long. For a moment, the weight lifted. Laughter from the playground echoed like a memory we hadn't made yet.

"I've always wanted to travel," Noa said, almost to herself. "To see places beyond Maryland. Beyond all this."

The image came easily—her hand in mine, the two of us blasting music on backroads, laughing with the windows down, maybe eating greasy pizza in some city we'd never been to before. Days unmarked by curfews or surveillance or fear.

"That sounds... unreal," I whispered. "Like something I'm not allowed to imagine. I've spent so long training myself not to think ahead—because wanting anything more always came with consequences. The future's always belonged to them. Not me."

She leaned into me, the warmth of her body cutting through the chill. Her voice softened as she said, "We'll make it real—adventures, chaos, whatever it takes. Just you and me."

And for the first time in a long time, I let myself believe.

That evening, when I got back to Headquarters, something snapped into place. Not loud—a cold, gnawing edge in the back of my mind that hadn't been there before. Like the whole building felt different. Sharper. More like a cage than usual. A cold, sharp resolve. I needed answers—about Dr. Foster's real intentions, about Dr. Bennett's endgame, and whatever the hell they actually wanted from me. The sterile corridors felt colder than usual, the hum of the fluorescent lights scraping down my spine. That sound always reminded me of test days—of being strapped to a monitor while they tracked every twitch and blink. I hated it.

Outside my door, the chessboard waited. Silent. Mocking. Another move made, another reminder that Foster never stopped playing. I stared at the board, my hand hovering over the pieces. This wasn't a game—not to me. It was a power struggle carved into pawns and queens. One misstep, and I'd lose more than a piece. I moved my knight. Bold. Risky. Then I walked inside.

The next morning came too fast. My alarm screeched through the quiet like it had a personal vendetta. On the screen above my desk, a message blinked.

Report to the top floor immediately.

My stomach dropped. Sixth floor. Dr. Bennett's domain. A whole level of marble, glass, and control—designed to remind you exactly who was in charge.

I changed out of my pajamas, every motion dragging with dread. The elevator doors hissed open, and I stepped in, pressing the button for the sixth floor. The climb was slow. Every glowing number overhead another step toward a trap I couldn't see yet. When the doors slid open, I was hit with that familiar cocktail of too-clean air and something faintly sweet—cinnamon. Out of place. Wrong.

At the front desk, the aide looked more like a mannequin than a person. Sharp bangs, unreadable eyes, not even a nod. She buzzed the glass doors open.

Inside, Dr. Foster and Dr. Lang stood like statues on either side of Dr. Bennett's desk. She was just as I remembered—tall, precise, terrifying. Her storm-colored eyes tracked my every step like a hawk circling something already wounded.

"Christopher," Foster said, voice clipped, all efficiency and ice. "You remember Dr. Bennett."

"I do." I nodded, keeping my face blank while my insides coiled.

She didn't bother with small talk. "I've heard quite a bit about your excursions in Annapolis," she said, tone razor-sharp. "Are you enjoying your brief moments of freedom?"

It was bait. I didn't bite. "Yes, Dr. Bennett." My voice was even. Controlled. Like they trained me.

She held my gaze, then gave the slightest nod. "We need to talk about your program and what comes next. Sit."

I sat. The chair was cold and unforgiving.

"Your Mark hitting zero is significant," she said. "It opens new avenues for research. We'll need your continued cooperation."

Each word felt like a chain tightening around my throat.

"What does this new phase involve?" I asked, fighting to keep my voice from shaking.

Dr. Lang glanced at his tablet, not pretending to care. "More in-depth monitoring. Regular tests. And we'll be observing your interactions with your... soulmate."

Noa.

My chest tightened.

"My interactions with Noa?" I repeated, too sharp. I didn't care.

Bennett's mouth curled—not quite a smile. "Yes. We've never had the chance to study the soulmate connection in real time. Ms. Mitchell's graduation will make it easier. She'll be relocated to Headquarters for ongoing observation. The preparations are already underway."

The room tilted.

They wanted her here. In this place. Under their eyes. Under their control.

"You want her at the Agency? To live here?" My voice felt hollow. "Why?"

Dr. Foster answered first, calm and clinical. "The soulmate bond is a variable with significant potential for longitudinal observation. With her relocation, we can document viability across multiple dimensions—psychological, emotional, physiological. It's a controlled environment for a complex data set."

"You make it sound like she's a lab rat," I snapped.

Dr. Bennett didn't flinch. "She'll be offered top accommodations in the dorms alongside yours, access to

86

Agency-sponsored higher education, and a secure administrative liaison position. We're not imprisoning her—we're providing structure. Stability. Purpose."

"Structure?" I echoed. "You mean surveillance. Control. That's what this is."

"She's already a subject of interest," Dr. Lang added flatly, eyes still on his tablet. "This is a logical progression in the data collection sequence. Integrating her into the environment streamlines long-term analysis." He paused, finally looking up from his precious data. "In layman's terms, this transition is inevitable. It's better she adapts now rather than later."

I looked at all of them, disgust crawling up my throat. For a second, I imagined flipping the table, smashing Lang's stupid tablet to the floor, shouting until someone actually listened. But I didn't. I couldn't. All I did was clench my jaw so hard it hurt and hope they didn't notice the way my hands were shaking.

"You act like this is logical. Clinical. But it's her life. Her entire future."

Dr. Bennett folded her hands. She paused long enough to let the silence weigh heavy before speaking again. "And being your soulmate, Mr. Hawthorne," she said with cool precision, "she'll understand the responsibility that comes with that. Or she'll learn. One way or another."

"She doesn't owe you anything," I said, my voice rising before I could stop it. I leaned forward slightly, too fast, too sharp. The words escaped before I could pull them back, before I remembered how dangerous it was to let them see how much I cared.

Bennett tilted her head slightly. "She owes us everything. Her entire life was mapped out the second she was born and connected to you. Her fate is not hers alone, Mr. Hawthorne. It's part of something bigger—something we've invested years into building. You may see it as control. We see it as fulfilling our duty to the world. What we do here ensures the survival—and evolution—of humanity. This isn't about personal freedom. It's about legacy."

For a beat, I couldn't breathe. The silence felt like a failure—mine. I should've said something. Should've fought harder. Shame curled up behind my ribs, sharp and restless. I was supposed to protect her. And I'd sat there. I wanted to tell her that she was wrong—that Noa deserved to choose her own life, not have it scripted by people who saw her as a variable on a spreadsheet. But I said nothing. Because anything I said would be used, twisted, documented.

Dr. Bennett's expression shifted, but there was something smug in her stillness—a slight tilt of her head, a glance toward Foster, like she was savoring a checkmate she'd seen coming all along. "Good. Your silence speaks volumes. Your cooperation is appreciated."

The meeting ended like a door slamming shut.

I walked out, the halls closing in with every step. The elevator ride down dragged like it knew I was suffocating. By the time I hit the third floor, my body was moving, but my thoughts were fire. Smoke curling under my ribs. Rage and despair tangled so tight I couldn't separate them.

They wanted to trap her. Wrap chains around her future and call it destiny. The same way they leashed me—soft words, hard walls, and a smile that always meant surrender.

The weeks slipped by, and the Agency's shadow crept in thicker than ever, sinking its claws into every scrap of air I thought I still controlled. The rare moments I had with Noa were shrinking—compressed between surprise room checks, blood draws that left bruises, and psych evals that always felt more like interrogation than concern. Silence had started to feel like something they monitored. Like if I held my breath long enough, they'd find a reason to take that too.

One Friday evening, before the start of Noa's spring break, we met at our usual spot in the park. Winter had finally loosened its grip, leaving behind thawed mud and sharp new green. The trees were trying—raw little buds clawing toward the light—and the air buzzed with birdsong, chaotic and defiant. Like they knew change was coming, and they were daring it to try.

"Noa," I said, taking her hand. "There's something I need to tell you."

She tilted her head, one brow arching, eyes narrowing with enough edge to make me brace. "Wow. That sounds totally reassuring. Please, go on."

I almost laughed. Almost. "It's bad."

She nodded once, jaw tight. "Okay. Go."

I drew in a shaky breath. "The Agency isn't just watching me anymore. It's worse. They're shifting focus. They want you at

Headquarters after graduation. Full-time. Monitored. Studied."

Her eyes flickered—shock first, then something colder. She blinked once. Looked away.

"They want to study us together," I said, voice lower now. "Up close. Controlled. They're calling it a long-term case study."

"So... I get to be the girl in the glass box." Her voice was flat. Tired. A little broken, a little biting.

"Essentially."

She didn't look at me. Stared at the horizon, arms crossed, wind tugging at her hair like it was trying to pull her out of this reality. "And they think I'll just say yes?"

"I don't think they were going to ask permission."

"Of course not." She turned to me then, eyes hard. "Because who can say no to the Countdown Control Agency... they expect everyone to just surrender."

I swallowed, throat dry. "They think everything they do is noble. Justified. That controlling those with Marks somehow serves the world. They dress it up in legacy and purpose, and most people believe them."

Silence pressed between us—tight and suffocating.

Finally, her shoulders dropped. "If being close to you means stepping into that place, I'll do it."

"Noa—"

"I'm not saying I want to," she said sharply. "But I'm not letting them isolate you again."

"I'm not asking you to," I replied. My voice was low, shaking around the edges. "But this isn't just about being watched. It's about being owned. They'll twist everything—our words, our time, our connection. They'll turn it into something clinical. Something theirs."

She made a sound—half scoff, half growl. "They want to drag me in like some docile experiment?" She spat the word like it tasted rotten, then clenched her jaw like she was holding the rest of it back.

I blinked. "Noa..."

"I'm not a lab rat, Christopher." Her voice cracked like flint—sharp, furious, hurting. Something in me pulled tight at the sound of it—shame maybe, or awe. I'd never seen her like this. Like she was becoming a firestorm of defiance aimed straight at the people who thought they owned us. "They don't get to poke and prod and act like that's all I am. Like I'm just another part of your story."

I opened my mouth, but she kept going, pacing now. "But if I say no... if I run... what happens to Ethan? Lucas? Who steps in when Mom spirals again?" Her voice dropped on the last part, like she didn't mean to say it out loud. Like it slipped past the armor before she could catch it. "Who makes sure they eat, sleep, get to school? If I disappear, everything falls apart."

She turned to face me, arms crossed, shoulders trembling. "And if I say yes, I walk right into the machine that's been eating you alive."

"Noa," I said, barely a breath. "We'll figure it out. Together."

She shook her head. "I hate that there's no right move." She paused, eyes flicking down for a second before locking back on mine. "But I won't just sit back and let them break us." Her voice wavered—only for a breath—then sharpened. She started pacing again, her words tumbling out under her breath like she couldn't stop them. "What can we do? If we screw this up, it's not just us who'll pay for it. My brothers... my mom... they'll be the ones left behind to deal with the fallout."

A rush of heat hit my chest as I realized what she meant—fear and adrenaline and something dangerously close to hope. "Wait... Are you thinking what I think you are? Are you serious?"

"Dead serious."

I squeezed her hand. "I know we talked about something before... but, I don't know. Can we really?" I hesitated. "Can we really give them the version they want to see... but behind the curtain, plan our escape?"

She nodded once, and for a second, her expression cracked—something fragile flickering in her eyes. "That's exactly what we can do. Whatever it takes, I'm with you."

"Then I guess we'll have to figure it out as we go. We're not going to live in a cage forever," I said, the words half a promise, half a prayer. My fingers tightened around hers, holding on like it was the only thing keeping me from unraveling.

She leaned into me, head resting against my shoulder. "I know. Just... don't try to pull some noble self-sacrifice crap. We get out together. Or we don't get out."

A breath I hadn't realized I was holding slipped out slow.

"Okay," I whispered.

As the sky faded from gold to deep, violet blue, we sat in the park while the world hushed around us. The stars blinked alive, one by one, like they were daring us to believe in something we hadn't had in a long time.

CHAPTER SIX

The Middle

Noa

The morning sun slipped through the curtains like it was trying not to wake me, casting soft stripes of light across the ceiling. I stayed in bed longer than I should've, eyes open, brain spinning. Spring break had finally arrived, but the pressure hadn't lifted. Always counting down. Always watching. The irony wasn't lost on me—I'd traded one countdown for another. Only this one didn't glow or pulse. It sat there, silent and waiting, like it already knew how the story ended.

Last night's conversation with Christopher looped in my head. The CCA wanted to bring me in after graduation. Not visit. Not observe. Bring me in—test me, monitor me, strip me down into data points. The idea made my stomach twist. A future I hadn't agreed to was already waiting for me, clipboard in hand, like I'd been penciled into someone else's schedule and no one bothered to ask if I wanted the appointment.

I turned my head toward the window. The light outside was golden and soft—too gentle for how harsh everything felt. I should've been thinking about Juilliard. About symphonies and packed concert halls. About closing my eyes on stage and getting lost in music and—no. I didn't let myself go there. Not now. Not when the future was already being rewritten without me.

Still, there was today. A day with Christopher. That counted for something. I let myself exhale, slow and careful, like if I moved too fast the moment would vanish.

I forced myself out of bed, jeans and a soft gray T-shirt pulled on more out of habit than energy. At the mirror, I ran a brush through my hair and caught my own gaze—eyes sharp, tired, but still holding on. There was a flicker of excitement in them. A flicker I didn't entirely trust—because wanting things always seemed to end with them being taken. But part of me still reached for it anyway.

Downstairs smelled like bacon and burnt toast. The kitchen clanged with noise—pans, plates, tension. Mom moved like every step cost her something—setting down the frying pan with a clatter that felt short of intentional, her eyes never lifting from the stove.

"Morning, Noa," she said, her voice clipped. The words hit the air flat, like she regretted letting them out the second they landed. "Make sure you pick up groceries after you're done playing house with your little CCA poster boy."

I reached for toast, keeping my voice even. "Yeah, fine. I'll be back by eight."

"And the laundry still isn't done," she added. "I don't care what time you get in."

"Got it." I didn't look at her. If I did, I might say something that would turn the whole morning into a war zone. She knew how to turn guilt into currency—and I was always broke. Scraping by on emotional coupons and expired apologies.

Ethan and Lucas were already at the table, arguing like it was

94

their job. Ethan's voice cracked as he insisted, "Captain America is way cooler than Iron Man—he throws a frickin' shield!"

Lucas rolled his eyes so hard I thought they might fall out. "Yeah, but Iron Man's got, like, rocket feet and a brain the size of a whole library."

The sound of them bickering grounded me in the best way—a clatter of voices that somehow steadied my heart.

"Don't have too much fun without me," I said, ruffling their hair. My voice caught a little at the end—so fast I almost missed it. They still needed me. And I hated how much I wanted to stay in this moment a little longer.

"We won't!" they shouted in sync.

I grabbed my bag and stepped outside, sunlight pouring down. A whole day with Christopher stretched out ahead of me.

And underneath the weight of everything else, I wanted it.

I really, really wanted it.

The spring air was crisp and carried the sharp scent of saltwater as Christopher and I strolled along Dock Street. The harbor shimmered beside us, sunlight dancing across the ripples as boats bobbed gently in their slips. Seagulls wheeled overhead, their cries sharp but oddly cheerful. The world felt open here, wide enough to breathe in—like maybe, for a minute, I could outrun the walls closing in at home. No expectations. No lists. Just salt air and space.

"Isn't it amazing how everything feels so fresh and new?" I nudged him gently with my elbow. "Like the world's shaking off winter and starting over."

He nodded, a soft smile tugging at his lips. "It is. Days like this make me feel like anything's possible."

The usual weight I carried didn't disappear—but with him beside me, it softened. Like the ache was still there, but for once it didn't crush me—it sat quietly in the background, letting me breathe.

Our conversation flowed as easily as the waves beside us—sometimes playful, sometimes slow and steady, like we were still learning each other's edges. We stopped at a waterfront cart and grabbed ice cream—mine was a swirl of salted caramel and chocolate, his a classic vanilla he claimed was his favorite.

I laughed. "Vanilla? That's such a cop-out. You know that's like saying your favorite color is beige, right?"

He raised an eyebrow, unbothered. "Beige is underrated. It doesn't have to try so hard."

We found an empty bench overlooking the water, the wooden slats warm from the sun. I curled one leg beneath me and took a slow bite, letting the cold sweetness melt on my tongue as sunlight soaked into my skin.

Christopher glanced at me between bites. "So what's something most people don't know about you? Something you love doing?"

"I've been on the swim team since freshman year," I said, staring out at the horizon. "But outside the pool or band hall, school's... rough. I don't really have any other friends besides Ami.

Everyone else..." I shrugged. "They don't get me."

"Why do you think that is?"

I let out a small laugh, more self-preservation than amusement. "I'm nerdy. Math and band nerd. Not the cool kind. People can be cruel when you don't make sense to them. Like being different is some kind of offense they have to punish."

"Ami's a bit different like that too, right?" he asked.

"Yeah, I guess. She's in marching band with me—color guard captain—and plays violin in concert season. But she's magnetic. People... like her. Sometimes it feels like I'm orbiting around her instead of standing beside her."

He nodded, gaze drifting to the water. "I've spent most of my life isolated from anyone my age, so this whole friendship thing is pretty foreign to me." He tapped a knuckle against the branded scar where his Mark used to glow. "And even now, I'm still under a microscope. But I had to do something to fill my time, so the Agency let me pick some 'productive hobbies.' I chose karate and chess."

"Karate and chess?" I raised a brow. "That's such a bizarre combo; it's kind of perfect for you."

He grinned. "It worked. Especially chess. Agent Harris—the one I mentioned before? We play sometimes. He's... different. I don't talk about him much, but he's one of the few people who doesn't treat me like a science project. But mostly, I have long, drawn-out matches with Dr. Foster."

I blinked. "Wait, the CCA's lead scientist?"

He nodded. "I've never beaten him. It's like he's playing something bigger than what's on the board. Like I'm always three moves behind and just don't know it yet."

"That sounds infuriating."

"It is. But it also keeps me grounded. Strategy. Patience. It helps when you're living in a cage."

I studied him, genuinely impressed. "I wish I had that kind of thing for myself."

"You do, with your music." His voice was warm but firm. "You're talented, Noa. Don't let anyone convince you otherwise."

The words hit something I didn't realize was sore. I let out a breath I hadn't realized I was holding. They settled in deep.

"Thanks," I said quietly. "That means more than you know."

He bumped his shoulder into mine. "Maybe we can teach each other. I'll show you some karate—and you teach me to swim."

I blinked. "You don't know how to swim?"

He shook his head. "Nope. The Agency didn't think it was worth the risk, I guess. Can't lose their precious lab rat to the sharks."

I laughed, but it scraped a little on the way out. "Then it's a deal. But I'm not making any promises about not drowning you."

"I'll take my chances," he said, eyes sparkling.

For a while, we sat there, shoulder to shoulder, the water lapping softly below us. Christopher leaned back on the bench and let out a breath that sounded too heavy for a day like this. "Do you ever think about how different things could've been? If none of this had happened?"

"All the time," I said. "I try not to, but the thought sneaks up anyway. Especially on days like this—when things almost feel normal."

"Yeah." His voice dipped low. "It messes with your head. Wanting something you've never even had."

"Freedom," I whispered.

He turned to me. "Do you think we'll ever really have it?"

I hesitated. Then nodded. "We have to believe we will. Otherwise... what's the point?"

He let out a soft laugh—not mocking, just tired. "Then we'll write our own story," he said, almost like he was testing the words on his tongue—half hope, half disbelief.

My chest tightened, but I smiled. "Yeah. Our own story."

And then we were quiet again. Not the uncomfortable kind—this silence felt sacred. Like a truce with the world. Like a breath we didn't want to let go.

Shoulder to shoulder, we watched the harbor breathe around us.

Evening came, and Christopher and I made our way to our last stop of the day. A short ride brought us to the curb of Ami's house, nestled in one of Annapolis's quiet, affluent neighborhoods. As we stepped out of the SUV, the air was crisp and invigorating, humming with the promise of warmth and welcome. Laughter spilled through the windows, soft light glowing from behind delicate curtains.

"Hey, you two!" Ami greeted us at the door, eyes

bright. "Come in, come in! Momma's just about finished with dinner."

Inside, we kicked off our shoes and lined them neatly by the door. The warmth of the Collins' home wrapped around me like a favorite blanket—comforting and familiar. It was the kind of place that made you breathe easier without realizing it. And as quickly, I felt guilty for doing so. Like comfort was something I hadn't earned.

The house was a thoughtful fusion of two worlds—woven silk tapestries and delicate paper lanterns shared space with dark wood bookshelves filled with worn volumes of British classics. A shoji screen, its frame carved with ivy-like patterns, separated the dining area from the living room, where a cozy armchair draped in a tartan blanket faced a minimalist tea set arranged with quiet precision. The scent of green tea mingled with old book pages and something savory drifting from the kitchen. It smelled like care. Like history. Like home.

Ami's parents, Professors Donovan and Miyako Collins, were busy at work in the kitchen, setting the table and finishing up dinner. Mr. Collins, always poised like he belonged in a debate hall, nodded politely as we entered—his salt-and-pepper hair somehow making him look more scholarly. Mrs. Collins moved with quiet elegance, her soft brown eyes catching mine as she smiled. She poured tea with a practiced grace, one hand steady on the pot, the other gently guiding the cups into place—every gesture as measured and intentional as her words. Everything about her—from the way she wrapped her apron to the calm steadiness in her hands—made me feel welcome before she spoke.

"Hi, Mr. and Mrs. Collins," I greeted with a smile.

"Hello there, Noa," Mrs. Collins said warmly, her soft accent turning my name into something almost melodic. She set down her spatula and wrapped me in a hug. "And Christopher! Oh, how lovely it is to meet you!"

Christopher froze for half a beat as she pulled him into an embrace, clearly not used to this kind of welcome. I couldn't help laughing at the startled look on his face.

"Please, make yourselves at home!" she said, already guiding us toward the dining area with practiced grace.

We settled around the table, the space alive with motion and energy. The clink of dishes, the scent of roasted vegetables, the warmth of laughter—it all created a rhythm, a pulse. Ami's family was lively and generous, and I could feel how much they wanted us to feel at ease.

But beneath that joy, there was something tighter, quieter—my fingers drummed silently against my knee, my jaw clenched without thinking. The nervous energy flickered between me and Christopher, too loud to ignore. This was the first time someone from my world was meeting him, and I could tell he was doing his best not to mess things up. I wanted to shield him from the tension—make it easier for him, but I didn't know how.

As I was settling into the rhythm of it all—the warmth, the food, the familiarity—I caught the shift in Mr. Collins. The atmosphere dipped, like the room had taken a quiet breath in. Mr. Collins, who taught current events at St. John's College, had a habit of sipping his tea right before lobbing a question like a verbal chess move—always probing, always skeptical. His firm distrust of overreaching government was practically stitched into the elbow patches of his tweed jacket. From the second we sat down, I saw it in his posture—the lean forward, the narrowed eyes. He was sipping his tea. Something was coming.

"So, Christopher," he began, tone polite but pointed. "Given your ties to the Countdown Control Agency, I reckon you might shed some light on their recent move to amend laws concerning the rights of those with a Countdown Mark. What's it like, then, rubbing shoulders with folks so keen on stomping over liberties?"

The air snapped silent. Ami's face flushed, and Mrs. Collins shot her husband a stern disapproving look. Christopher froze, caught mid-reach for his glass of water. His hand hovered for a second too long, and his eyes flicked toward Mr. Collins before quickly darting away.

"Uhm..." He hesitated, that awkward half-smile tugging at his lips. "I guess it's intense sometimes. I don't really have any say in that stuff, though. You could say it's above my pay grade."

Mr. Collins leaned in, unimpressed. "I must say, I've been utterly fascinated by the CCA since their inception in 2001. Their operations are veiled in secrecy, yet they ballooned into this immense structure practically overnight. Alarming, wouldn't you say?"

Ami looked mortified. "Papa, please. You promised you wouldn't interrogate him."

Christopher's smile slipped slightly, but he didn't fold. "The Agency's goal is to study and better understand the Marks, understand how they fit in the next step of the development of society." His voice was careful—too careful. Scripted. Like every word had been drilled into him.

Mr. Collins tilted his head. "And the restrictions? The policies that strip away choice—do you find them justifiable?"

Christopher glanced at me. A flicker, like he was checking if I was still in his corner. Then he replied, "The Agency believes those measures are necessary for the safety of those with Marks—and for society's long-term well-being."

It was technically a good answer. But it didn't feel like him.

Thankfully, Mrs. Collins stepped in, gentle but firm. "Let us not turn this into a policy forum, my dear. Tonight is for food and company—not for placing our guests on trial."

"My love," Mr. Collins replied, straightening his silverware. "That's precisely what I'm doing—getting to know him, in the only way a proper Brit knows how: with a healthy dose of skepticism and pointed questions."

He might have continued, but the look Mrs. Collins gave him was sharp enough to stop time.

Conversation shifted. Lighter, easier. Christopher kept his posture apparently relaxed, but I could see it—his shoulders were too still, his eyes too focused. Every now and then, his fingers twitched against his thigh, like he was holding something back—words, nerves, maybe both. Mr. Collins watched him with quiet suspicion the rest of the meal.

After dinner, while Christopher helped Mrs. Collins with the dishes, Ami tugged me gently toward the back door. I hesitated—part of me reluctant to leave him in there alone—but Ami murmured that her dad had gotten all the interrogating out of his system for the night. We stepped out onto the back porch, where fairy lights strung overhead glowed like fireflies, casting golden halos on the garden below. The scent of lavender and cherry blossoms and damp earth drifted up as we sat on the steps, the quiet a welcome contrast to the tension still clinging to my ribs.

We found our spot beneath the cherry blossom tree, its pale petals fluttering down like soft confetti, catching in our hair and brushing the tops of our shoulders. The hush of the garden wrapped around us.

"Noa," Ami said quietly. "You seem really happy."

I turned toward her, searching her face. "I am, I think. Or at least... I want to be."

Ami didn't smile, not really. Her expression tightened in that way she got when something didn't sit right. "But you've been... I don't know. Different lately. Distant. Is everything okay?"

I looked down, tracing the edge of a petal that had fallen into my lap. "Yeah. Everything's fine. Just... a lot on my mind."

She let out a small huff. "You always do that."

"Do what?"

"Say you're fine when I know you're not. You've been doing it since we were ten. Don't think I forgot how you hid that fractured rib for two days because you didn't want to miss the science fair."

I laughed, caught off guard by the memory. "I won first place."

"You also nearly passed out during your presentation." She nudged my shoulder. "You don't have to do that with me—not now. Not with this."

I nodded slowly, swallowing hard. "It's just... complicated. Everything with Christopher, and my mom, and the twins. I'm trying to hold it all together."

Ami's voice softened. "I get that. But I miss you. I miss us. The late-night phone calls, the way we used to plan out our futures like we had any clue what we were doing."

I smiled, but my throat tightened. The words stirred something sharp beneath my ribs—the ghost of a future I wasn't sure I'd get to live. I blinked hard and looked away, not ready to let her see the tears edging at the corners of my eyes. I took a quiet breath, grounding myself, then looked back at her with a wobbly smile. "You mean when we were going to move to New York and become famous poets?"

"Or open a bookstore where we'd only sell banned books and overpriced lattes."

I laughed. "I still think that would've worked."

Ami looked at me for a long moment, her eyes shining. "I know things are changing. But I don't want to lose you in the process."

"You won't," I said, more certain than I felt. "I'm still here, Ami."

"Promise me?" she whispered.

"Promise," I whispered back, pulling her into a hug. "I'm still here, Ami."

But even as we walked back inside, the weight of that promise pressed on me—a tightness coiling in my chest, each step heavier than the last. Because I wasn't sure if I could keep it—not with the way my world was closing in around me.

I woke up with the shouting still ringing in my ears. Not like a memory—more like a bruise that hadn't faded. Not overnight. Not even a little.

The argument started the second I stepped through the front door. She was already mad that I came home late, but last night? She went nuclear. Her voice had cut through the quiet like glass breaking.

"You only think about yourself!" she'd screamed, slamming the hallway door so hard the frame rattled. Her face twisted—eyes wild, lips curled. She didn't look like her. Not really.

"I'm not your maid," she'd spat when I tried to explain. The words hit harder than any slap. I stood there, frozen, while her voice echoed off every wall. By the time I made it to my room, my hands were shaking, my throat raw. I went to bed with guilt clawing at my stomach—and woke up with it still there.

Downstairs, the clanging of pans made everything worse. I crept into the kitchen, hoping to grab cereal without being seen. Burnt toast punched me in the face the second I walked in. Mom stood stiff by the toaster, not looking at the smoking bread. Her back was straight. Too straight. Like her spine was angry. But under that anger, something looked... tired. Worn thin in a way I couldn't name.

She turned, and her face went cold. Stone cold. "I want to meet this Christopher," she said. Flat. Like she was reading from a list. But I felt the hook behind it. Guilt dressed up like concern.

My heart pounded. My fingers found my hair and tugged like that would keep me steady. "Mom, I don't know if that's a good idea."

She didn't blink. "You're my daughter. You live under my roof. If you're spending time with him, I have a right to know who he is."

"Mom, please." I was already unraveling. "Now's not a good time—"

"Why not? Are you ashamed of me?"

"No," I said too fast. I winced. "It's not that. I just... I don't want him to see this part of my life. He's already dealing with enough. I don't want to add to it."

"Add what? Me?"

I swallowed hard. "Yes. You. The way you treat me. I don't want him to see that."

Her expression faltered—only for a second. Then rage took over.

"How dare you," she whispered. Her voice shook. "After everything I've done for you..." It got louder. "I put food in your stomach, a roof over your head. That ain't easy. And this is how you repay me?"

Tears blurred my eyes. I stepped back without thinking, curling in on myself. "Mom, I'm sorry. But you don't understand. You don't know what it's like to watch you love Ethan and Lucas and just... tolerate me. I can't keep doing this."

"Then leave," she said, voice like frost. "If you think I hate you so much, think you're too good for this family, then go. But don't expect me to welcome you back when you end up with nothing."

The words hit like a punch to the gut. I couldn't breathe. My feet moved before my brain caught up. I ran. Up the stairs. Into my room. Shut the door. I collapsed on my bed and buried my face in the pillow. It smelled like old tears and fabric softener. The sobs hit hard—sharp, shaking, like my body was trying to cry it all out at once. How did it get this bad?

I thought of Christopher. The way he listens. Really listens. The way he shows up with quiet kindness like it's no big deal. Like it's easy. He sees me. And he doesn't flinch. I wouldn't let her ruin that. He had enough darkness of his own. I wouldn't drag him into mine.

Then I saw Ethan and Lucas. Their wide eyes. Their questions. My baby brothers caught in the middle of something they didn't cause and couldn't fix. If I left... who would protect them? But staying was killing me. Like rust. Slow. Inevitable. I had to find a way out. One that didn't lead to another kind of cage.

Spring break flew by, and suddenly, school was back in session. Midterms came and went. I got through them fine, when everything felt like a blur. Every day started to blend together—bits of time with Christopher snuck in like secrets, always under the CCA's watchful eye. Hallway buzzers. The scratch of pencils on scantrons. Those stiff, uncomfortable chairs that squeaked every time someone shifted. I was both relieved and on edge.

Home wasn't much better. So I threw myself into my schoolwork. Hard. Becoming valedictorian wasn't only a title—it was an escape plan, and I was so close to grabbing it. Juilliard still felt like a dream, but one I could still reach someday if I kept moving, kept acing every test and turning in every assignment. Every small win felt like proof that maybe, just maybe, I could still build something better for myself when I could leave the CCA behind. It was the only thing in my life that felt like mine to choose.

One night, I was half-done with my homework when I heard it: that soft tap-tap of rocks hitting my window. My heart jumped. I rushed over.

Christopher.

He was grinning up at me like a kid in a movie. I cracked the window, trying to keep my voice low. "What are you doing here?"

"I had to see you," he said. His voice floated up on the warm air, but there was tension under it—like part of him knew this was reckless. Knew it broke rules. "Can I come up?"

I nodded, heart thudding. "Be careful."

He climbed the tree like he'd done it a thousand times. Smooth. Quiet. Then he was in my room, and everything felt still for a second. We stared at each other—until he pulled me into a hug that nearly knocked the air out of me.

"I missed you," he whispered, breath brushing my ear.

"You saw me yesterday," I mumbled into his chest. He smelled like fresh soap and something earthy I couldn't name—but I knew it. It grounded me in a way nothing else did. With him, everything went quiet. No shouting, no walking on eggshells, no CCA shadows creeping behind my thoughts. Just this. Just calm.

"I don't care," he huffed. "I miss you the second we're

apart." His voice caught at the end, like the words cost him something. Like saying them out loud made them more real—and more terrifying.

I rolled my eyes. "That was so corny," I said, nudging him lightly with my elbow. "You rehearsed that in front of a mirror, didn't you?"

His grin curved, but it was shaky. I could feel his heartbeat against mine, a little too fast. Like he was nervous about more than the climb up the tree.

We sat on my bed, the room washed in moonlight and the soft glow from my bedside lamp. He looked nervous—his fingers twisting in the hem of his sleeve, eyes flicking toward mine and then away. But serious.

"Noa," he said, "there's something I've been wanting to ask you."

My heart skipped. "Okay...?"

He pulled a tiny velvet box from his pocket. Inside was a silver necklace. A heart-shaped locket, polished to a soft sheen, delicate but weighty in my palm. It was inlaid with tiny emeralds—my birthstone—each one set like dewdrops along the edge. The silver was etched with an intricate pattern of ivy and wildflowers curling from the edges toward the center, as if the vines were reaching for each other. In the middle, an engraving: a crescent moon tucked behind the petals of a blooming iris. It looked like something out of a fairytale. It caught the light like it had been made to find it. I opened it—and a tiny folded paper slipped out.

"Read it," he said quickly.

I did.

WILL YOU GO TO PROM WITH ME?

My whole face lit up. My hands trembled as I held the note, and my throat tightened so fast I could barely get a word out. I blinked hard, but the tears still came—soft, hot, unstoppable. "Yes," I said, laughing and crying at the same time. "Of course I will."

He exhaled, like he'd been holding his breath for hours. "Thank you. You have no idea how happy that makes me."

"Please," I sniffed, wiping at my cheeks. "Like there was ever a chance I'd say no. You bribed me with sparkly things."

"I knew the locket would win you over."

"It did," I admitted, pretending to inspect it. "Though I gotta say, if you'd gone with a full marching band and fireworks, I might've said yes louder."

He laughed under his breath. "Next time, I'll rent a parade."

I picked up the necklace, brushing his hand as I took it. "It's perfect," I whispered. "Will you help me put it on?"

He nodded. His fingers shook a little as he fastened it around my neck. The locket rested against my skin, cool and weightless and somehow everything.

"You know prom is still a month away, right?" I asked, teasing.

"Do you want me to take it back?" he asked, raising a brow with a smirk that almost didn't look like him—relaxed, playful, like the weight he usually carried had slipped off long enough to joke.

"No!" I laughed, covering it with my hands. "It's mine now."

"Thought so," he grinned.

We sat there, tangled up in each other. His arms around me. My head against his chest. The rhythm of his heart and the quiet of the room settled something in me. But in the quiet, I kept listening. For footsteps. For the creak of a floorboard. For anything that meant this was about to be taken away.

"Does anyone know you're here?" I asked softly.

He hesitated. "Only Harris. He said he didn't see anything."

I let out a breath. "That's... not the same as a yes, I guess."

He smirked. "You didn't ask how I got here—again."

I narrowed my eyes. "Okay, yeah—how did you even get here, anyway? There's no way one of your drivers dropped you off."

"Of course not," he said, all mock-offense. "You were too busy ogling me last time to ask."

I scoffed. "Right. Totally lost in the depths of your soulful brooding."

"You said it, not me."

I nudged him with my shoulder. "Seriously. How?"

"Taxi," he said with a shrug.

My eyebrows shot up. "A taxi? From CCA Headquarters to my house? Do you have any idea how expensive that is?"

He leaned back on his hands. "Yeah, well. I have one very unlimited government-issued credit card. Hooray for the misappropriation of federal funds."

I stared at him, half-laughing. "Aren't you worried about getting caught?"

He looked at me, softer now. "Not really. It's worth it."

"No." Too fast. "I—I don't want you getting in trouble. For

me."

His voice dropped, soft but firm. "You're not trouble, Noa."

I didn't say anything. I didn't have to. He knew.

This felt real. Like the life I always wanted—the normal kind. Promposals, laughter, whispered promises in the dark. For once, I wasn't thinking about the CCA's grip around our lives or my mom or the weight of everything. Just this. Just him. And for a split second, I let myself wonder if I was allowed to want this. If it was something I'd earned... or something I was borrowing until the world took it back.

The normalcy of it all made me want to cry. Because it wasn't only sweet. It was rare. Precious. A glimpse of what life could be like. What it should've been all along. And still, guilt tugged at the edges—Ethan and Lucas were down the hall, still stuck in the same chaos I was trying to escape. Wanting this felt selfish. But I wanted it anyway.

The rest of the night passed in hushes and laughter and kisses that felt like secrets. A whispered joke that made him laugh so hard he had to bury his face in my pillow to not wake the rest of the house. The soft sound of his thumb tracing my knuckles. The quiet click of the locket clasp as I turned it over in my hand, again and again, like I couldn't believe it was real. And I held onto it like it might disappear by morning.

CHAPTER SEVEN

The Unforgiven

Christopher

I wandered the maze of corridors long after lights out, my footsteps echoing enough to remind me I wasn't supposed to be here. Not technically. But rules at Headquarters always came with a thousand exceptions—especially for someone like me.

It was never truly quiet in this place. Somewhere, someone was always walking, typing, monitoring. But at this hour, everything softened. The hum of the panels, the buzz of overhead sensors, the distant shuffle of boots—they all faded into a kind of artificial stillness. I knew these halls like muscle memory. I didn't have to think to navigate them.

I wasn't exploring. I was avoiding. Sleep wasn't going to happen, and staying in my room meant sitting still long enough to feel everything pressing in. I wasn't interested in that kind of collapse.

The air here always smelled sterile—like metal and bleach. Cold. Impersonal. I stayed close to the walls, pressing my palm flat against the cold metal whenever footsteps echoed too close. I ducked under the sweep of security cameras, slipping past motion sensors with breath held and body tucked tight into shadow without tripping a single alert. I'd had practice. A stolen badge lived in my back pocket, swiped from a careless technician years ago. It still worked. It still gave me access to places I wasn't supposed to see. And it still felt like the only thing I'd ever taken for myself.

Noa was studying. Finals. Focused. Distant.

It made my chest ache more than I wanted to admit. I hated how quiet the world felt without her voice—without her grounding me, from miles away. How loose the floor beneath me felt without her anchoring it. I told myself to knock it off, that I was being pathetic, that I didn't need anyone that badly. But the ache didn't care.

I replayed our last conversation—soft promises passed between stolen minutes. A life beyond this place. A future where we could exist without protocol dictating how we breathed. It sounded ridiculous when I thought about it too hard. Dangerous, even. Like wanting it was a mistake I didn't know how to stop making. But still, I wanted it. Needed it.

I turned a corner—and my heart stuttered. Voices. My breath caught in my throat before I recognized them.

"...can't keep this from him forever, Ezekiel. Him not knowing the truth could be altering our results."

Dr. Bennett!

I pressed myself flat against the wall. Ahead, the hallway dipped into shadow—enough to disappear if I stayed still.

Dr. Foster's voice came next, cool and clipped. "We've kept it from him this long, Alice. Telling him now would only complicate our research. He needs to remain focused on the program."

My skin went tight, but I forced myself still—shoving the reaction down, flattening it into quiet. Every muscle buzzed with the wrongness of it, but I couldn't afford to feel. Not yet.

What truth?

Their footsteps grew louder. I backed deeper into the dark.

Dr. Bennett again, voice lower and uncertain. "He's our main test subject, the only one we have unfiltered access to. I just... I'm not sure how much longer we can justify this. If he found out some other way, Ezekiel, he might—"

Foster cut her off. "Your feedback has been heard, but no—Christopher must never find out. He's too important. Too unstable. And frankly, too naive to handle it. The truth would only derail everything I—we—have built."

I didn't breathe. Couldn't. Their voices trailed off with their footsteps. But the silence that followed felt heavier. Like the hallway itself was waiting to see what I'd do.

My hands curled into fists, nails biting into my palms. My jaw locked tight, like my body was trying to hold in something it didn't have words for.

Test subject. Unfiltered access. Truth I wasn't allowed to know.

I thought Dr. Bennett was the one in charge. But Foster's tone hadn't been deferential—it had been final. Like this had already been decided.

I stayed frozen long after they disappeared, heart pounding in my ears, legs locked like they'd forgotten how to move. The hallway lights flickered once—a stutter—but it made everything feel more unreal. They were hiding something. Something big. Like I didn't have the right to know what I was, what had been done to me. I'd spent nineteen years doing exactly what I was told—silent, useful, compliant—and none of it had earned me the truth. Not even a piece of it.

A burn started in my chest—slow, then blistering.

I needed to know.

Now.

The rest of the night—and most of the next day—blurred together. I moved through it like a ghost. Briefings. Exams. Meals I rarely touched—pushed around on the tray until the heat bled out and everything tasted like cardboard. My body went one way while my mind stayed glued to that hallway—Foster's voice, Bennett's silence, every fragmented word I couldn't unhear.

By lights-out, I wasn't even pretending to sleep. I lay in bed, staring at the ceiling, every muscle tense. My thoughts ran in circles. I'd replayed that conversation a hundred times, but I still couldn't make sense of it. Their voices echoed in my head—calm, calculated, inhuman. Like I was a system glitch. A failed prototype. Not a person.

Noa was the only thing that kept me tethered to now. Her voice. Her fire. Her relentless sarcasm. And yeah, maybe I was leaning on that too much. Maybe I was getting soft. But right now, she was the only part of this place that felt real. But she had another exam, and I wasn't about to dump this on her. Not until I knew what *this* was.

Fear? Anger? Numbness? I felt it. All of it. And for a second,

I hated myself for it—like feeling anything at all made me weak. Like I should've been able to shut it down, bury it, stay sharp. My chest tightened, jaw clenched so hard it hurt. But I couldn't stop it. Couldn't control any of it.

I sat up, rubbing my hands over my face. I couldn't stay here. I had to move. Do something.

Headquarters at night was dead quiet. The air felt heavier. Like the whole place was holding its breath, waiting for something to snap. I kept close to the walls, moving through shadowed hallways and blind spots I'd mapped out years ago. The badge I'd hidden for months pressed against my thigh with every step, like it knew this moment was coming.

Down the stairwell. Deeper underground. Each level dropped the temperature a few more degrees. My footsteps echoed off the metal steps, sharp and hollow. Cold bit at my fingers, at the back of my neck, like the walls themselves didn't want me here. The basement didn't try to feel human. It was concrete, steel, and secrets.

I found the lab—same reinforced door, same security reader. My fingers shook as I swiped the badge.

Beep. Click. Door open.

Inside, the lab was dim and humming with idle machines and sleeping screens. The air was too sterile, too quiet. I moved quickly, pulling open drawers and folders—nothing useful. Everything was organized to keep people out. Then I saw it: a cabinet, locked.

I hesitated, pulse loud in my ears. Then I reached for the paperclip I always kept tucked in my sleeve.

One try. Two. Snap.

The cabinet creaked open. My name stared back at me from the top file. My whole body locked up. I reached for it slowly, trying to steady my hand even though it trembled. Like touching it too fast might make it disappear—or worse, confirm everything I feared.

I opened the file. And everything broke. I didn't scream. Didn't cry. I stood there.

The words on the page blurred, then snapped into focus. And they made sense—too much sense. Things I thought I knew twisted themselves sideways. Conversations. Tests. Silences I hadn't questioned until now. My entire life reassembled itself into something unrecognizable.

I couldn't think. I couldn't breathe. Then—footsteps. I slammed the file shut, shoved it back in the cabinet, and relocked it with shaking fingers. Backed away from the desk. The doorknob turned. I didn't move. Didn't blink. Then silence. Then footsteps retreating. I didn't wait. I ran.

Up the stairs. Down the hall. The shadows swallowed me. My chest ached, lungs on fire, pulse ringing like static. I made it back to my room. Shoved a chair under the knob. Dropped to the floor. My hands wouldn't stop shaking. My thoughts spun like static in a locked room—loud, dizzying, no way out.

I wasn't okay. I didn't know if I'd ever been okay. And I wasn't sure I wanted to go back to pretending I was.

I stayed up most of the night, unable to shut off the war in my head. Anger flared hot, curling my hands into fists before I noticed. Betrayal buzzed under my skin like static, itching to erupt. But underneath it all was something heavier—grief, thick and suffocating, pressing into my chest like concrete. Not grief for a person. For the version of my life I thought I had. It wasn't perfect, but at least it felt like it was mine. Now, even that was fake.

By morning, I was wrecked. Exhausted, strung out, fingers twitching from too much adrenaline and not enough sleep, eyes dry and burning. Still wired with purpose—or maybe clinging to the idea of it. If I stopped for a second, everything might crash. Whatever this place thought it owned in me—it didn't. Not anymore. I had to get out. I had to figure out how deep this lie went. And I had to keep Noa safe.

The cafeteria buzzed like usual. People talked over each other. Trays clattered. The sharp smell of coffee mixed with something warm and fake. I sat off to the side, picking at my food, not really tasting anything. The noise felt distant, like I was underwater—muffled voices, people moving in slow motion, a dull pressure behind my eyes.

Noa's face kept flashing through my mind—her dry humor, the way she looked at me like I wasn't a lost cause, like maybe I could be more than a CCA mouthpiece. She was the only thing that felt real—the one person who cut through the static and made time slow down. When she looked at me, it was like gravity shifted. Like I actually existed. But she didn't know the truth. I didn't really know myself.

After breakfast, I headed to the fourth floor, like my schedule dictated. Lang was waiting, clipboard in hand, stiff as always.

"Good morning, Christopher. Ready for today's tests?"

"Sure," I said, managing something that sort of passed for a smile. "Let's just get it over with."

Same old routine—blood draws, reflex tests, memory prompts. Lang barely looked at me. Jotted notes and spoke like a machine. But something in me had shifted. Something he couldn't measure.

He turned to his computer but carelessly left a file on the desk. My name was on the tab. I swallowed hard, palms going damp, a chill running down my spine as the weight of it hit me. Was this smart? Stupid? Did it matter anymore?

"Dr. Lang, can I ask you something?" I kept my tone casual.

He looked up, annoyed. "What is it?"

"I've been having trouble sleeping. Anything you can recommend? Something mild?"

Lang sighed and started typing. "Expected, given the recent transitions. I'll authorize a low-dose sedative. Wait here."

As he stepped out of the lab into his adjoining office, I moved. Slid the file into my bag, zipped it closed like nothing happened. My heart thundered—vision tunneling, throat tight, ears buzzing faintly like my body already knew this could go bad fast.

"Thank you," I said when he came back in and handed over the prescription.

"Follow the dosage," he said without looking. "You'll report in again in two days."

I left, the file feeling like a brick in my bag. I couldn't read it here—not in a hallway, not with people around. I needed somewhere quiet. The fifth-floor library came to mind—nobody ever used it. Cold, quiet, forgotten.

The lights hummed softly overhead. The air smelled like paper and dust. I found a corner, sat down, and opened the file. Pages and pages of charts. Bloodwork. Behavior reports. Then—

"Developmental History and Genetic Modifications."

The words punched the air out of my lungs. I read everything. They'd altered me—before I was even born. I didn't understand all the science behind it. But from what I could tell, every strength, every weakness, every decision was somehow mapped out—I wasn't only observed. I was designed. Built. I wasn't a person. I was a product.

My hands shook. My jaw locked. I felt like I was gonna throw up—stomach twisting, skin clammy, the urge to gag climbing my throat. I hated myself for it. All the training, all the years of discipline, and I was falling apart over a few pages of truth. Weak. That's what it felt like. And I had no idea how to stop it.

Then I heard the door. I slammed the file shut, shoved it in my bag, and ducked between the shelves.

Dr. Bennett had walked into the library. What in the world was she doing here? Did she know I took the file? How could she?

She moved slow, scanning like she already knew someone was hiding. I held my breath, crouched low. Her eyes passed over my row. I didn't wait. I slipped out the far end, every step calculated, quiet.

Back in my room, I locked the door behind me and slid to the floor, phone already in hand. My thumbs flew.

We need to meet tonight.

My hands wouldn't stop shaking. Noa was the only person I knew I could trust. And after what I'd read, I needed her more than ever—though part of me hated that, too. Needing someone felt dangerous. Thinking it made my shoulders lock up. But I couldn't. Not with her. She was the only part of this that hadn't broken.

The truth had burned everything else down. All that was left was the wreckage—and her.

CHAPTER EIGHT
The Pretender

Noa

The spring night was warm and still, the stars twinkling above like a thousand tiny diamonds. As I hurried down the familiar path to our meeting spot, anticipation thrummed through me, making my breath come faster and my fists curl at my sides. I kept adjusting my sleeves, a nervous habit I couldn't seem to break, each step quickening my heartbeat. The moonlight filtered through the branches of the tall oaks, casting playful shadows on the ground. Every rustle of the leaves and crack of a twig heightened my senses, but I pressed on, knowing Christopher was waiting for me.

If he'd snuck out at three in the morning, something was seriously wrong. More so that he asked to meet here instead of showing up at my window again. To say I was worried was an understatement. When I reached our secret spot, I spotted Christopher's silhouette leaning against the trunk of our favorite tree. His face was half-hidden in shadows, but the tension in his posture was unmistakable.

And the rest of him—his hair was a mess, his clothes rumpled, eyes too wide like he hadn't blinked in minutes. He looked unhinged in a way that made my stomach drop. Not because I was scared of him. Because I wasn't. I was scared for him.

Seeing him like that filled me with dread—my stomach dropped and my chest clenched all at once. My pace faltered for half a second before I forced myself forward, pulse racing. Whatever he had discovered wasn't small.

"Noa," he called softly, his voice not much louder than a whisper but laced with urgency. I quickened my pace and joined him, catching the tremble in his hands. I hesitated for a second, unsure if he wanted me close, then stepped beside him and leaned against the tree. The bark was rough against my back, grounding me. I didn't say anything yet—stayed still, heart pounding, waiting for him to speak.

"What happened, Christopher? What's going on?"

He was shaking. Not hands—his whole body. Like he couldn't hold it in. He stepped away from the tree and started pacing, his movements sharp and restless. His breath hitched like he'd been holding it too long.

Then he took a breath, locking eyes with me. "I found out something huge. The Agency, Dr. Foster, Dr. Bennett... they've been hiding things from me. It changes everything."

The wind stirred the leaves above us, stealing his words into the dark. I saw the weight in his eyes, the pressure threatening to break him. "Tell me," I said, trying to keep my voice steady. My throat tightened, and I shifted my weight from one foot to the other, suddenly aware of how rooted he looked—even in his unraveling. My jaw clenched, a quiet reflex against the panic curling in my chest.

"I snuck into Dr. Foster's office last night," he said, the words tumbling out so fast they almost blurred together. He was pacing again, shoulders tight, movements jagged. "Found a file with my name on it. My parents aren't dead." He stopped suddenly, like the weight of it caught up to him mid-sentence. "My mom didn't die in childbirth. My dad didn't die in a car crash."

"What?" I gasped. "They're alive?"

"No," he shook his head. "I'm sure whoever Samuel and Judith were, they're dead. If they ever existed."

"I don't get it... What exactly did you find?"

"Samuel and Judith Hawthorne aren't my parents." His voice dropped to a whisper. "My real father is Ezekiel Foster. My mother is Alice Bennett. Dr. Foster and Dr. Bennett are my parents."

The words hit me like a punch to the gut. I stepped back, hand flying to my mouth. "What? How... how is that possible?"

"They lied to me my entire life," he said, voice cracking. "With all the genetic altering, I wasn't born—I was made. I'm not their son. I'm their... project."

The air between us went still, too thick, like breathing might snap something. We didn't speak. Didn't move. Stood there in the dark, shoulders brushing, both of us struggling to stay upright under the pressure. I reached for his hand, squeezing it tight, trying to anchor both of us. My throat felt tight, useless. Nothing I could say would fix this. "Oh, Christopher, I'm so sorry," I said softly, barely more than a whisper. "They didn't just lie—they took everything from you. Your past. Your parents. Even your name." My voice trembled. "And now you're the one left to deal with the fallout."

He nodded, jaw tight. "We have to get out of here, sooner

126

rather than later. I can't stay under their control. But we need a plan—something careful, something they won't see coming. We can't just keep talking about it anymore, we have to act."

"What can we do?"

He scanned the shadows, though I'm not sure why. By now, he was so loud everyone within a couple of miles could have heard him. His pacing had turned frantic, each step hitting the ground. His breaths came short and sharp, his chest rising and falling like he couldn't catch up to everything crashing through his mind.

"I don't know! I don't know anything. What else are they hiding? What was the point of all those tests? What else did they do to me? And what does this have to do with their supposed agenda, researching the Countdown Marks? Why all these laws for us with Marks, and only us? I don't understand any of it anymore!"

His voice cracked at the end. He shoved his hands into his hair and let out a sharp, frustrated breath before turning and punching the trunk of the tree hard enough to make the bark splinter. He stayed like that, shoulders heaving, forehead pressed to the bark like he was trying to hold himself in place.

"We can't run until I know more," he said finally, voice lower now. "If I can find something that incriminates them—something solid—we might be able to get out without them coming after us."

"You know I'm with you," I said quickly, then hesitated, the words catching in my throat. A flicker of guilt twisted in my stomach—because as I said it, part of me was already thinking of my brothers. Already wondering what it would cost. "But I have to think about my brothers, too. I don't know how I could leave them behind."

His face fell. "Noa, you might have to. They're too young. We'll be lucky to get out at all, let alone with anyone else. If we can come back for them, we will. But right now, we have to focus on surviving... But I'll understand if you can't come with me. I know what they mean to you."

He looked so defeated, like he was bracing for me to walk away. I stepped closer, heart twisting. "I can't leave them," I whispered. "But I also can't abandon you. I don't have an answer yet... but we'll figure it out. Somehow."

The night deepened around us, silence stretching long and heavy. But in that quiet, something shifted.

Christopher slid down the trunk of the tree until he was sitting with his back against the bark. I followed, settling beside him in the grass.

"I'll start small," Christopher said. "Look for gaps. Stuff they leave out. Reports left open. Offhand comments they don't think I'll catch. I won't do anything obvious—I want to see how deep this goes. If they could hide the fact that the two biggest players in the CCA are my parents... what else are they hiding? From me? From the public?"

I nodded. "Just don't get caught."

"I won't," he said, but the tight line of his jaw said otherwise.

"I remembered something," I said slowly, then paused. For a second, I wasn't sure if it was worth mentioning—if it would sound stupid or like I was grasping at straws. But the memory had been nagging at me ever since he started asking all these questions—all the whys and hows that didn't have answers. "A couple months ago, on the bus... some girls were talking about Jessica Simmons—she's a junior. Or was, I guess. They said she got pregnant, and the guy wasn't her soulmate. Supposedly, the CCA got involved."

His eyes sharpened. "What happened to her?"

"Depends who you ask. One girl said she was forced into some kind of procedure. Another said she ran. But no one saw her after that."

He was quiet. "You think the Agency did something to her?"

"I don't know," I admitted. "Back then it just felt like gossip. Or some horror story parents make up to keep us in line, make sure we followed the new laws. But now? I don't know."

Christopher looked at me, stunned. His eyes darted away like he couldn't quite hold my gaze. "Before now, I never would've believed the Agency would hurt someone," he said, his voice lower, almost ashamed. "I didn't think the way they treated me was necessarily wrong. It was just... normal." He rubbed the back of his neck, staring at the ground. "My normal." He paused, voice cracking. "But now I don't know what to believe."

I squeezed his hand. "Then believe in me," I said, the words catching before they fully left my mouth. I wasn't sure I believed in myself half the time. "In us." My voice was softer now. "We'll figure this out. Somehow."

He nodded, then hesitated. "If I find anything solid, I'll text you first. If something happens..." His voice trailed off for a moment. He looked away, jaw tight. "I'll find a way to reach you. Maybe convince Harris to get a message to you." He paused again, then met my eyes. "Just promise you won't come looking."

My chest tightened. "You better stay in one piece," I said, aiming for a joke, but it came out too sharp—too raw. My voice cracked halfway through, the fear bleeding into the space between us before I could swallow it down. "Or I'll break into that ugly headquarters myself just to slap you."

That earned a faint smile. "Noted."

We sat in silence again, the kind that hums with everything unsaid. We didn't have it all figured out. Not even close. But we weren't frozen anymore. We had a place to start. And maybe that should've been comforting—but it wasn't. Not really. It was the only option we had left that didn't feel like giving up.

Ami and I pulled into her driveway after school. My brain was scrambled—pulled in a dozen directions at once. The ride had been quiet. I couldn't focus on small talk, not with everything Christopher had told me still ricocheting in my head. Stuff about the CCA. The soulmate experiments. How they'd watched him his whole life like he was some kind of science project. My hands were freezing though my chest burned. I couldn't catch my breath—like my body couldn't decide if I should run or curl into a ball.

Ami parked and turned toward me, brow furrowed, her eyes scanning my face like she could see the chaos I was trying to hide. "You seemed off today during band practice. Everything okay?"

I forced a smile. Tried to sound normal. "Just a lot on my mind. Finals. College applications. The usual."

My fingers picked at the frayed seam of the seatbelt, eyes fixed anywhere but her face. My chest ached like my body knew I wasn't telling the truth, even if technically, I hadn't lied. I didn't want to push her away. But letting her in? That felt like a different kind of danger.

"You sure that's all?" she asked, clearly not buying it.

I barely processed the question—my attention already hijacked by a text from Christopher.

> Found something.
>
> Need to meet.

"I just... need some air," I said, maybe cutting her off, maybe not. "Actually, would you mind giving me a ride somewhere?"

Ami blinked. "Right now?"

"Yeah," I said, trying to keep my voice casual. "I just really need to clear my head."

Ami frowned. "But I thought we were going to study for the physics test." Her voice dipped, sarcasm threading through the words—but there was something else there too. Something soft and a little hurt. "You said you wanted to go over the practice questions together."

"I know," I said quickly. "I'm sorry. I just—can we do that tomorrow?"

She scoffed. "You know we already had plans for a girls' night tomorrow..."

"Yeah, right. I knew that, of course. I meant at school, homeroom or something." I tried not to sound irritated, but the edge still slipped out. Heat climbed up my neck—I knew I was brushing her off. And the worst part? I didn't know how to stop. The urge to explain bubbled up, but I swallowed it down. Saying too much felt just as dangerous.

"Can I have the ride, or do I need to just walk from here?"

She stared at me, her lips pressed into a thin line. "Where am I even taking you?"

"Just drop me a few blocks from Madison and Fifth. I'll walk from there."

Ami's brow scrunched. "That's not even close to your house."

"I know. It's fine. I just need some space. Please?"

She didn't answer right away. Sighed and put the car in gear.

"You're meeting Christopher, aren't you?" she asked, fingers tapping the steering wheel like she couldn't sit still. She didn't look at me.

I didn't answer right away. "It's important."

"Seriously, Noa? We had plans." Her voice cracked—barely—but I heard it. She stared at her lap, hands gripping the hem of her hoodie like it might slip away if she didn't hold on tight. "You blow me off the second he texts and now want to be dropped off in some random spot like it's nothing?" Her voice wasn't loud, but the frustration was thick. "This is getting really weird."

We didn't speak again until she pulled up to the curb.

"Seems like everything's important when it's about him. I

know he's your soulmate and all, but I don't know... Something's off. And it all started when you met him."

That hit harder than I expected. I turned away, guilt flaring in my chest. She wasn't wrong—and I hated that she noticed. "It has nothing to do with him, okay? I promise. And I'll still come by tomorrow. Girls' night."

She nodded, jaw tight. "Right."

I hesitated, then opened the door. "Thanks for the ride."

Her voice dropped. "Just don't forget who's been here the whole time." Her eyes caught mine—for a second—and it felt like a challenge. Like she was daring me to prove she still mattered. Then she looked away, jaw clenched like she'd said more than she wanted to.

I shut the door before I could answer, her words clinging to me like thorns.

As I walked away, the warm evening air wrapped around me, but it didn't help. Not with the way everything pressed against my chest. Ami had every right to be upset. And yeah... she was probably right. The deeper I got into whatever this was with Christopher, the more distance I was putting between us. I hadn't realized how bad it had gotten until now.

From the outside, I probably looked like a cliché. The girl who ditched her best friend the second a boy looked her way. My throat tightened. Shame twisted in my stomach, sharp and tangled. And maybe part of me hated how much that image fit. I didn't want to be that girl—but I didn't know how to be anyone else right now. I felt stuck in a part I never asked for, and walking away felt impossible.

But this wasn't about that. This was bigger. It had to be.

Still didn't mean it didn't hurt.

I told myself I was keeping her safe. That the truth would only put her in danger. But deep down, I knew that wasn't the full story. I wasn't only protecting her—I was locking her out. And if I kept doing that, I was going to lose her.

The tension with Ami. My mom breathing down my neck. My brother looking at me like I had answers I didn't. It wasn't only the weight of all of it—it was how lonely it felt underneath. Like something had hollowed me out. I was still showing up, still smiling, but I felt like glass—one wrong word and I'd crack. I was surrounded by people, but somehow still invisible. Still carrying everything alone. And that was before you counted the mess with Christopher and the CCA. It felt like I was trying to hold up the whole world on my shoulders.

As I walked away, I could still feel Ami's concern trailing me like static. Our friendship had always been solid. Familiar. The kind of safe that didn't need explaining. But now? There was a crack running down the middle. Not big enough to shatter things, but enough to feel it. And I kept walking. Didn't slow down. Didn't look back. Because if I did, I might have to admit I'm the one that created the crack in the first place.

My heart pounded with a mix of anticipation and dread. The park felt different tonight—wet, unsettled. Rain had started right after Ami dropped me off, light at first, now more of a mist that clung to my jacket and dampened my hair. The pavement glistened, and the trees dripped around me. It wasn't cold, not exactly, but cool enough to raise goosebumps and keep my shoulders tense. Every rustle, every shift of wind prickled against my skin, like the night itself was warning me.

Christopher was already there when I arrived, leaning against a tree, arms crossed, posture rigid. He looked like he was made of tension. Something about the way he held himself made me feel steadier and more on edge all at once—like if he could keep it together, maybe I could too. He looked wrecked—hair tousled, dark shadows under his eyes, like sleep hadn't visited in days. I'd seen him yesterday, but somehow he looked worse. When his eyes met mine, there was clarity. Determination. And beneath that, barely visible—fear.

"What did you find?" I asked, voice low and rough at the edges.

He nodded. Rain tapped lightly on the tree canopy above us, threading through the silence. It stretched between us, tight and fragile.

"I think so. I found a report," he said finally. "Internal research summaries. Mostly redacted. Buried under medical labels and some kind of genetic jargon."

I didn't know what half of that meant. I didn't need to. The way he said it—like it had punched a hole in everything he believed—was enough.

"Dates that don't match up to public record," he continued. "And something about genetic trials that started before Marks even existed, before I was born."

His jaw clenched. But there was something steady in his eyes—calm, almost defiant. Brave, maybe. Or reckless. I couldn't tell. All I knew was that it scared me more than if he'd looked afraid.

"It's not concrete, not yet," he said. "But it's something. Enough to know they've been hiding way more than I thought. And if I can get into Dr. Bennett's office, I might be able to piece together enough to get us out. To make the Agency back off."

My stomach twisted, and my eyes went wide. "Do you mean you want to try and blackmail our way out?"

He didn't answer. Just held my gaze with that steady, unreadable look—like he'd already made peace with this idea... but I hadn't. I shifted my weight, arms folded tight across my chest like they could hold something in. The panic stayed behind my ribs, but barely. A chill crept up my spine. I gripped my arms tighter, trying to steady the tremble in my hands. I forced myself to breathe.

"What would be the next step?"

He raked a hand through his hair, started pacing, his boots kicking up water as he moved. The rain had picked up—steadier now, heavier in the quiet spaces between our words.

"Her office has a secure file cabinet. I saw it last time I was called in. If there's anything real, it's in there. Tomorrow night, there's a scheduled system maintenance. Security protocols will drop for a few minutes—that's my window."

He looked at me then, really looked. Reached out and took my hand. The contact jolted something in me—like my fear had been running under the surface, and now it had a place to land. My fingers curled into his without thinking. It didn't make the panic go away, but it made it quieter.

"I've got this, Noa. I'll be careful. I promise."

"Christopher, if they catch you..."

My voice cracked. The thought of him locked away—or worse—made my lungs seize. I blinked hard and angled my face away from his, like if I could keep my face still enough, maybe none of it would happen. Then I forced my expression to stillness, shoved the panic down deep, and met his eyes again.

He squeezed my hand tight. "I won't get caught. I have to do this."

The silence after those words didn't settle. It hovered. It pressed against my skin, waiting to ignite.

We stood there in the dark, our backs to the same tree, the bark slick with rain, the damp starting to creep through my jeans. The plan unfolded between us in whispers. Timelines. Exit points. Backup contingencies if something went wrong. All of it built on the hope that no one would see him slip through the cracks. If someone heard him. If he dropped something. If one of those cameras turned back on too soon. All it would take was a second—and they'd take him, and I wouldn't know until he didn't come back.

I hesitated, fingers digging into my palm before I spoke. "You'll need to be invisible," I said, my voice barely audible. "No noise. No second chances."

He nodded once. "I know. I've been watching so much over the years. I've mapped out their routes, Dr. Bennett's habits. If

I'm wrong about the timing—"

"Then you don't go."

His eyes met mine again. That same storm brewing in blue—pulling me in and pushing me back all at once. I couldn't tell if I felt drawn to it or afraid of getting swallowed whole.

"I have to, Noa. I don't know if I'll get another chance like this. They haven't done a maintenance this big in years. I don't know when I'll get another shot."

My chest tightened with every step we mapped out. The rain fell harder now, more insistent, dripping from my hair and running down the back of my neck. Every risk he brushed past like it didn't matter was like the rain soaking through our clothes—constant and ignored.

"Well... then I guess you better not get caught," I whispered, more to myself than him.

We didn't say anything after that. We didn't have to. The air between us said it all—quiet and heavy. Only there was no stillness now. Rain pattered steady against the leaves and the ground, building in rhythm like a warning before the downpour. It slicked the grass and blurred the edges of everything, the way his fingers flexed once against mine and then went still. Every part of me was on edge, but I didn't pull away.

It had become clear—this wasn't only about escape for Christopher. This was about the truth. My heart was hammering, because what came next wasn't only risk. It was change. The kind that doesn't let you go back. The kind that tears things open. If this worked, it could set us free—or ruin us. I didn't know what scared me more: him getting caught, or him pulling it off. What if the truth shattered everything we thought we knew? What if trying to fix it broke it worse? What if there wasn't something better—another kind of cage, wearing a different name?

The evening sky was a tapestry of deep blues and purples as I walked up the path to Ami's house. Laughter and music floated through the open windows, wrapping around me like a warm embrace. Tonight was supposed to be a girls' night, a chance to relax and distract myself from the chaos that had become my life. But it was hard to push aside the nagging worry about Christopher—how long he'd be gone, what he might find, what might happen if something went wrong.

My breath caught without warning, and I checked my phone again even though I knew it wouldn't buzz. Seeing the blank screen made the ache sharper. My stomach felt tight, and I kept clenching and unclenching my hands like that might trick my body into relaxing.

It didn't help that there was still something off-kilter between Ami and me. We hadn't argued, not really, but her words in the car yesterday stuck with me—the way she wouldn't look at me, the quiet in her voice that didn't feel like comfort. I could still feel the crack between us. It hadn't blown up into anything, but it left something unsettled, a quiet ripple beneath the surface. We hadn't really spoken much since then, and I worried about what I was about to walk into.

Ami greeted me at the door with a bright smile, her energy infectious. "Hey, Noa! Come on in. We've got popcorn, movies, and way too much candy."

It was like she'd hit reset, like none of yesterday's tension had happened at all. Part of me wanted to bring it up—clear the air—but I didn't want to ruin the chance at normal, either. I tried to match her smile, but it took effort. Maybe I felt guilty. Or maybe I really needed tonight to feel normal.

"Sounds perfect," I said, following her inside.

Inside, the warmth and coziness of Ami's home enveloped me like a layer of warmth I hadn't realized I needed. The living room was filled with soft cushions, fairy lights twinkling overhead, and the aroma of freshly popped popcorn wafting through the air. Familiar, safe. Almost enough to believe nothing had ever been wrong.

With her parents out for the evening, we had the run of the house. We settled onto the couch, a pile of snacks between us, and started Titanic. We never actually made it through the whole thing on girls' nights—it was too long, and we always got distracted. But for some reason, we kept trying. It had become a tradition. One of our favorite BCM movies. Before Countdown Marks.

Ami nudged me with her elbow. "Think we'll actually finish it this time?"

I smirked. "Not a chance."

She laughed, and for a moment, it felt like we were still us.

As the movie played, I watched Rose and Jack fall for each other in the span of days, drawn together by nothing but instinct and timing. No glowing numbers. No guarantees. Only chaos and connection. It was wild to think people used to live like that—falling in love without knowing whether it was right or lasting. Guessing. Hoping. Choosing.

Countdown Marks gave us answers, but I wasn't sure they made anything easier. Maybe we'd gained certainty—but lost the wonder. Was it better now that people knew? Or had the Marks made everything worse?

I tried to lose myself in the storyline, but my mind kept drifting back to Christopher. The scenes blurred as thoughts of the night's dangers crept in. I found myself shifting in my seat like I could somehow shake the thoughts loose.

Ami must have sensed my distraction because she paused the movie and turned to me, concern etched on her face. "Noa, are you okay? You've been so quiet all night."

"Sorry, Ami," I sighed, struggling to balance honesty with the need to protect her. I had to tell her something, I couldn't keep lying to her. "It's just... I had another fight with my mom."

Ami's eyes softened. She tucked one leg beneath her and leaned in slightly, her voice quieter than usual, like she didn't want to press too hard. "What happened this time?"

I looked down at my hands, picking at an imaginary thread on my PJs. "She doesn't understand what I'm going through. We argued about my responsibilities at home, and it got pretty bad. And she wants to meet Christopher, and I don't know how to handle it."

Ami leaned in, her voice gentle. "What did she say?"

I took a shaky breath, the memory of the argument still

fresh. "She said some pretty awful things. Essentially, I'm selfish for not helping out more, that I'm too focused on Christopher and school, and that I'm letting everyone down." I couldn't bring myself to tell Ami about Mom's cruel ultimatum to leave the house and never look back.

Ami's face twisted in sympathy. "Noa, that's so unfair. You're juggling so much already."

"I know," I whispered. "I feel like I'm being pulled in a million directions. She doesn't see how much pressure I'm under. And then she demanded to meet Christopher, like that would solve everything."

Ami looked uncertain, biting her lip like she wasn't sure if what she was about to say would help or make things worse. "I've never had a fight like that with my parents. I can't imagine how hard it must be. But maybe she just wants to understand what's going on with you?"

I shook my head, the hurt still raw. "It didn't feel like that. It felt like she was trying to control me, to make me feel guilty for wanting something more. The things she said... they really hurt. And I'm tired of people thinking they can control me."

"What do you mean? Who else is trying to control you?"

My breath caught. I hadn't meant to say that much. I scrambled to recover, trying to sound casual. "I... I didn't mean it like that. It just feels like everything's already decided for me. Here's your soulmate. Graduate. Go to college. Check all the boxes. I feel like I'm disappearing inside someone else's plan."

Ami reached out and squeezed my hand, her touch warm and reassuring. I wanted to melt into it, to let it undo everything tightening inside me—but part of me flinched anyway. Not from her, but from how exposed I suddenly felt. Like kindness made everything real in a way silence never could.

"I'm so sorry, Noa. I wish I knew what to say."

Tears welled up in my eyes, and I blinked them away, tilting my head back and biting the inside of my cheek. I dug my thumbnail into the edge of my sleeve, focusing on the sting instead of the ache behind my eyes—anything to keep it together. "Thanks, Ami. It just sucks, you know? I want to be there for my brothers, too, to help out my mom, but I also want to have my own life. Is that so wrong?"

"No, it's not wrong at all," Ami declared firmly. "You're allowed to have your own dreams and your own life. Your mom should respect that."

I nodded, feeling a little better. "I just don't know how to make her understand. Every time we talk, it ends in a fight."

Ami sighed, looking thoughtful. "Maybe... you need to find a way to show her. Not just tell her but show her how much you care about your family and your dreams... I don't know; it's a thought."

I gave her a small smile. "Thanks, Ami. I'll think about it. It helps to talk about it."

She returned the smile, and for a second, things felt normal again—almost. Like maybe that weird tension from earlier had melted into the popcorn and candy between us. But my chest still felt tight, and every time she laughed, I caught myself wondering if she meant it—or if we were both pretending not to notice the crack still sitting there between us.

"Anytime, Noa," she said brightly. "That's what friends are

for."

Her voice was light, maybe genuine—but something in me paused. Like I wasn't sure if she meant it the way she used to. Or maybe I didn't know how to accept it without wondering what was between the lines.

We resumed the movie, but the distraction only lasted so long. My thoughts kept drifting back to my brothers, Ethan and Lucas, and the harsh reality that I might have to leave them behind. The idea tore at my heart, but I knew I had to find a way to protect them from the CCA's reach. The guilt sat heavy, making it hard to sit still. I found myself half-present, fidgeting with the edge of my sleeve, glancing at my phone.

We ended up turning the movie off prematurely, as predicted, and Ami jumped up and grabbed a board game from the shelf. "How about a round of this? It'll be fun, and it might take your mind off things." I agreed, grateful for her effort to lift my spirits. We played and laughed, the game providing a temporary escape.

My laughter came easily enough, but it always felt a beat too loud, a little too eager. I kept sneaking glances at Ami, watching for any flicker of tension that might rise to the surface. But she was smiling, focused, like nothing had ever cracked between us—and maybe that made it harder. Like the silence between moves said more than either of us was willing to admit. When we laughed, the tension never really left. It lingered between us, thin and quiet, like the frayed edge of something we were both pretending wasn't coming undone.

Finally, as the night wore on, Ami asked one of the

questions I had been dreading. "Noa, what's really going on with Christopher? You've been so on edge lately. Is there something you're not telling me?"

I took a deep breath, the urge to confide in her almost overwhelming. "Ami, I wish I could explain everything. But it's complicated. Just know that Christopher and I are dealing with something big, and it's not something I can share right now."

Ami's eyes softened with concern. "Is it... sex? Is he pressuring you? I'll totally beat him up for you if you need me to!"

Her sudden outburst made me burst into laughter, which was exactly what I needed. "No! It's nothing like that, I swear."

As the night came to an end, I found myself grateful for Ami's support, steady and real, even if a little broken beneath the surface. I curled up in my usual nest of blankets beside her bed, staring at the ceiling in the dim light. I was utterly unable to stop thinking about Christopher—wondering if he was safe, if everything had gone according to plan.

I tried to force myself to sleep, knowing tomorrow would come with new complications. But for now, I held tight to the fragile calm Ami had offered me, even if it only lasted a few hours.

CHAPTER NINE

Behind Blue Eyes

Christopher

I was in the middle of my weekly karate session—one of the few activities around here I actually enjoyed. The dojo-style training room smelled like sweat and disinfectant, the soft thuds of movement echoing off the polished hardwood floor and mirrored walls. They'd built it just for me—or so they said. One of the few "freedoms" I'd been allowed to choose. But nothing around here ever really felt like a choice. Everything had limits. Conditions. Hidden expectations dressed up like generosity. This room was yet another way to make me feel like I had control—when all it really did was remind me how little I actually did. Their version of generosity, dressed up like care.

One of the automatic doors slid open, and an agent stepped inside—black suit, crisp white shirt, black tie, and an almost invisible earpiece curled behind his ear like something out of Men in Black. He looked straight ahead, unreadable. One of my "security" detail. They were all robots to me. Security detail was a joke. They weren't securing anything except my obedience.

The agent crossed the mat and leaned to whisper something in my instructor's ear. The man nodded once, then turned to me with a strange tightness in his jaw. "That's it for today, Christopher. You've been summoned to Dr. Foster's office. Immediately."

My pulse skipped—more like lurched. My body reacted before my mind caught up, like some conditioned response buried too deep to unlearn. One summons and I was already bracing for punishment.

I wiped sweat from my brow as I grabbed my phone from the bench, my fingers twitching before I could still them. The alert glared up at me, and I tightened my grip like my phone might fall if I let the panic win.

> REPORT TO DR. FOSTER'S OFFICE. IMMEDIATELY.

No explanation. No context. Only those six words, pulsing like a warning shot through my chest.

The hallway outside felt colder than it should've, the artificial air brushing against my damp skin like a warning. It settled into my chest, echoing the dread already clawing its way up my spine. I took the elevator down to the first basement level, the doors sliding open with a soft ding. As I stepped into the basement, the omnipresent hum of machinery filled the air—a constant reminder of the facility's cold efficiency. I walked past Foster's lab until I reached his office. As the door closed behind me, a sense of foreboding settled over me like a second skin.

"Sit down, Christopher," Dr. Foster commanded, his voice stern. I sat, a hollow feeling growing in the pit of my stomach.

"Why have you been visiting the same spot at the park multiple nights in a row?" he asked, his tone calm yet threaded with an unyielding tension.

My mind raced, searching for an excuse. How did they know? I had been so careful. "I... I just like the view," I stammered, attempting to sound nonchalant.

Dr. Foster's penetrating gaze felt like it could see straight through me. "Don't lie to me, Christopher. We know everything. You're being tracked. Surely you know that by now."

His words hit me like a physical blow. *Tracked?* How?

My mind scrambled for answers until something clicked. That shot. Weeks ago, in the lab with Dr. Lang—he'd jabbed a syringe filled with some clear fluid into my arm. No warning. No explanation. A muttered line about protocol and a sharp sting that stayed with me longer than it should've.

I'd chalked it up to routine discomfort. Another test. Another needle. I was distracted, too. I had just met Noa a couple hours earlier. But now that I think about it, and the way Lang avoided eye contact... it was obvious. It hadn't been routine at all.

What did they do to me?

My stomach turned. The room tilted slightly, like my body couldn't decide if it was going to collapse or run. A wave of nausea rose in my throat, bitter and paralyzing, as panic clawed its way up my spine. They'd been watching me the entire time. Sneaking out to the park in the middle of the night, or going to Noa's without permission.

...my break-in to Foster's lab.

My chest tightened, panic surging as I understood—they knew everything. They knew I'd broken into Dr. Foster's lab. Did he know I knew the truth?

What felt like hours of reeling was only a couple minutes. I forced myself to breathe, to focus. Shoving the panic down was muscle memory by now—compartmentalizing had kept me going this long. I couldn't afford to unravel, not here. Not in front of him. This was a test, another play of the chess board. I needed to win this struggle with Foster.

"I don't know what you're talking about," I lied, but my voice wavered.

Dr. Foster sighed, disappointment flashing across his face. "You can't hide from us, Christopher," he said, voice smooth but clipped—like control was a language he'd mastered. *"The Agency is always watching."*

My mind spun with the implications, and I fought to rein in my anger. How could Foster sit there so calmly, so detached? How could he do this to me, his own son? I fought back the red sitting at the edges of my vision that came from the reminder of being his son.

"Always *watching*, huh?" My voice dripped with sarcasm. "Like our games of chess? Always one step ahead, right?"

Dr. Foster's expression remained infuriatingly calm. "It's important to stay vigilant, Christopher. You should know that better than anyone."

"Why?" I demanded, my voice rising with anger. "Why do you do this? Why treat me like some experiment?"

Dr. Foster's eyes narrowed slightly, his fingers lacing together as he leaned back in his chair, perfectly composed. His tone stayed steady. "You are important, Christopher. You were the beginning; you started all of this."

For a second, I wasn't sure if it was supposed to be comforting—if maybe this was his version of reassurance. Like calling me the beginning was some kind of legacy I was supposed to be proud of. But coming from him? It didn't feel like pride. It felt like ownership. Like I wasn't a person, only property he'd had a hand in creating.

What he said next only confirmed it. "Sometimes, sacrifices are necessary for the greater good."

The word 'sacrifices' sent a shiver down my spine. Memories flooded back—those cold, dark rooms where I'd been isolated for "misbehavior," the long nights spent alone with my thoughts. All for the "greater good."

"Sacrifices," I echoed bitterly. "Is that what you call locking your own son in a dark room for days? Treating your own son like a lab rat? Lying to me, *telling me both my parents were dead?*"

Flashes of those nights hit me all at once—curled on the concrete floor, stomach hollow, the hum of the vent the only sound in the dark. No light. No warmth. Only silence and the weight of being forgotten.

"Am I just another piece on your chessboard?"

Dr. Foster didn't flinch. He didn't react when I said I was his son.

For a moment, I thought he might. Some desperate, pathetic part of me still hoped he'd say something, that he'd admit the lie—recognize me as something more than a test subject. But the silence said everything. That sliver of hope shriveled and turned to ash.

"Discipline is necessary," he stated dismissively.

I clenched my fists, anger bubbling beneath the surface. But I knew better than to lash out. I'd learned the hard way what that bought me—dark rooms, days in isolation, torture disguised as discipline. Losing control gave them power.

"And now?" I asked, my voice trembling with controlled rage. "What now?"

Dr. Foster's gaze was steady and unyielding. "Now, you continue with your duties. You get closer to Ms. Mitchell. After she graduates, she will join you here at the facility. We will continue to monitor and examine both of you as you grow closer and eventually create more children of your own for us to research."

His candor stunned me into silence. He pointed to the door like I was an afterthought he dismissed. No parting words. No glance back. The space between us said more than he ever had.

I stumbled out, the weight of it all hit like lead in my stomach. The hallway to the elevator felt off—too bright, too narrow. The lights buzzed louder than usual. I kept walking, but my mind was still stuck in that office—trapped between rage and the terrifying clarity of knowing I was never getting out.

I crept up the emergency stairwell, each step slow, deliberate. My chest was tight with adrenaline, but not the sharp kind that made you move faster—it was cold, steady, clenched low in my gut. Fear had long since stopped feeling like panic.

Now it hummed under the surface, a familiar pressure. The concrete walls pressed in, the air thick with recycled tension and institutional silence. Every footfall echoed louder than it should've.

I waited. Counted the seconds. Then it happened—the emergency lights flickered on, casting everything in a cold, red-tinted glow. Maintenance had started.

Perfect.

I slipped through the sixth-floor door. The reception area was deserted. Stripped of personality. Sterile. I didn't stop. Kept moving until I reached Dr. Bennett's office.

My fingers trembled as I pulled out the lockpicks I'd stashed from one of Harris's supply runs. I'd never asked why he gave them to me. Maybe I didn't want to know. Trust was fragile in this place—fleeting. Still, the tools were real, cold and sharp against my skin, and right now, that counted for something. I forced myself to focus—counted each click, each tiny resistance, each spike of anxiety that nearly made me stop. When the lock finally gave, I pushed the door open and stepped into the dark.

The office was cloaked in shadow, lit only by the faint, buzzing emergency lights. Shadows crawled across the walls. Papers sprawled across the wood surface like discarded secrets. I hesitated for a beat—then crossed the room in two long strides, the tension in my shoulders tight enough to snap. Every part of me was wired to move quickly, quietly, like getting caught was only a breath away.

I moved fast, pulling out the camera I'd borrowed from Noa—an old-school point-and-click. My fingers were steady, despite the hammering of my pulse. I snapped quick photos of every drawer, every document I could reach. The silence pressed in, broken only by the soft clicks of the shutter. My grip was slick with sweat, and I had to force my hands to stay steady. Each breath felt thin. But I kept going—one photo, one breath at a time.

Then came the footsteps. Slow, heavy, getting closer. My pulse spiked as my stomach lurched. I dove beneath the desk, curling up tight, breath caught in my throat as the door creaked open. A figure stepped inside. For one suspended second, fear took over everything—sight, sound, thought—until he stepped into the red light.

"Christopher?" Harris called out, voice low.

His eyes found mine beneath the desk. No panic. No raised voice. That quiet tension he always carried, like everything he said was coded.

"What are you doing here?" His whisper was rough with urgency.

I hesitated. Then—because I was too tired to lie and too desperate to stall—I told the truth.

"I needed to know what they're hiding from me."

His jaw tensed. A beat. Then he nodded.

"Follow me. Quickly."

We moved back into the stairwell. Shadows swallowed us whole. Neither of us spoke. The silence between us wasn't awkward. It was loaded. Unasked questions. Unspoken fears.

When we finally stopped—tucked into a blind spot between floors—Harris turned.

"I know you're wondering why I didn't turn you in," he said, voice low, careful. "But there's no time to explain everything."

I nodded. "Yeah. That thought crossed my mind. Among others."

He scanned the hallway, then met my eyes again.

"They're tracking you. That health monitor Dr. Lang gave you?" Harris glanced over his shoulder, making sure no one was in earshot. He gestured to the clip on my belt. "It's not a monitor. It's a recording device. They've been listening. Watching. Everything."

The floor shifted beneath me. A sharp wave of nausea surged up before I could steady myself. I staggered, caught myself, heart pounding in my ears like a warning drum.

"They've heard... all of it?"

"Everything." He pulled something from his pocket—small, black, unremarkable. "This jams the signal. Scrambles audio. Disrupts the feed. But you can't use it too often or they'll notice. Save it for emergencies."

He pressed it into my hand. It felt heavier than it looked.

"How did you get this?"

"Doesn't matter. It's yours now. I've got another."

I stared at the device. A sliver of power. A crack in the walls around me. It wasn't freedom—not yet—but it was the first thing that felt close to it in a long time. And that was enough to shake something loose inside me.

"Why are you doing this?" My voice came out quieter than I meant.

Harris hesitated. Then, simply: "Because you deserve more than this. And I don't agree with half of what they're doing." He paused, barely a breath. "If you want out, you need to be smart."

"How did you know I wanted out?" I asked.

Harris didn't answer right away. His eyes scanned mine, like he was calculating how much to say.

"You've been different lately. Watching more. Talking less. You flinch every time someone says your name over the intercom."

I let out a short breath. "I didn't think anyone noticed."

"Most don't. I've been paying more attention."

"Why? Actually, it doesn't matter right now." The words spilled out before I could stop them. "Noa and I... I can't stay here. Noa can't live here. But I don't know how we get out."

Something shifted in his expression—his shoulders slackened slightly, and his eyes lost their usual sharpness. Softer. Sadder.

"I have ideas. But not now, not here. Give me a few days. Keep your head down until then."

My voice felt raw when I spoke. "I want to trust you, but—"

He held up a hand. "I get it. Just don't make the mistake of thinking this changes everything. Not yet."

I pocketed the scrambler, feeling its weight settle in my pocket like both a promise and a question. It grounded me, solid and cold against my leg, but it also lit a quiet spark of unease—because power, even a little, always came with strings. But for the first time in days, things didn't feel so final. A part of me still braced for the catch.

The route to Noa's house was familiar—comforting in theory, but my stomach told a different story. Tension curled in my gut like a second spine, but I forced my face to stay neutral. I couldn't let it show—not here, not now. If I gave it room, it would swallow everything else. I had to protect her. Had to find a way out of the Agency's chokehold. The weight of it pressed down, as I tried to keep my breathing steady. Not that it mattered with a suit in the driver's seat. I couldn't have a thought without someone watching it happen.

I knocked three times. Calm. Controlled. Not desperate. Like that would actually fool anyone if they looked close enough. Noa opened the door, surprise lighting her face.

"Christopher, hey!" Her eyes widened and then, in the next second, she threw her arms around me. Hard. Like she'd been holding her breath since the last time we talked. "You're okay. You're actually okay."

I hugged her back, pressing my face into her shoulder. "I'm fine."

She pulled back, eyes narrowed now. "Then why didn't you tell me you were fine? You went full Mission Impossible last night and then ghosted me."

"I didn't exactly have time—"

"Yeah, well, you'd better make time next time," she said, but her voice had softened. "And also, I told you not to come during the day—are we just ignoring vampire protocol now? I don't need you and my mom in the same zip code."

"I know," I said, glancing past her shoulder, scanning instinctively. "I'm sorry. I just... I needed to see you. Your mom isn't home, right?"

She shook her head. Relief melted into her features. "No, she and the twins are at the movies. We've got the place to ourselves."

The door clicked shut behind me. The house smelled like lavender and cookies, warm and soft and painfully normal. Earth-toned walls. Framed photos of Noa and her brothers. It felt like something I might ruin by standing in it.

We sank into the couch, cushions swallowing us. I pulled out the audio scrambler Harris had given me, pausing for half a second as my eyes flicked toward the corners of the ceiling—imaginary cameras, imaginary ears. Then I flipped it on. A soft buzz filled the room.

Noa leaned forward, brow furrowed. "What's that?"

"It scrambles audio—keeps them from recording us. Harris gave it to me. We can't use it often, though. They'll notice."

"Recording us?" she echoed, eyebrows shooting up. "Cool, cool. So should I grab the tinfoil hats, or do we accept we're starring in the world's least fun reality show?" Her voice dipped into disbelief, but her posture went still. "Seriously though—what's going on?"

I hesitated, then took a breath and let the words fall out.

"They've been tracking me, listening in. Everything. They've heard it all."

"How?"

"This device Dr. Lang gave me?" I pulled it from my pocket

and held it up between us. "He said it was to monitor my health. It's not. It's a listening device. They've been using it to record everything I say."

Her eyes shimmered, but she blinked fast, jaw tightening as she looked away like the act of holding it in was muscle memory. She reached out and gripped my hand like she could pull me back from wherever I was spiraling.

"Christopher, this is... insane. Of course you're bugged—this is our life now, right?" She rolled her eyes, but her voice steadied mid-sentence. "We are not panicking. We breathe. We plan. And if this is the part where you decide to carry the world on your back again, I'm gonna smack you with a throw pillow. You're not doing this alone."

I held her hand tighter, grounding myself in her steadiness. It scared me a little—how much I needed it. How much I needed her. But I didn't let go. "We stay smart. From now on, I'm coming during the day. No more sneaking out at night. I know that means I might run into your mom, but we'll deal with it if we have to. We need to act like everything's normal."

She nodded slowly, jaw clenched. "Okay, but we need more than vague hope. What's the actual plan? Or are we trusting that your mysterious maybe-ally doesn't spontaneously combust or dip out mid-crisis?"

"I'm... working on it. Harris seems to have something brewing, I think. He said he needs at least a few days. Until then, we keep things quiet. No weird behavior. No risks." I met her eyes, steadying myself with the promise. "We're getting out, Noa. I swear it."

She held my gaze like she believed me more than I believed myself, and that trust hit hard—like a weight I hadn't asked for but couldn't ignore. It made me want to be worthy of it, even if I wasn't sure I could be. "I trust you. But we're doing this together, Christopher. If things go sideways, you don't shut me out. Got it?"

I tried for a smile. "Maybe we can try to enjoy prom next weekend while we wait for Harris to come through?"

A small laugh slipped out of her, sharp at the edges but real. The kind of laugh you let yourself have when survival means pretending, at least for a little while. The tension thinned, if only a little. We spent the next hour talking about nothing and everything—her panic of not having a prom dress yet, who was on prom court, how bad the punch would be. Pretending the world wasn't on fire.

CHAPTER TEN
High Hopes

Noa

The town pulsed with life, voices overlapping, the occasional honk slicing through the hum of a warm, too-bright spring day. Window displays glittered with sequins and pastel silks, and the air was thick with the mingled scents of street food grease and sweet-blooming lilacs. It was less than a week until prom, and somehow—because we'd procrastinated like champs—this was the day we were finally dress hunting.

Ami and I strolled down the busy sidewalk, her arm occasionally brushing mine. The first boutique we entered looked like it had been dipped in frosting. Racks of soft-hued dresses gleamed under warm lighting, and some delicate piano piece trickled from hidden speakers, trying way too hard to sound effortless. Ami lit up immediately, already tugging at hangers with glitter in her eyes.

I followed, plastering on a smile that already felt like it was starting to split at the seams. Like I'd been holding it too hard, for too many days, and now faking it felt like work. Guilt pricked at the edges—Ami didn't deserve the version of me that was half-present. But faking it was safer than explaining the storm I didn't have words for. I wanted to want this—this whole day—but anxiety coiled in my chest. And the whole shopping-last-minute-for-a-prom-that's-tomorrow thing? Not exactly soothing.

"Look at this one!" Ami's voice sparkled as she held up a shimmering gown. It caught the light like it knew it was the main character.

I nodded, forcing a grin that barely made it to my eyes. "It's beautiful. You should try it on."

As she disappeared into the fitting room, I wandered, fingertips grazing fabric like maybe touch would ground me. But my brain kept circling back to Christopher—to everything he told me yesterday. We were being watched. Always. Every time the boutique door opened, I flinched.

Ami twirled out of the dressing room in the sparkling gown. "What do you think?"

"You look amazing," I said. And this time, it wasn't a lie.

We kept hopping shops, laughing at the awful poofy dresses and weird feathered monstrosities. Her joy tugged me along like a playlist I didn't expect to vibe with—bright, catchy, pulling me in before I realized I was nodding along. It felt foreign—borrowed, almost—and I knew it wouldn't last. But for a few minutes, I let myself believe in it. Pretended it was mine, too.

Then I saw it. *My* dress.

Soft, simple. Not flashy, just—me. It felt like something I could melt into without pretending. I hesitated. My mom hadn't given me a cent for prom. She barely acknowledged I was going.

Ami must've seen my face fall. "My parents gave me their credit card for today. For both of us," she said, her voice gentle but firm. "Let's find you something perfect."

161

My throat thickened. I nodded, took the dress into the fitting room, and slid it on. When I looked in the mirror, something inside me shifted. It was a rare, quiet joy. A flicker of excitement.

I stepped out, and Ami's eyes went wide. "Noa, that dress is everything. You have to get it."

Blushing, I whispered, "It feels... right."

We found shoes, accessories. She went full glam with glittering jewelry, and I picked simple earrings that didn't try too hard. For a little while, it felt like us again, like any other day. Normal. Safe.

Hours later, we slid into a booth at a cozy little diner tucked between a florist and a record store, the kind of place that smelled like waffle batter and melted cheese. A plate of fries sat between us, half-devoured and gleaming with grease.

Ami gushed about her date—how they were planning a late-night drive along the coast after prom, maybe stopping at the beach to watch the sunrise. "He's obviously not my soulmate," she laughed, "since my Mark's still ticking. But come on—tell me that doesn't sound like something out of one of those old BCM romance movies."

I smiled, but only barely. My head was too loud. It felt like trying not to cry in the middle of a crowd—tight throat, eyes burning, everything knotted up in my chest. Like if I said one honest thing, it would all come spilling out.

"Noa, are you even listening?" Ami's voice cut through the noise in my head, sharp enough to slice through my spiral.

I blinked. "Sorry—what?"

"This is the third time I've had to yank you out of whatever mental black hole you're stuck in," she scolded. "Seriously, Noa—if I'd known I was signing up for essentially solo shopping and one-word answers, I might've brought somebody who'd actually enjoy being here. Are you seriously going to sit there and pretend nothing is wrong?

I flinched. "It's not about you. I swear. I'm just... stressed."

Ami scoffed, the sound small but pointed. "You said that last time. And the time before that. I believed you when you said it was about your mom. But now? It feels like you're shutting me out again." Her voice cracked slightly. "What is going on?"

I couldn't look at her. I stared at the fry basket instead, picking at a soggy piece I had no intention of eating. "Nothing, I guess. I... can't talk about it."

"Is it nothing, or is it you can't talk about it?" She raised her voice a little. "I think it's more you won't talk about it." She grabbed another fry and stuffed it in her mouth a little too forcefully, like chewing might keep her from saying something she'd regret... and that hurt more than I expected. "I'm trying, Noa. I'm trying to give you space. But you keep pushing me away and then acting like I'm the bad guy."

"Because if I tell you the truth, everything between us might fall apart." The words came out quieter than I meant, my fingers tightening around the hem of my sleeve. My stomach flipped, shame prickling under my skin. I was so afraid of her knowing the truth. I couldn't put her in danger. I wouldn't be able to handle it if something happened and I was the one that caused it.

That stopped her. She stared, jaw tense, emotion flickering in her eyes. "Then at least give me that. Let me be upset, or confused, or whatever. Just... let me be there."

I swallowed hard. "I want to. I... can't. Not yet."

A beat passed. Then another.

Finally, Ami reached across the table. Her fingers closed around mine—not as easily as before, but still there. "Can you promise me you will tell me everything soon? I feel like I'm losing my best friend, like you're going to disappear."

I nodded, managing to whisper yet another lie, "I promise."

We finished our fries in silence. Not awkward—heavy. Ami slowly nudged the plate away, her fingers toying with a crumpled napkin. The only sounds were the faint hum of the diner and the occasional clink of cutlery from nearby tables. She stared down at her phone, scrolling without really looking, and I picked at a spot on the edge of the table, not sure how to fill the space between us. We paid the bill and headed toward her car. She offered me a ride, but I shook my head. "I think I'll walk. Need to clear my head."

She hesitated. "Okay. I guess I'll drop your dress and such off later, then." Her voice faltered near the end like she wanted to say something else, maybe call me out one last time, but she swallowed it down and looked away instead.

I watched her car disappear, then turned the opposite direction. My thoughts swirled, loud and tangled. My steps quickened without me meaning to, arms folded tight across my chest. I nearly walked straight into a light pole, only stopping when a dog barked nearby and jolted me back into my body. The day had started with sparkles and laughter—but secrets don't stay buried forever. And I was running out of space to hide them.

My room was quiet enough to feel unreal. Lavender drifted from my diffuser and a melancholic playlist I didn't remember turning on. My bedside lamp glowed warm, but it didn't reach the storm inside me.

Christopher sat beside me on the bed, close enough to touch but not pushing. His cologne mixed with the lavender, and I wanted to bury myself in it—hide inside the safety of that scent. He didn't say anything at first. Just waited.

"Noa, you've been so quiet since I got here," he said finally, voice low and careful. "What happened yesterday?"

I let out a shaky breath, dragging a hand through my hair. "Ami and I had a fight. She's frustrated because I've been distant, and I can't explain why. I keep replaying everything I said, wondering if I could've said it better—if I made it worse by not being honest. It's tearing me apart."

My throat tightened. I blinked hard, but the sting built anyway, and the tears came, hot and fast, slipping down my cheeks before I could stop them, blurring the room into soft shapes. "She's my best friend, and I hate lying to her. And my brothers, and..."

Christopher reached for my hand, and I let him take it. His touch grounded me. Warm. Steady. Real.

"I'm sorry, Noa," he said, his voice thick. "I'm sorry this is so hard. That my messed-up life has ruined yours—"

"No, Christopher," I cut in, shaking my head fast, a cold jolt running through me at the thought of him walking away—of losing the one person who truly saw me if I didn't say it now. "No. I love you. I wouldn't change any of this if it meant I didn't have you."

His breath caught. "You love me?"

I laughed through my tears, that kind of half-laugh you give when everything hurts but one thing is still good. "Of course I do. Isn't it obvious?"

His eyes locked on mine, something flickering in them—like hope trying to surface after being buried too long. "I love you, too," he said. "I'd love you even if you weren't my soulmate."

He leaned in, and I met him halfway. The kiss was intense—soft and overwhelming all at once. When he pulled back, I was still crying.

"We'll get through all of this, okay?" he said.

"Okay," I whispered, glancing at my branded scar, the remnants of my Countdown Mark. I remembered the jolt when it hit zero, how everything had shifted. That moment felt like a different lifetime.

Christopher glanced at me, his expression tightening like he felt the air change between us. "Are you sure about dinner? I know you've kept your mom pretty distant when it comes to me."

I nodded. "I'm sure. I want you to meet my brothers while things are... before... before things change."

The quiet crept back in. This time it didn't feel warm—it pressed in like a closing door. I broke. The weight inside me cracked open, and the sobs hit before I could stop them.

Christopher reached into his jacket and pulled out the audio scrambler, flicking it on. A faint buzz filled the room, like a shield locking into place.

"It's okay. We can talk now," he said. "Let it out."

And I did. Everything came pouring out in between sobs. "I'm scared, Christopher. I don't know how I'm supposed to keep lying to Ami. Every time I look at her, I feel like the worst version of myself. Like I'm choosing this life with you over someone who's always chosen me. And my brothers—they don't know what's coming. I see them every day, help them with their homework, make their dinner... like everything's normal. How am I supposed to leave them behind? Whether it's the CCA stealing me away, or we find some way to escape, either way... they are losing me. How am I supposed to live with that?"

He pulled me close, and I sank into him like I might disappear if he let go. "I know it's hard. But we're keeping everything from Ami and your brothers to protect them. If they knew, they could become targets, and we honestly don't know what the Agency could do." He lifted one hand and gently wiped the tears from my cheek with his thumb, his touch achingly soft. "For now, all we can do is take things one day at a time. Harris is supposed to be giving me the plan in a few days," his jaw tightened. Like he needed to believe it as much as I did.

I wiped at my face with the sleeve of my hoodie, the fabric scratchy against my skin. "I wish it didn't have to be like this. I wish we didn't have to hide and lie and pretend everything's fine."

Christopher's fingers moved gently through my hair. "I wish that too. But I think we're close. Once we're out, we can stop pretending."

Christopher brushed his fingers lightly across my knuckles. "I can't imagine how hard it is for you—bottling everything up all the time, not able to talk to your best friend about any of it. I can only assume that it all feels... impossible."

Something sparked in my brain—a flicker, but it straightened my spine before I realized it. "What if we wrote everything down? In journals. We could keep them here, pass them back and forth. So I could get it out more. It would be safer than talking out loud, right?"

He nodded slowly. "That's actually smart. We could track everything, too—what we know, what we're planning. No risk of being overheard."

"I'll get us some tomorrow," I said. The idea made the weight ease, at least a little. "Even when we can't talk out loud, we'll still have a way to get things off our chests."

Christopher's smile was soft and tired. "And maybe one day we'll look back on them—on all of this. See how far we've come"

I looked at him, my breathing finally slowing, the storm inside me settling into something almost still. "Thank you, Christopher. For being here. I don't want to think about how much you had to fight to be here in the middle of the week."

"Well, this is important. So where else would I possibly be?"

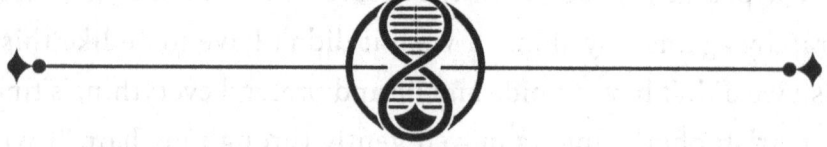

The smell of roasted chicken filled the house—thick and warm. I set the table carefully, like maybe if the forks were straight and the napkins folded just right, everything else would stay under control. Bread baked in the oven. My stomach churned.

Christopher was about to meet my mom and brothers.

I glanced at him. Gave him a smile that felt like paper—thin and shaky. Guilt flickered behind it. I was the one pulling him into this—into the minefield I'd been walking my whole life. And he didn't know where the explosions were buried. He smiled back, but his jaw was tight. We were both trying.

The table was dressed with our best dishes—the kind that came out only for holidays and apologies. Silverware clinked gently as I adjusted it. The sound felt too loud. Golden lamplight spilled across the dining room, casting soft shadows on old family photos. Moments frozen in time. The kind where we were all smiling and no one was yelling. A different life.

"Dinner's ready! Can someone help me bring the food to the table?" Mom's voice called from the kitchen—too bright.

"I'll help," I said quickly, heading in. Christopher followed.

Heat blasted from the oven. We carried dishes into the dining room, the weight of them heavier than it should've been. Everything in the house felt like it was holding its breath. Ethan and Lucas were already seated, eyes wide and curious.

"You must be Christopher," Ethan said, grinning. "Noa talks about you a lot."

"Ethan!" I hissed, face burning.

Christopher chuckled, some of the tightness in his shoulders easing. "Nice to meet you, Ethan. Lucas. I've heard a lot about you guys too."

Mom walked in with the last dish and set it down. "Hello, Christopher. I'm Caroline. I've heard a lot about you."

"Nice to meet you, Ms. Mitchell," he said politely.

"Please, call me Caroline." She smiled. "Let's eat."

For a while, it was fine. Small talk. The twins chattered. Mom laughed at something Ethan said. We made it through dinner. Then Mom brought out dessert—chocolate cake from a box. The boys didn't care where it came from; it was chocolate, and that was enough. I thought, for a moment, that the night might be a success.

That's when she poured herself a glass of wine, and my stomach twisted. My heart kicked up—fast and jittery. I watched the glass tilt, the red liquid curling inside like it already knew what came next. I didn't breathe. I didn't blink. Waited. I knew this routine. The flicker in her eye. The soft click of the glass on the table. And the sharp turn that always followed.

It was only one glass. But I knew that look. I'd seen the way it flickered before things turned. Her smile tightened. The laughter dulled. I felt it in my chest first—like the air had shifted.

Then she set her fork down.

"Noa, it's a miracle you're actually here for dinner. You're usually so busy with your 'activities.'"

The word sliced. My body stiffened.

"What does that mean?" I asked, though I already knew.

"It means you're never home. Always off doing who-knows-what. It's like you can't wait to get away from us." Her voice had turned sharp. Acidic.

"I help out," I said—almost whispered—trying to keep my voice steady. "You know that."

She looked right past me and zeroed in on Christopher. "And

you, young man, what exactly are your intentions with my daughter? I don't care about this soul-whatever business, or Marks, or fate, or any of that nonsense. That may work somewhere else 'cause of those people you work for or whatever, but I don't believe any of it. So let's drop the fairy tale and get real—what do you want from her?"

Christopher met her gaze, calm. "I care about Noa. I want to support her and the future she wants for herself in whatever way I can."

Mom's smile vanished. "Support her? How? By pulling her away from this house? From her responsibilities? She knows I'm sick, and she already does the bare minimum as it is," she scoffed. "And what future? She'll be lucky to get a job at the diner I work at."

My chest tightened. Shame prickled at the back of my throat. I wanted to disappear—melt into the floor, crawl under the table, anything to get away from the way she said it. Especially with Christopher and the boys right there.

"Mom, that's not fair—"

Christopher's hand slid over mine under the table.

"Caroline," he said, voice level but firm, "Noa's doing her best. There's no reason to speak about her like that."

Silence fell—hard and fast. Mom blinked, then narrowed her eyes.

"Excuse me? I don't recall asking for your opinion on how I speak about my daughter."

Christopher didn't flinch. "I won't sit here and listen to anyone disrespect her, no matter who they are."

The air snapped.

"You need to leave. Now," Mom said.

I stood with him, fists clenched. But the look she gave me—icy and absolute—froze me in place. Christopher's hand squeezed mine once, then let go. He mouthed, it's okay, before walking toward the front door. Mom followed, like she wanted to be sure he left. She slammed the door behind him. The echo stuck in my chest.

"That's not fair, Mom," Ethan said, voice hot. "Christopher's right. Noa works hard. You should appreciate her."

Mom whipped around. "Enough! Both of you—go to your rooms. You're grounded."

Lucas stood. "But I didn't—"

"Go," she snapped.

The boys gave me heartbroken looks before trudging upstairs.

I didn't move. I was frozen—heart hammering, stomach flipped. I wanted to go after him, to say something, anything, but my legs wouldn't work. Not with her still watching me like that.

"You didn't have to do that," I said quietly.

"This is my house," she said. "I can do whatever I want, and I don't have to hear your lip about it."

I stood. My voice didn't shake—but somewhere underneath the anger, the words caught on a thread of guilt. What would this mean for Ethan and Lucas? What if I left and they had no one?

"Fine. But I'm done. I'm done being treated like a problem. I don't want you at my graduation. And after that? I'm leaving. For good."

Her eyes widened. I didn't wait. I climbed the stairs, every step

172

feeling like I might collapse. Ethan and Lucas sat near the top, eyes wide, faces pale. They'd heard what I said about leaving—I could see it in their eyes.

I ran past them. Slammed my door. Collapsed onto the bed. And I sobbed. The weight of everything—the secrets, the fight, the thought of leaving my brothers—crashed down on me all at once.

The school buzzed with energy on the last day of senior finals. Hallways pulsed with the clatter of lockers, the shuffle of sneakers, and voices layered over one another—swapping answers, summer plans, half-hearted goodbyes. The air was heavy with relief and unease, the scent of sweat tangled with blooming flowers from the courtyard windows. I wove through the crowd, noise swelling around me, amplifying the chaos already storming inside my chest.

Three days had passed since the horrific dinner. Since the wine. Since the slammed door and the piercing silence. Since the twins' faces—wide-eyed and frozen—after they heard my announcement of leaving and never coming back.

I hadn't spoken much to anyone since, except Christopher. The silence from Ethan and Lucas felt louder than anything—like grief, or worse, like blame. Sometimes I wondered if I made the right choice. If standing up to her had cost me more than I could afford. But I couldn't take it back. I wouldn't.

My brain kept the night on a never ending loop. The wine, her voice, that slam of the door. I tried to will it away, tried to anchor myself in the present. Get through the day. Get through finals. I clenched my pencil so tight my fingers ached, forcing my eyes to the notes in front of me. My foot tapped out a frantic rhythm under the desk. Breathe, I told myself. Breathe.

In each class, I sank into each seat as low as they would let me. My classmates chattered around me, laughter bubbling up in bursts, but it all felt distant. I couldn't focus. Couldn't think. The words on the pages blurred and twisted. The ticking of the classroom clocks dug into my nerves—each second dragging its feet and flying past all at once.

Lunch came too fast. And not fast enough.

I spotted Ami across the cafeteria, laughing at something her friend, Sarah, said. Her posture was all confidence—perfect ponytail, easy grin—but there was tension in the way her fingers curled around her fork. She wasn't eating, dragging the tines across her plate, shoulders a little too stiff for her smile to be real.

I walked toward her before I could lose my nerve—half-expecting her to turn away, to pretend she didn't see me. My heart thudded hard against my ribs, and I hated how much I needed this to go well.

"Hey, Ami," I murmured, hovering at the side of the table.

She looked up. Her smile dimmed.

"Hey, Noa."

Sarah, sneered at me. "Oh look, it's the loner. Did you get lost on your way to the library?"

"Maybe she's here to borrow a personality," another girl said

174

with a smirk, not even bothering to lower her voice.

Ami stiffened, her eyes flicking to me and then quickly away. Her grip on her fork tightened, knuckles paling, but she didn't say anything. I felt a sting of hurt but tried to ignore it. "Can we talk?" I asked Ami, glancing at her friends, who fell silent, watching.

Ami pushed back her chair and stood up without saying a word. She grabbed her tray and led me toward the quiet stretch of wall near the vending machines, her pace brisk but steady. "What?"

I swallowed hard. "I'm sorry. I know I've been distant. And I know you're tired of hearing that—I would be too." My eyes burned, and I blinked fast, hoping she wouldn't notice. "I keep pulling away, and every time I think I can try to explain, I panic." I rubbed my arms, suddenly cold. "I tell myself that it's safer to keep everything locked up, even when it hurts." My voice wavered. "But I miss how it used to be. I do. I... I don't know how to be okay right now."

She crossed her arms, eyes scanning my face. "I don't get it, Noa. You have your soulmate! But somehow it's like everything has been off balance ever since you met him. And shutting me out isn't the answer. That's not how we do things."

"I know. I don't want to lose our friendship."

"Then talk to me."

"I can't. Not all of it. Most of it isn't really my story to tell. We've been friends for so long—I really need you to trust that if I could tell you everything, I would."

She was quiet for a beat.

I hesitated, then exhaled, fingers curling into my palm to hide the tremble. "Something happened. And it changed everything. I'm not ready to talk about it yet, and I'm not sure how much of it I can talk about. I'm not being dramatic or flaky or hiding for no reason. I... I'm trying to figure out how to breathe through it all right now."

Ami's expression cracked a little. "Okay," she said softly. "But I hate this guessing game. It's too stressful and honestly, not like you at all."

"I'll tell you what I can as soon as I can. I don't want to lose you while I'm processing everything." It was the best I could give. A half-truth soaked in guilt.

The bell rang.

"Final exam of the day," I said, voice thin.

"Good luck," she murmured. It was soft. Honest. Her hand brushed my arm—brief, tentative—but I think it said everything she didn't say out loud.

The last test passed in fragments. Questions blurred on the page. I tapped my pencil against the desk, the steady beat the only thing keeping me anchored. My hand cramped from gripping it too hard, and I blinked, realizing I'd been staring at the same sentence for too long. Every tick of the clock buzzed in my ears—each second a reminder that time was moving whether I could keep up or not. I turned in my paper, heart pounding harder from dread than relief.

Outside the classroom, my phone buzzed—a text from Christopher. Seeing his name made me relax a little.

Prom tomorrow! ILY! :)

I read it twice, three times, catching everything between the lines. That he cared. That after the disaster at dinner earlier this week, he still wanted to show up for me. It was the kind of simple thing that used to mean nothing. Now it felt like everything.

My breath caught. Prom. Tomorrow. Something so normal it almost felt wrong to want it. Like I didn't deserve a night of glitter and music after everything I'd said. Everything I'd left behind. I hoped Ami was still okay with our plans to get ready together. We have been dreaming about prom night since freshman year. That felt like a lifetime ago.

When the final bell rang, the hallway swirled with noise, teachers shouting reminders, and seniors cheering like the future wasn't a gaping unknown. Lockers slammed open like gunshots. Someone whooped near the stairwell. Confetti—or more like torn-up notebook paper—fluttered through the air. It smelled like sweat, cheap cologne, and too many dreams. The end of the school year for us seniors. Of childhood. Of this chapter in our lives.

I gathered my things, hands shaking. Every step felt heavy with what I couldn't say. With what came next. I was so ready to be done with this place. So ready to walk out those doors and never look back. But I wasn't ready for whatever was to come next.

CHAPTER ELEVEN

Going Under

Christopher

L ast night's dinner kept replaying in my head—the sound of Noa's voice, the way her mother wielded words like a weapon. It gutted me. To think she'd lived her whole life under that roof, with a woman like that. And in a strange, backwards way, I was almost grateful I hadn't known until recently how cruel parents could be. At least when you grow up in a cage, you don't expect love to feel soft.

I hated how different our lives were—and how similar. Two different kinds of pain. Two different prisons.

A flicker of memory surfaced—the first time the Agency felt off. I was twelve, maybe thirteen. I'd finished my lessons early and doubled back through the labs instead of heading to my dorm. Lang's door was cracked open. I should've kept walking, but curiosity got the better of me.

Inside, I saw a projection of code pulled up on a screen. It was labeled 'Control Subject 3.' Lang and Foster were arguing in low voices. Not discussing—arguing. And when Lang spotted me in the doorway, his face went flat.

He didn't yell. Just walked over and quietly shut the door in my face. No explanation. No follow-up. Nothing.

I kept waiting to be punished, or questioned, or even

acknowledged. But no one ever said a word. That was the moment I knew there were things they didn't want me to see. Things I was never supposed to know.

Now, years later, I recognized the silence for what it was. Not absence—but warning.

Harris waited for me in a quiet corner of the building—one of the blind spots I'd mapped out ages ago. I registered the risk he kept taking just to meet like this. The alcove was dim and quiet, the kind of place you only found if you wanted to disappear. The walls were lined with shadows, and the air felt cooler—like even the heat didn't want to stick around this part of the Agency.

He scanned the hallway with that same precise stillness—part soldier, part ghost. When he finally gestured for me to follow, I slipped behind him into a small, dimly lit room. Just a table and a few chairs. The air was stale. Old. Like even time forgot this part of Headquarters existed.

"Christopher," he said, voice low. Controlled. "Things are getting more dangerous. The Agency's tightening security across every level."

My pulse kicked up. I ran a hand through my hair. "I want this tracker out of me," I muttered—then immediately looked away, jaw tight. I hadn't meant to say it like that. Not out loud. Not where someone could hear the crack in it. "It's like... I can't breathe without them watching. Every move I make, I can feel them."

Harris's expression softened—not pity, just understanding. Which was rare for him. He didn't let much show. That he let even this flicker through told me how serious things were. "I know. It's invasive. Dehumanizing. But I've been working on a solution. It won't be easy—but I think it's possible. We have to be careful. Smart."

His words were like a rope tossed into deep water. I grabbed on—too fast, too desperate—and immediately hated that I had. Hope felt dangerous. Fragile. Like something that could be yanked away the second I started to believe in it. My chest tightened, and I glanced at the floor, grounding myself before the feeling could pull me under. My hands curled into fists before I realized I'd moved. "I just want out. And I want Noa safe. Away from all of this."

Harris reached into his pocket and pulled out a small device—sleek and unassuming. I blinked. For a second, it didn't feel real. Like something out of a spy movie. Hope and danger wrapped in a piece of plastic no bigger than my palm. Matte black, with a single blinking light. He placed it in my hand.

"This is a decoy signal generator. Once we remove the tracker, this will take its place. It mimics the original. The Agency won't know you're off their radar. Go ahead and take it with you, so it has time to sync up with your locations and routine. That way, it'll be primed and ready to take over once the tracker in your arm is disabled."

I turned it over in my palm. It was light—too light for something that carried this much weight. My fingers curled instinctively around it, like gripping it tighter might make it real.

"And the removal—it won't trigger anything?"

Harris shook his head. "I snuck into IT and rewrote some protocols. Took a while to bypass the retinal security—had to piggyback on a maintenance override. Risky, but it worked. There won't be a ripple. But we have to be precise."

I nodded, meeting his eyes. "Thanks, Harris. But seriously—how'd you even manage to get into IT? The fifth floor's a fortress unless you're headed to the library." I tried to keep it light, sarcastic, but the tension in my jaw gave me away. Half of me hoped he'd joke back.

A smirk flickered across his face. "I have my ways."

He rested a hand on my shoulder—solid, grounding. I froze for a second, not used to that kind of contact. The instinct to pull away was immediate—ingrained. But I didn't. Maybe part of me needed it more than I wanted to admit.

"Trust me. I have a plan—or at least the beginnings of one."

He hesitated just long enough that I knew whatever he said next was more than a theory.

"If the pieces fall into place, there's a window right after Noa's graduation. Her class has a big grad party planned at the lake—bonfires, music, the whole thing. I was at a briefing with your security detail about it this morning. There will be Agents there, watching, but it's a big class. If we time it right, you and Noa could slip away before anyone notices you're gone. I'm already setting things in motion."

Something in my chest pulled tight.

"You really think it could work?" I asked.

Harris nodded. "I wouldn't bring it to you if I didn't. But you and Noa will need to be ready. No second-guessing."

I nodded once. Sharp. Certain. For the first time, it didn't feel like hope—it felt like action.

When I stepped back into the hallway, the air felt different. Heavier. The walls pressed in, concrete and sterile, but somehow more suffocating than ever before. Voices drifted through the corridor—muted but sharp. Snippets of conversation about preparations for Noa's relocation echoed off the walls. The words hit me like a punch to the ribs. I staggered a half-step back and had to brace a hand against the wall, breath caught mid-lung. It took everything not to let it show.

The fear didn't spike. It sank—quiet and deep. My stomach dropped, fingers tingling with that strange numbness that came when panic tried to claw its way out and I forced it back down. I swallowed it on instinct, forcing my mind to shift gears. I needed to move, plan, react—before the feeling had a chance to bloom into something that could slow me down.

Deep, cold, and heavy.

I knocked once—soft, careful—before slipping into Noa's room. I could hear crickets buzzing faintly outside her window, their rhythm clashing with the thick hush of her room. String lights glowed along the walls, casting everything in amber. The scent of lavender and old books lingered. Photos. Notebooks. A worn stuffed animal near her pillow. It felt like her—warm and lived-in.

She sat on the edge of her bed, legs tucked in, shoulders curled protectively inward. Her eyes lifted as I stepped closer—relief flickered first, then a flash of guilt, like she'd betrayed something sacred by needing me there.

I sat beside her, my fingers brushing hers. The contact steadied me more than I wanted to admit. A flicker of instinct told me to pull back—enough to reestablish the walls I'd spent years building—but I didn't. I let it settle.

"Hey," I whispered, giving her hand a small squeeze.

"Hey." Her voice almost didn't make it past her throat. "I'm glad you're here. I needed to see you."

I nodded. We didn't need to name the weight between us. "I know. It's been a rough few days."

I hesitated, then added, "How did finals go?"

She gave a half-shrug, eyes still distant. "I turned everything in. I don't remember most of it. Just felt like I was going through the motions."

"That still counts," I said gently. "Are you happy to be done?"

She gave a dry, humorless laugh. "Happy? I don't know. I thought I would be. But now it feels like one more thing ending. One more door closing."

I nodded, letting the silence fill in the rest. There wasn't anything I could say to make it less true.

She looked down, her fingers curling into the blanket like she could anchor herself there, and the room held its breath with her. "I've been thinking about Ami a lot. I hate lying to her so much. I feel like I'm losing my best friend."

Her phone buzzed on the desk. Ami's name lit up the screen. Noa flinched. Just a fraction, but I saw it.

I pulled the audio scrambler from my pocket. Flipped the

switch.

"Just to be safe," I murmured. The hum it gave off was faint but grounding. "I get it, Noa. I do. But we can't risk telling her. The more people who know, the more dangerous this becomes—for everyone. We keep Ami safe by keeping her out."

She swallowed, her throat bobbing, eyes rimmed with unshed tears. I could see the guilt bleeding through—like she thought letting Ami go, for now, made her a terrible friend. "I know you're right. It's just so hard. She's always been there. Every step. And now I have to lie and pretend that nothing is wrong. She's not stupid, and she knows me so well. She knows something is seriously wrong, and she's tired of waiting for me to let her in. And I don't blame her for being mad. I probably would be, too, if the roles were reversed."

Her voice cracked. I pulled her into me without thinking. She trembled—silent, small, and aching—as her fingers clutched the front of my shirt. For a moment she went rigid, like her body hadn't decided whether to lean in or pull away. And then she exhaled, letting herself fold into me, and I held her until her breathing steadied.

It felt like we were always stretched thin. Holding it together long enough for the other to fall apart. A silent rhythm we never talked about but always followed. Not out of choice. Out of necessity.

"Listen," I said, easing back to meet her eyes. "It won't be forever. When we've gotten—when we're safe—we'll figure out a way for you to reach out and tell her everything."

She nodded slowly. A breath in. A longer one out. I brushed

a piece of hair behind her ear. "We'll get through this. Together. We're almost there. I talked to Harris. Right now, the idea is we leave the night of your graduation—during the big party at the local beach. Everyone will be distracted. It's the perfect cover."

That flicker of hope returned in her eyes. Fragile, but real. "Graduation's only two weeks away."

I didn't hesitate. "That's the plan. We leave the night of graduation."

Her eyes switched from hope to fear in an instant. "That's in two weeks. Christopher—two weeks."

She gripped the edge of the bed like the floor might drop out from under her, then pushed to her feet. She started pacing, shallow breaths scraping her throat as her eyes darted to the window, like she needed an exit.

I reached for her hand again, steadier this time. "I know. I feel it too. It's fast. But we'll be ready."

She shook her head slowly, panic threading her voice as her hands started to shake. One lifted to her mouth, thumb pressing hard against her lip like she was trying to hold the fear in physically. "What if we're not? What if we think we're ready, but we're not and we—fail?"

"We can't afford to fail—not with what's at stake," I said. "Not this. Not when it matters most."

She didn't say anything, but the tightness in her shoulders gave enough for me to see she believed me. At least a little.

She blinked, like she was still trying to believe it. "Okay. We can do this, right?"

"We can do this," I said. "We will."

I switched the scrambler off. The silence that followed felt louder than the hum.

After that, we pulled out our journals—no more words, only scratched notes passed between us. We wrote for nearly an hour.

Every detail mattered now. For me, it wasn't only a plan—it was survival. And she felt it too. That shared urgency. That silent understanding that we wouldn't get another shot.

A sense of unease settled over me as I approached the entrance to Headquarters. Armed guards patrolled in greater numbers now, their sharp gazes cutting through the night. Every step closer made the weight in my pocket feel heavier—like the devices Harris had given me were made of stone. For a moment, I wondered if I'd made a mistake trusting him. If he'd slipped up. If this was all about to blow up in our faces.

Bright white lights flooded the exterior. Surveillance cameras tracked me with blinking red eyes, their mechanical whirring louder than it should've been. It was warm out, but a chill crawled down my spine. The rhythm of the guards' boots echoed, syncing too perfectly with my pulse.

At the door, one of the guards stepped forward, expression carved from stone. "Routine check," he said, voice flat and unmoved. My stomach tightened. I braced without meaning to, breath shallow, mind already running through a cover story on loop. I forced myself still as his hands moved over my jacket, pausing too close to the wrong pocket.

"What's this?"

He held the scrambler between his fingers, his grip too firm, gaze flicking up to meet mine with a sharpness that sent a fresh jolt of panic through me.

I kept my voice casual. "Just a fitness tracker. Helps me count my steps."

He stared at me for a beat too long. Then, with a grunt, he tossed it back. "Stay out of trouble."

I nodded and walked inside, limbs heavy with adrenaline. The corridors had never felt this tight. Armed guards lingered around every corner, eyes sharp and movements too precise. I moved carefully, noting every camera, every flicker of motion. Sweat clung to my palms. I wiped them on my jeans and kept walking, caged by the silence and the constant awareness that I didn't belong.

They weren't only being cautious. This was a response. They'd detected the scrambler. Maybe not fully, but enough to know someone was interfering. Maybe they were testing me. Watching how I moved, how I reacted. Maybe Harris was compromised. Maybe I was. Foster knew. Bennett knew. They had to, right? Unless I was imagining it. Unless this was what it felt like to finally snap. They weren't going to wait to catch us—they were laying traps.

I passed a cracked office door. Voices filtered out—low and clipped, one laced with a familiar edge of authority. "...relocation is set for the night of her graduation... after the grad party... ready for the new tests." The words landed like a punch. My jaw tensed.

I hovered for half a breath, but the risk of being seen loomed. I kept walking. I didn't want them to catch me listening.

By the time I made it to my room, my hands were trembling. I shut the door and leaned against it, chest heaving. The sight of my bed, my desk, the scattered pieces of a life that never really belonged to me—it all felt colder now.

I collapsed onto the mattress, chest tight and vision blurring at the edges, trying to breathe through the panic. My fingers curled into my blanket, gripping hard like it could tether me back to solid ground. Noa. Prom. The escape. There was too much to plan, too many things we had to get right. Too much going on at once. But I kept thinking about her—how badly I wanted to give her something beautiful before everything shattered. And part of me hated myself for it—for wanting more when survival should've been enough. I knew it was selfish. I wanted it anyway. One night of magic—one night where none of this existed.

Then I saw it. A red light blinking from the ceiling, tucked behind the fixture. My whole body froze, instinct screaming to move, to run—but I couldn't. A cold sweat broke across my back, breath held so tight it burned in my chest. I stayed still, breath caught somewhere between fear and fury. I sat up slowly, ice in my veins.

A camera.

When had they installed it?

If they'd seen Harris.

If they'd heard anything...

Our entire plan could be blown before it started.

I stood in a field of wildflowers, the golden sun casting a warm glow over the landscape. Noa's laughter filled the air, a sound so pure and joyous it made my heart ache—and twist. Part of me didn't trust it. Like I was trespassing in someone else's happiness. Like I didn't deserve to be in it. She was beside me, her black hair cascading down her shoulders, her eyes reflecting fierce determination softened by bliss. For a moment, everything was perfect.

Then the ground fractured beneath us with a deep, echoing crack—like the earth itself was splitting open. The sound rang out sharp and thunderous, then shattered into the brittle chime of breaking glass. The field shattered around us, slicing through my skin as I fell. I reached for Noa, but she was already gone—swallowed whole by the darkness in a blink, her laughter still echoing like a ghost. Cold wind rushed past, howling, taking the echoes of laughter along with it. I tumbled through weightless black, shards spinning around me, cutting, vanishing. Seemingly endless.

Surgical lights flickered overhead—too bright, too cold. The scent of antiseptic seared my throat, sharp and chemical, choking me with memories I didn't ask for. My stomach turned, nausea curling deep, as if my body remembered what my mind had tried to forget. Suddenly, I was strapped to a metal table, limbs paralyzed, muscles twitching. Shadows moved in jagged patterns, voices echoing off invisible walls.

"The subject is stable. Proceed with the next injection," said Dr. Foster's voice—disembodied, everywhere at once, like it had sunk into black abyss around me and wormed its way inside my skull.

The lights blinked out, and suddenly the table was gone—the straps vanished. I was beneath soft, golden light, sitting next to a tree. Noa's head rested on my shoulder, her presence grounding me. "I love you, Christopher," she whispered.

Then her image blurred and I was thrown back under the lights.

A baby cried from across the room. Storm clouds roared. I saw him—small, trembling—surrounded by figures in lab coats. Something twisted in my chest. Somehow, I knew that cry. I knew that face. It was me. Dr. Foster loomed over the infant, his frame too tall, limbs bending at wrong angles, face flickering in and out of focus like a corrupted file. His eyes stayed fixed—flat, hungry, inhuman. "Increase the dosage," he commanded. A dark blue glow of a Countdown Mark pulsed on the baby's tiny arm—on my arm.

I screamed, but thunder swallowed my voice.

I was a boy again, staring through thick glass at Foster and Bennett. They smiled, but their eyes were wrong—sharp, unreadable. "Your parents," a voice whispered behind me, dry as bone. I turned. No one was there.

Scenes fractured like mirrors—flashes of Noa strapped to a gurney, fear raw in her eyes. Foster and Bennett circled like vultures. I couldn't move. Couldn't speak. All I could do was watch. The helplessness hollowed me out, left me screaming inside while my body stayed silent.

"The subject shows promise," Dr. Bennett murmured, her tone clinical—dispassionate, like she was commenting on a lab rat instead of a person. It made my skin crawl.

I'm back in the field again. But now the wildflowers were wilted and blackened. The sky hung low, heavy with smoke. Noa stood among the dying stalks, her outline flickering.

"Save me," she whispered. Her voice barely reached me over the rising shriek of sirens.

A lab swallowed the field whole. At the center stood a massive hourglass, its frame scorched and ornate, its glass fractured. Inside, a single tree clung to life in the upper chamber while a cracked city crumbled below. Red threads bled from the cracks, writhing like living things. They wrapped around the tree and sank into the buildings like veins with a pulse, twitching as if feeding something deep beneath the surface. The sand was running out.

"Don't let them do this to me, Christopher," Noa's voice echoed.

The fractured hourglass groaned. A web of fresh cracks split through the glass with a deafening creak—each one splintering deeper, more jagged. Red light pulsed behind the fractures.

I could hear Foster's voice echo alongside the splintering glass, "The subject is responding well. Begin the next phase."

With a final, earsplitting crack, the hourglass shattered. Black sand poured out in a violent rush, devouring everything in its path. The sky. The lab. The tree. The city.

Noa.

I ran—down endless corridors, alarms blaring. The walls bled light—harsh, burning, alive. It pressed into my eyes, seared my skin, like it wanted to peel me open from the inside. Noa's screams curdled through the air, raw and inhuman.

I reached a door. Burst through. Found only the table. The lights. The straps.

Flickering scenes collided—Noa and I dancing under stars, her laughter fracturing into screams, my Mark glowing like an open wound. I stared at it, transfixed—its glow pulsing like a warning, like a brand. Fate. Control. Surveillance. The one thing I could never outrun. Foster's eyes. The hourglass. The sand.

"Noa," I whispered. "Please."

The world broke apart. I fell.

Her voice reached me like a distant heartbeat. "Christopher..."

I hit the ground. Light exploded. Glass and sand rained around me—shards slicing the air, nicking my skin, catching flickers of the nightmare in their fractured reflections as they fell. My scream tore through the chaos while the sand buried me alive.

Before the sand swallowed me whole, I saw the shattered remnants of the hourglass—red threads coiled around the pieces, burning like fire.

I woke with a gasp, drenched in sweat. My heart pounded in my ears. The room was dark, silent—except for my ragged breathing. My hand shot to my arm before I could think, fingers scrambling for my Mark like it might still be glowing.

It was only a dream, I told myself.

But it felt like more.

It felt like a warning.

CHAPTER TWELVE

Dancing Queen

Noa

Ami's bedroom was a whirlwind of activity, every surface covered in curling irons, makeup palettes, and discarded clothing. And for once, I was grateful for the noise. The buzz. The distraction. It was a relief—so different from the strained silence of the last few times we'd hung out. For the first time in what felt like weeks, it felt like maybe Ami had really forgiven me. Like maybe we were okay again. I hoped it would last. I didn't let myself breathe too deep, afraid I might shatter it. Like if I acknowledged it too loudly, it might all disappear.

Normally, her room was a study in order—Mrs. Collins' OCD reflected in every meticulous detail. But tonight, it had become a vibrant mess, buzzing with the energy of a night we'd both imagined since freshman year. The air was thick with the scent of hairspray and floral perfume—sweet and cloying, almost too perfect. It clung to the back of my throat, making my stomach twist slightly. Like part of me already knew this moment was too fleeting to hold. "Dreams" by The Cranberries played low in the background, its nostalgic hum threading through the chaos.

Ami's bed was buried in the aftermath of getting ready—discarded hangers, makeup brushes, the backup dress options we'd both vetoed in earlier chaos. Jewel-toned fabrics still spilled onto the floor like waves, remnants of indecision and excitement. In the middle of it all, she stood before her full-length mirror, curling a strand of hair with practiced ease. Her dress—a bright electric blue, floor-length gown—hugged her figure and shimmered under the dim light. The fabric whispered as it moved, slick and almost weightless beneath her fingers. Bold and unapologetic, like her. The dress flowed behind her with every movement, sleek and dramatic, making her look like a starlet stepping out of a dream. The purple glow of her Countdown Mark glinted faintly down her arm, a steady pulse against her skin.

I sat across the room at her desk, smoothing the skirt of my emerald dress with trembling fingers. It matched the locket Christopher had given me—a small, perfect thing that rested over my heart. My dress was simple and timeless. It was floor-length, with a soft, graceful silhouette. The skirt swept the floor with a subtle elegance that made me feel older—and softer—all at once. The earrings and heels matched the silver of my locket, completed the look, but it was the locket itself that made me feel the most beautiful.

"Hold still," Ami chirped, turning from the mirror with a sparkle in her eyes. She crossed the room to fix a stubborn curl near my temple, her fingers steady, gentle. "You look amazing, Noa. Seriously. Come look."

She pulled me to the mirror, making me face myself. The emerald dress clung to me just right, its silky fabric catching the light like water and feeling cool and almost unreal against my skin, pooling slightly at the hem in soft waves. The bodice was fitted, with delicate pleating that cinched at the narrowest part of my waist, and slender straps that framed a gently scooped back—elegant and daring enough to feel grown-up without trying too hard. Loose yet defined curls framed my face, soft and natural, and a dusting of silver shadow made my hazel eyes glint with something shy of confidence. The locket gleamed against my skin. A tether. A promise.

"Christopher is going to lose his mind when he sees you," Ami said, beaming as she gave a playful spin and threw her arms wide like she was presenting me to an invisible audience. Her voice was pure theater, loud and dramatic, like she was narrating the climax of a movie.

I smiled, though a quiet ache stirred beneath my ribs. "Thanks. You look incredible too."

Ami twirled, her dress catching the light and scattering reflections across the room like stars. "Can you believe it? It's our prom. Then graduation in two weeks... Everything's about to change."

The future. For her, it shimmered with promise—her Countdown Mark almost at zero, her life waiting to begin. For me, it felt like a race against time. A door closing fast behind me. I felt the sting of something I didn't want to name—envy, maybe. Or guilt for feeling it at all. I forced a nod. "Yeah. It's going to be amazing."

The doorbell rang. Moments later, Mr. and Mrs. Collins appeared, camera in hand and faces glowing. Mrs. Collins immediately began straightening our dresses and smoothing flyaways, clicking her tongue at the smallest imperfections. Her smile was warm, but her eyes scanned like a checklist, needing everything right before the shutter clicked.

"Alright, girls, time for some pictures!" Mrs. Collins chirped. We followed them outside, where Christopher and Ami's date, John, waited for us.

Christopher was leaned up against a sleek black limo, its polished surface catching the glow of the setting sun. The limo, provided by the CCA, gleamed too perfectly. We both knew the agents inside weren't only chauffeurs—they were escorts. Watchdogs. I caught Christopher's eye, and for a moment, the glamour fractured. We didn't have to say it. We both knew this was another leash.

Part of me wanted to rip it off, to defy it right there in front of them. But mostly, I felt tired. Like no matter how far we ran, they'd always find another way to tighten the grip. But I tried to push past that fear, at least for tonight. He looked stunning—tux crisp, hair perfectly tousled—and when his eyes landed on me, I let everything else fade away.

"You look... incredible," he murmured, like he couldn't believe I was real.

"You clean up pretty well yourself," I murmured, heat rising to my cheeks.

Ami squealed, dragging John toward the limo, her dress trailing like a comet behind her.

"Alright, everyone, line up in front of the limo!" Mr. Collins called, waving his hand like a traffic cop who moonlighted as a prom photographer. His voice had that unmistakable dad-tone—somewhere between overly enthusiastic and awkwardly formal. Mrs. Collins clicked away, capturing the moment in rapid fire.

Ami turned to me after, practically vibrating. "Ready?"

"Ready."

John offered Ami his hand, guiding her into the limo. They looked like they belonged in a movie—flushed with youth, full of promise.

Christopher took my hand. His touch was warm and grounding, a steady anchor against the wild flutter of nerves in my chest. That simple contact made me feel like I wasn't unraveling. He, too, helped me into the limo, and as we settled into the plush leather seats, I caught a glimpse of Ami laughing in John's arms.

For a second, I wished I could trade places with her, be as carefree as she was.

The limo's interior wrapped around us like a silk cocoon. Soft leather seats cradled us in comfort, and dim, ambient lighting cast a glow across the cabin. It should've felt luxurious. Safe. But instead, it felt surreal—like I'd stumbled into someone else's life and wasn't sure how long I'd be allowed to stay. The distant hum of the city faded into a low murmur as we glided through the streets. "Young Folks" by Peter Bjorn and John played softly through the speakers, its carefree rhythm brushing against my nerves like a memory I couldn't quite hold.

Ami and John sat beside us along the curve of the L-shaped bench, their faces flushed with excitement. Ami practically bounced in her seat, her dress catching the light with every movement. John watched her with pure joy in his eyes, his hands clasped neatly in his lap, posture straight but relaxed. He looked like a golden retriever in a tux—absolutely thrilled to be here, soaking in every second without a care in the world. For a moment, the joy almost felt contagious.

"This is amazing!" Ami beamed. "I can't believe we have a CCA escort. This feels like something out of a movie!"

Christopher and I exchanged a glance—brief but weighted. The presence of the agents in the front seats didn't need to be addressed between us. It hung there, quiet and constant, like static beneath the music—an invisible hum that made my skin prickle and the back of my neck tighten. I felt it in my spine, in the way my posture straightened without meaning to. The surveillance I could never quite shake. A reminder that nothing we did was unobserved.

"Yeah," I said, summoning a smile that felt a little too practiced. "Definitely a night to remember." I wasn't sure if I meant it or if I wanted Ami to believe I did.

John nodded. "It's not every day you get to arrive at prom in style. I mean, look at this limo! It's got lights in the ceiling and everything. I half expected a mini bar—or at least a cooler with a couple beers."

Christopher's hand slid into mine while he rolled his eyes, halfway ignoring John. His thumb grazed my skin like a silent question. "You doing okay?" he asked, low enough only I could hear.

I nodded, though my heart thudded against my ribs. "I'm

trying to enjoy the moment," I whispered back, "but it's hard not to think about... well about everything else."

He gave my hand a gentle squeeze. "I know. But tonight, let's focus on us. Let's make this something good to hold onto. Just for us."

I leaned into him, letting the contact root me in something steady. My skin tingled, my breath hitched. The windows framed streaks of city light, each one a glimmer of the outside world we didn't belong to tonight. The music kept playing—light, bouncy, indifferent to everything we were carrying.

Ami's laughter spilled into the car—bright, unburdened, almost startling in its purity. She turned to me, eyes wide with joy. "Noa, we're gonna dance all night. No worries, no stress. The music and us."

I smiled, drawn into her glow. "I wouldn't have it any other way."

When the limo rolled up to Martin's West, my breath caught. Twinkling lights framed the building like stars had stitched themselves into the night for this. For a second, I froze, caught between wonder and dread. It looked like something out of a fairytale—but I wasn't sure I belonged in one. Students moved in waves at the entrance—flashes of color and laughter and anticipation.

Christopher helped me out, steadying me with both hands. The moment my heels touched the pavement, camera flashes exploded around us. I blinked into the lights, the sound of shutters a harsh reminder: we weren't only another couple. Not to them. Sometimes, with all the chaos in our lives already, I forgot about how public our soulmate pairing had become.

"Smile," Christopher whispered, his voice soft but edged with something protective. Not a prompt—but a shield. A way to tell me he had me, when all those lenses stared too long.

I looked at him—and smiled. For him. For us. It wasn't affection—it was defiance. A silent dare to the world watching. But beneath that, a flicker of fear curled tight in my chest. Because I wasn't sure how long we'd get to keep this.

We stepped forward, hand in hand, into the shimmer and noise of it all. My heart buzzed like electricity—part thrill, part dread. This was our night. However long it lasted, I was going to feel every second of it, even if the feeling carved me open.

Martin's West was transformed into a dreamlike ballroom bathed in light, the theme "Timeless Moments" reflected in every detail. Twinkling fairy lights draped from the ceiling like strands of stardust, casting a soft, enchanting glow across the space. Giant clocks adorned the walls. Hourglasses filled with glittering sand shimmered at the center of every table, refracting the light like something caught between magic and memory. The room pulsed with energy—laughter, perfume, music—every beat vibrating beneath my skin. My heart raced, and a shiver ran down my arms like static, each note of the music tightening and releasing my breath in waves.

As we walked in, the opening notes of "Shut Up and Dance" by

WALK THE MOON filled the air, the bass line thrumming through the floor and up into our bodies. The music wasn't too loud—loud enough to make everything else fade. It was impossible not to feel swept up in it, pulled into something bigger than myself, something weightless and fleeting.

Christopher's hand never left mine as we wove through the crowd, the stares and whispers curling around us. Phones were already raised. Eyes tracked our every move. It felt like walking into a spotlight—equal parts celebrity and specimen. I recognized faces—people who had gone to school with me for four years and barely spared me a glance. Now they watched like I was something new, something worth paying attention to—because Christopher Hawthorne was on my arm. I smiled on instinct, lips tugging upward as if muscle memory could mask the weight settling into my chest.

My hands trembled slightly, betraying what the smile tried to hide—a fault line beneath the surface, pulsing with pressure. It wasn't enough to break, but enough to hurt. It didn't help that there were CCA agents stationed at every corner, every entrance. Their presence was suffocating—an invisible force field that shaped the edges of the night.

We found a place near the dance floor, and I tried to breathe. The space shimmered with gowns and tuxes, bursts of laughter, perfume that clung too thick to the air. It was beautiful—too beautiful. Magic turned suffocating by the weight of everything beneath it. I told myself to take it in, to memorize the feel of it—because there was no guarantee we'd get a night like this again.

Somewhere in the chaos, Ami and John had made their way to the dance floor. Her blue dress sparkled like diamonds, hair catching in the lights as she laughed at something John said. She spotted me and waved, mouthing "Come join us!" with all the ease of someone untouched by surveillance. I nodded, but my feet didn't move. Guilt tugged at me—Ami was glowing, twirling in that blue dress like nothing could touch her, and here I was, drowning in secrets I hadn't been able to tell her.

Christopher leaned in, his breath warm against my ear. "You okay?"

"Yeah," I said—too quickly. "Just trying to take it all in."

He smiled, gave my hand a gentle squeeze. "Let's make some memories."

I let him pull me onto the dance floor, letting the music take hold. Lights flickered above us, painting everything in golds and blues, strobing shadows across Christopher's jaw and the edge of my vision. I let the rhythm carry me, even if the worry still clung like a second skin. The CCA, the escape plan, the secrets. All of it hovered at the edge of the music.

Ami's laughter rang out—bright, full, unguarded. It pulled at something in me. I remembered a summer night when we'd laughed like that—laying in the grass, pointing out constellations we made up ourselves. Back when everything felt simpler. Safe. This moment felt miles from that. I used to laugh like that. I used to think we'd always have each other, no matter what. But secrets change things, even if you don't mean them to.

When the music dipped into something slower, I turned—maybe to breathe, maybe to ground myself—and saw

Rosalyn in the crowd. She stood with a small group, her dress sleek, her eyes sharp as they scanned the room. I hadn't noticed her much since that last class before everything changed. She looked different tonight—calmer, maybe. Her gaze caught mine for a fraction of a second; too quick to read, but heavy enough to stick. Like she knew more than she let on. A flicker of unease stirred in me. I didn't know whether I felt threatened, or curious. Maybe both.

I mumbled an excuse and headed toward the punch table. As I reached for a cup, I bumped into a boy with sandy blond hair standing next to his date. "Sorry," I muttered.

He smiled and extended a hand, easy and polite. "Thomas," he said, his voice warm and casual, the kind that instantly put people at ease.

I shook it, surprised by the gesture—and the unexpected charm. "Noa."

His date offered a warm smile, her hand resting lightly on his arm. Something about the ease between them made my chest tighten—not jealousy, exactly, but a quiet ache. A longing for that kind of simplicity, the kind that didn't come with a thousand strings pulled tight around your every move. They looked happy. Like everything around them made sense. Thomas stood with easy posture, shoulders loose, expression open—like nothing around him could shake his center. It struck me how at ease he was with his date, how naturally they fit together—even with the obvious turquoise glow of Thomas's still-moving Countdown Mark pulsing faintly between them.

"It was nice to meet you," I said, clutching my cup a little tighter than necessary. I nodded and turned away, feeling the strange ache of something I couldn't name.

Christopher found me a moment later and tugged me gently back into his orbit. As a slow song filled the room, his hand settled on my lower back and I melted into him, letting the music soften everything sharp.

I laid my head on his shoulder and closed my eyes. His heartbeat thudded steady beneath my cheek, and the warmth of his body wrapped around me like a shield. I let myself lean into it, memorizing the weight of his presence—how it grounded me when everything else was spinning.

For a moment, it all felt far away—the agents, the pressure, the weight of what came next.

Just music. Just him. Just now.

As the night wore on, the music slowed to a gentle rhythm, and Christopher pulled me close for another dance. I was finally starting to let myself relax. I wasn't bracing for what came next or looking over my shoulder—I was just… here. With him. With Ami. Even with John, who kept making her laugh. For a few minutes, it felt like maybe it was okay to be in the moment, to laugh without fear clawing its way up my spine. Like maybe I didn't have to carry it all, all the time. Like maybe tonight could be mine. A memory to fold into the corners of my heart, carry forward like armor into whatever came next.

When the song ended, I felt a gentle tug on my arm. Ami stood there, cheeks flushed, eyes bright with something that looked like laughter—until I really looked.

"I need a break," she said, breathless. "Come with me?"

I nodded, though a knot twisted in my stomach. "Sure."

We slipped out of the main hall, the noise and strobe lights fading into something muffled and distant. Outside, the world felt slower. Softer. The warm night air kissed my skin, laced with the sweet scent of the beginning of summer. But underneath the quiet, there was a tension—like the hush before a storm, too still to trust. My skin prickled with the sense that something was coming, even if I didn't know what yet. Somewhere, someone laughed—high and unburdened. The stars above blinked quietly, too far away to care.

For a second, I could almost pretend we were two friends stealing a breath of quiet from prom night.

Ami turned to me, her gaze cutting through the dark. The lightness in her expression dropped away.

"Noa, I'm not doing this again," she said, arms crossed as she shifted her weight from one foot to the other. There was a sharp edge to her movements—it was clear she'd been holding this in too long. "Not tonight. Watching you fake your way through the whole prom... You've been distant all night, and earlier too, when we were getting ready. It's like you're here—but not really here."

I swallowed hard, the weight of her voice pressing against my ribs. "Ami... please don't push."

Her brows pulled together, frustration laced with something sharper. "I get that you and Christopher are soulmates or whatever," she said, her voice tight—half hurt, half sarcastic, like she was trying not to crack. "But it feels like there's no room for anyone else in your life anymore. What happened to us?"

Her words didn't sting—they lodged in my chest, my breath catching hard, a cold rush flooding my veins, stuck in the space where laughter used to live. And beneath the hurt, guilt twisted sharp and sudden. Maybe she was right. Maybe I had pushed her out without meaning to, and now I didn't know how to pull her back in.

"Ami, I'm sorry. I never meant to shut you out. It's just—"

Tears pooled in her eyes. She turned her face slightly, letting out a shaky breath that sounded more like a scoff, as if mocking herself for letting it show. She blinked them back like it would stop them from falling.

"I don't care what it is, Noa. You should trust me enough to not keep pushing me away. Not after everything."

I reached for her, but she stepped back, and the air between us snapped cold. It felt like the floor dropped beneath me—like I was unraveling from the inside out, threads pulled loose with no way to gather them back in.

"Ami, please. I wish I could tell you everything. But I can't."

She flinched, and when she spoke, her voice cracked down the middle.

"So do your promises mean nothing now? First it was 'when you're ready,' now it's 'you can't?' Well, I don't know if I can promise to keep pretending things are fine when they're clearly not."

Her voice broke something open in me. My throat burned, and

I had to fight the urge to bolt—to disappear into the dark and pretend none of this was happening. The pressure swelled in my chest like a wave I didn't know how to outrun or contain.

"Ami, I love you. You're my best friend. But there are some things I can't share with you."

She took a shaky breath, her shoulders sinking as her hands curled into fists at her sides.

"Then I hope you know what you're doing. Because I'm done. Maybe after graduation, it's best if we… go our separate ways."

The words sliced clean through me. I flinched before I realized it, the world narrowing to a single point of pain in my chest. Time stuttered. Sound dulled. I wanted to stop her. I wanted to hug her until it made sense again. I wanted to promise I'd explain everything—that I'd find a way to keep her safe and still keep her close.

Part of me wanted to say something—anything—that might undo the damage. But another part whispered that staying quiet was safer. That if I said much more, I might break the last thread holding us together. So I stood there, trying to convince myself that silence was protection.

"Ami, please… I don't want to lose you."

Her eyes held mine for a long second, searching—maybe for hope, maybe for something I couldn't give her. Then she shook her head slowly, like the answer had already sunk in.

"I think you've already lost me."

She turned and walked back inside, her shoulder brushing mine as she passed—one last flicker of contact before the distance settled between us. She didn't look back. Kept walking, swallowed by the light spilling from the hallway.

I stood there, frozen. Every step she took echoed like thunder in my bones. My chest felt hollow.

Somewhere inside, the opening notes of "Fix You" by Coldplay floated through the door, cruel in their irony.

The stars blinked above me—silent, indifferent. My heart broke quietly beneath them. I didn't fall apart—not completely—but something inside me pulled tight. I clenched my jaw, forcing myself to stay upright, to keep breathing, to not collapse under the weight of what I'd lost. I wiped my tears with the back of my hand, the air stinging against my damp cheeks, and drew in a breath that didn't steady anything.

I leaned against the wall, trying to collect myself, but guilt still tugged at the edge of my thoughts—Ami's voice echoing louder than the music. I hadn't meant to hurt her. I wasn't sure how we'd gotten here, but the ache of that fracture pulsed beneath everything else. The warm air clung to my skin but did little to quiet the riot in my chest. What was supposed to be a night of magic and memory had splintered into something sharp—another reminder of the sacrifices we were still making. The moon above didn't care. Its light brushed against my skin—cool and indifferent—making me feel both seen and small, as if the universe was watching but would offer no comfort. It hung there, pale and untouchable, casting its indifferent light across a world that kept asking too much of us.

Footsteps. A familiar presence. Christopher approached slowly, his steps quiet against the ground. He said my name gently—like a question, like he was asking permission to step into my world. Then he appeared beside me, his expression already laced with concern.

"Noa, are you okay?"

I shook my head. The words wouldn't come.

He pulled me into his arms without waiting for permission. My knees almost buckled with relief, the weight of everything catching up to me all at once. "I'm here," he whispered—soft, steady, like the only truth that still mattered. One hand rubbed slow circles against my back, grounding me without asking for anything in return.

I hesitated for half a second—unsure if I deserved the comfort, unsure if I could let go enough to feel it. Then I buried myself in his warmth. My hands clutched at the back of his jacket like it might anchor me to the earth. His heartbeat was a quiet metronome against my cheek. Solid. Real. I didn't know how long we stood like that, but I wasn't the first to let go.

When I finally pulled back, my cheeks were wet, though my mascara hadn't budged. Small victories. I swiped at the tears and tried to breathe like the world wasn't caving in.

"Thank you," I said, voice ragged but true.

He gave me that soft, crooked smile—one touched with something else this time. Sadness, maybe. Or quiet awe. Like he was memorizing the way I looked in this fragile moment. He brushed a strand of hair from my face. "Always."

For a while, we didn't speak. Stood there with the weight of silence pressing in. Then Christopher slipped his fingers through mine and tugged gently.

"Dance with me?" he asked, voice low and hesitant—like he wasn't sure if it would be enough, but wanted to try anyway.

My breath hitched. I nodded. "I'd love to."

He led me a few steps away from the building, away from the dull thrum of music and laughter spilling from inside. I was about to ask where we were going when he pulled out his phone, set it on the ground, and tapped the screen.

The opening chords of "You and Me" by Lifehouse floated into the air—soft, haunting, familiar. The music settled into my bones like something I'd always known, loosening something tight in my chest. It was the sound of maybe. Of almost. Like a memory I hadn't lived but somehow still missed. The melody wrapped around us like a lullaby from another lifetime. He pulled me in, and we began to sway beneath the stars.

The world receded. The tension, the ache, the fracture lines across my chest—they all went quiet, and for a second, I didn't trust it. Peace didn't come without cost. But then his touch grounded me, and I let the moment hush everything else. Moonlight spilled across the grass, silvering everything it touched. Moving through it felt like slipping into a dream—like the edges of reality blurred enough to make me wonder if we were still tethered to the world at all. It felt sacred, this moment.

Christopher's arms circled me like they were made for it. I melted into him, letting my head fall against his shoulder. The lyrics soaked into my skin, echoing every unspoken hope I hadn't dared name aloud.

I didn't think about the CCA. Or the cameras. Or the way everything could fall apart tomorrow.

For once, I didn't need to.

In his arms, I let myself believe—though part of me whispered not to. That it wouldn't last. That we didn't get to have forever. But I clung to the moment anyway, desperate to feel something that wasn't fear. That we could have this. That maybe fate hadn't stolen everything.

As the song continued, something in me softened. The weight didn't disappear, but it felt lighter somehow. Like maybe love didn't make the fear go away—it made it feel less impossible to carry.

When the music ended, we didn't move. We stood there, holding on.

The stars blinked above us, silent and impossibly far away.

I tilted my head to look up at him. His eyes were dark with emotion, reflecting all the things we hadn't said yet.

"No matter what happens," he whispered, "I love you."

A tear slipped free. This one didn't sting—it felt clean. "I love you, too," I said, the words steady as my heart thudded beneath them.

He leaned down, forehead to mine, and for a moment we breathed together. Then his lips brushed mine—soft, certain, aching. His hand cupped my cheek, warm and steady, as my breath caught in my throat. The world fell away—not in a dramatic rush, but in a slow, quiet unspooling—until there was only him, only this. It felt like both a question and a promise. A kiss full of quiet promises and trembling fears and everything we hadn't been allowed to say.

When it broke, we stayed like that. Wrapped in the hush. Suspended between the stars and the reality waiting for us. I knew, deep down, this moment could fall apart way too easily. We weren't invincible. But in that moment, I almost believed we were.

Chapter Thirteen

Resistance

Christopher

The atmosphere of Headquarters felt like it was closing in on me, the blinking red light of the surveillance camera above a constant reminder of the Agency's grip on my life. The digital clock on my nightstand glowed 2:00 AM, its harsh red numbers slicing through the darkness and casting unsettling shadows on the walls.

Sunday turned into Monday like it didn't matter—another night under lockdown. The memory of dancing with Noa still lingered—the feel of her hand in mine, the way she leaned in when the songs slowed, like she didn't want it to end. I couldn't stop replaying it.

I lay on my bed, staring at the ceiling, trying to quiet my mind. Each thought was a fragment of the escape plan I needed to finalize with Harris interrupted by my thoughts of Noa. My mind kept drifting to a future I didn't know if I deserved—something almost close to freedom, maybe peace—a life free from the Agency. Fear, hope, and determination swirled inside me, impossible to separate.

A faint rustling of fabric caught my attention. I turned my head slightly, heart pounding. The door creaked open, and Harris slipped into my room under the cover of darkness. His movements were precise and cautious—but there was something different tonight. His shoulders were tense, his jaw tight. For a second, his eyes flicked toward the camera in the ceiling before settling on me. He closed the door behind him with a soft click.

"Hold on," Harris whispered, reaching into his pocket to pull out his audio scrambler. The device emitted its signature soft buzz, masking our conversation from prying ears. Harris glanced over his shoulder, his jaw tightening as he adjusted the device like he'd done it a hundred times, but this time, there was a tension in his movements—like he was waiting for something to go wrong. He had been using it sparingly due to increased Agency suspicion, so tonight had to matter.

Harris moved to a shadowed corner, his voice barely above a whisper. "Stay still, act like you're asleep. We need to talk about tomorrow night."

Harris leaned in, his expression serious. "I need you to meet me in this hidden room on the second basement level tomorrow night. We'll remove the tracking device then. It's crucial we're not seen together. Use the service stairs—avoid the elevator. There are limited cameras in those stairways, so keep off to the side and an eye out for patrols."

His voice was tight. This wasn't a drill, and if we messed it up, that was it. Game over.

"They've tightened security," Harris continued. "They're on edge, and any mistake could blow everything. You need to stay focused."

I nodded, forcing the motion to look natural as panic buzzed beneath my skin. I could feel it rising, pressing against the inside of my chest, but I shoved it down—habit, instinct, survival. The pressure hit me hard, but I wasn't supposed to feel it. Feeling was dangerous. So I didn't.

Before he could step away, I lowered my voice. "Where exactly is it? The room."

Harris hesitated for a beat, then answered, "Take the service stairs all the way down. You'll reach a maintenance corridor—mostly abandoned. There's an old storage door with a keypad that's been broken for years. Push hard on the left side of the frame—it'll pop open. From there, follow the hall until you see a flickering overhead light. The room's tucked behind it. It looks like a janitor's closet, but it's soundproofed. No one ever goes down there."

I nodded once, committing every detail to memory like my life depended on it. Because it did.

Harris's voice dropped lower, a hint of protectiveness threading through the tension. There was something in the way he said it—like he wasn't giving instructions, but trying to shield me from the fallout he knew was coming. "Stay alert. And remember, trust no one."

His warning sent a shiver down my spine, and I instinctively glanced at the blinking red light above the door. What if they knew? What if this was all being recorded, dissected, cataloged for punishment later? My thoughts spiraled before I could stop them—long enough for the training to kick in and shove it all into the back of my mind like it didn't matter. The danger was real. I could feel it crawling under my skin, but I couldn't let it show. I met Harris's gaze, determination mirrored in his eyes.

"I understand," I replied, my voice steady despite the fear gnawing at my insides.

Harris had basically become the one person I didn't question—not because I trusted easily, but because he hadn't let me down yet. Right before he left, he paused for a second, like he was about to say something but thought better of it. I found myself watching him go without meaning to, like if I looked away, something would snap loose inside me.

Harris slipped back into the shadows, disappearing into the night. I laid back on my bed, the room falling into silence once more. The severity of everything pressed down on me, tightening across my chest like a vice, making it hard to breathe. But under the flicker of the red light on my ceiling, there was something else too—a single breath that didn't feel as heavy. A flicker of hope I didn't trust, but couldn't ignore.

The halls were quieter than usual as I slipped out of my room—too quiet. Every step down the stairwell echoed. I stuck to the shadows, taking the service stairs two at a time, the cold concrete pressing against my palms when I leaned into corners to avoid the line of the cameras. This part of Headquarters always felt different—like the walls didn't breathe. My heart thudded harder the deeper I went, each step carrying me closer to a line I couldn't uncross.

By the time I hit the second basement level, the air felt

heavier, thick with the scent of dust and rusted metal. The hallway stretched ahead like something forgotten, dim and too still. The only sound was the faint hum of overhead lights—no footsteps, no voices, only silence thick enough to choke on. I reached the door Harris described—a beat-up storage frame with chipped paint and a keypad that hadn't worked in years. I pushed hard on the left side. It gave way.

The room looked like it hadn't been touched in forever—until you saw the maps. They covered one wall, dotted with red pins, black lines cutting through cities like scars. A metal table sat under a single light, covered in tools, papers, scraps of old tech. Harris stood at the edge of it, waiting, his arms crossed tight and jaw clenched, looking like he hadn't slept in days. His eyes didn't leave the doorway until I stepped through.

"Close the door behind you," he said, voice low, eyes already scanning the hall behind me. He powered on the audio scrambler, its buzz filling the room like white noise in my skull. "We don't have much time."

He nodded to the stool in the center of the room. I sat. My hands clenched my knees—automatic, like my body was trying to lock itself in place.

"Let's get this tracker out of your arm," Harris said, voice even but tight, like he was trying to sound calm for my sake. He grabbed something off the bench that looked like it belonged in a horror movie. "This isn't gonna be pleasant, kid. So take this and bite hard."

He handed me a thick strip of leather. I didn't ask questions. Just nodded, shoved it between my teeth, and braced—like I'd been trained for this. No hesitation. Follow the order, take the hit, survive.

The pain was immediate. Burning, sharp, deep. It hit the same place in my mind as every punishment I had ever endured, designed to break you down. My body remembered before I did. Like fire and glass burrowing into muscle. My jaw locked around the leather, breath ragged through my nose. I focused on the wall—the lines, the pins, anything but the way it felt when the tool dug deeper through my muscles.

Sweat dripped down my spine. My nails dug half-moons into my thighs. I couldn't stop the twitch of my legs, the silent curse in my throat.

I glanced at Harris. His hands didn't shake. His face was all focus and tension, brows low, eyes narrowed. I caught something behind it, though. Worry. He didn't say anything except, "Just a bit longer, Christopher," voice low and tight. Not commanding—something gentler, like he needed me to believe it too.

Eventually—finally—he pulled out the chip. A tiny piece of metal that had watched my every step over the last few months. He dropped it into a small containment unit like it was toxic.

"It's out," Harris said, and I could hear the relief under the flatness of his voice.

He glanced toward me. "You still have the decoy tracker?"

I nodded and pulled it from my pocket—the matte black device Harris had given me almost two weeks ago.

"Good," Harris said. "That thing should have already taken over. Don't forget to ditch it when you're ready to disappear. It'll keep them looking in the wrong direction—if we're lucky."

I shoved it back in my pocket. It felt heavier than it should—like it wasn't tech anymore, but every decision waiting to blow back in my face. Every risk.

Harris unrolled a map across the desk and tapped a spot near the beach. My heart kicked a little harder. I leaned in, trying to focus, trying to stay steady.

"I'll stash a car here—nothing flashy. Keys will be in the wheel well. At the grad party, once you leave the tracking device and the 'health monitor' behind, you and Noa head straight here. Got it?"

I nodded, tracing the route with my finger. Memorizing everything.

"And the safe house?"

He tapped again, farther inland. "Cabin in Patapsco Valley. About a forty-five to fifty-minute drive from Sandy Point, if traffic's light. No tech. I'll meet you there, then move you both somewhere safer."

He handed me one last thing—a grey box, about the size of my palm.

"This is a signal jammer. Blocks video, audio feeds, Bluetooth, the works... Use it when you leave, use it while you wait. Don't turn it off. I'll leave it for you in the glovebox of getaway car."

I met his eyes. "Thank you, Harris." I hesitated, the rest of it caught in my throat. He didn't need me to say it—he already knew.

He placed a hand on my shoulder, firm and steady. "We're in this together now, Christopher." He paused, like he wasn't sure how much to promise. "I'll do everything I can to get you and Noa to safety."

I stepped into the elevator, the metallic doors closing behind me with a finality that echoed the dread building in my chest. This wasn't a routine summons—this felt like something else. Like we'd been caught. Hauled into a room, stripped of everything, with Harris nowhere in sight and no one to blame but myself. I'd seen enough to know that's how it would go. As the elevator began its ascent, I felt the familiar pull of gravity, a physical reminder of the tension coiling within me. My hands clenched and unclenched at my sides, a subconscious attempt to dispel the nervous energy building with each passing second.

Why now? Why this meeting? Had someone seen me with Harris? Had they found the hidden room? The questions tumbled over each other in my mind, each one feeding my unease. The last time I was on the sixth floor, I'd come searching for answers—quiet, desperate, reckless. Now, I was being dragged back into her world without warning, and the timing couldn't be worse.

The thought of facing her now, after everything, sent a shiver down my spine. She wasn't a mad scientist or the head of an overwhelming government agency—she was my mother. That fact was both bewildering and infuriating. The betrayal stung deeper than I cared to admit. My shoulders tensed, jaw locking tight as I shut it down—fast. Stuffed it into the same locked drawer where I kept everything I didn't have time to feel. Anger was easier. Anger gave me something to hold onto while I figured out how to face her. How do you confront the person who orchestrated every lie, every invasive control over your entire life?

As the elevator slowed, I forced a breath through my nose, steadying the panic that threatened to crack open inside my ribs. I needed to stay sharp. Calm. Cold, if I had to.

When the elevator doors slid open, I stepped into the office reception area and immediately clocked the secretary. Different from the last one—a petite woman with dark hair pulled into a bun so tight it looked painful. She looked calm. Too calm. Maybe the rumors were true—no one lasted long under Dr. Bennett.

She glanced up, her expression unreadable. "Christopher," she said, setting aside a stack of documents. "Dr. Bennett is expecting you. One moment."

I nodded once. My heart kicked faster as she slipped into the office, the door left slightly ajar. Moments later, she returned, holding it open. "You can go in now," she said.

I stepped inside. The door clicked shut behind me.

Bennett's office looked exactly as I remembered—cold, clean, curated. The air smelled faintly like disinfectant and old paper, with a mix of artificial cinnamon. The towering bookshelves. The mahogany desk. And her, sitting like she owned the air in the room. It made my skin crawl.

She looked up, a soft smile on her face. A trap in silk. Her eyes flicked over me, sharp and clinical. My spine straightened instinctively, shoulders locking tight, like I could hide something by bracing hard enough.

"Christopher," she said, cool and precise. "Thank you for coming."

I stayed near the door, arms stiff at my sides. "Did I really have much of a choice?" I said, voice flat and low, the bitterness contained beneath the surface.

She didn't flinch. "Please, sit," she said, gesturing lightly toward the chair without moving an inch from her rigid posture. Her voice stayed smooth, but there was no warmth in it—the suggestion of control dressed up as courtesy.

"I'd rather stand."

There was a flicker in her eyes—something sharp—before she smoothed it out. "Very well. I wanted to talk about your future. You're approaching a pivotal moment."

I folded my arms. "Is that so?"

Bennett leaned forward, elbows resting on the desk like we were having some kind of heart-to-heart. "I know you've been struggling with the truth about your origins," she said, her tone warm but empty—carefully placed, perfectly rehearsed. "I want you to know, despite everything, my priority has always been your well-being."

I nearly laughed. "You've done a great job showing that, mother."

Her eyes flickered. But she didn't bite. "The world outside these walls is dangerous. The Countdown Control Agency offers protection. Guidance. A future."

"A future as a pawn?"

"Not a pawn," she said, voice hardening. "A leader. Someone who can help shape what's next."

For a second, I wanted to believe her. But it was automatic, the way my mind yanked me back. The newly formed scab on my arm throbbed like a warning. Hope didn't survive long in places like this—not for people like me. I heard Harris's voice in my head. Saw the chip on the table. Felt the scab forming on my arm.

"What about my choices?" I asked, the words rough in my throat. "Do they matter to you?"

She hesitated—long enough to notice. "Your choices matter more than you realize. The influence you wield carries a weight of responsibility."

I didn't trust the sincerity in her voice. Not when it was wrapped in so much strategy. "Why now?"

Dr. Bennett stood. "Because it's time you understood the role you have in this world." As she said it, she rose from her chair, spine straightening, voice gaining the faint edge of command beneath the calm. "We're not your enemy, Christopher. We're your family."

Family. I nearly choked on it.

"Family protects," I said coldly. "They don't surveil and control."

Her expression shifted—softening, a little, her head tilting and her hands uncurling slightly from where they rested on the desk. "I only want what's best for you. Like any mother would."

I turned away, the ache in my chest twisting tighter. "I need time to think."

"Of course." Her voice dropped, almost gentle. "Just remember—I'm always here."

I didn't look back. I walked out, the door closing behind me.

The hallway felt colder. I clenched my fists to keep from shaking, swallowing the heat behind my eyes before it could turn into something I couldn't control. Every step away from her office felt heavier than the one before.

CHAPTER FOURTEEN

Bittersweet Symphony

Noa

The kitchen felt like a ghost town. No squabbling over cereal boxes. No clatter of pans. Just silence—the kind that pressed into your chest and made you feel like the only person left alive.

I poured cereal into a bowl, the clink of the spoon against ceramic louder than it had any right to be. Morning light spilled through the window in long, pale streaks, catching the dust in the air like it was frozen mid-fall. Today was graduation day. My stomach dropped the second I thought it, like my body was trying to reject the idea before it could land. It felt like standing on the edge of something I couldn't name.

I sat down at the table, spoon in hand, and my thoughts drifted backward, to my birthday a little over a week ago. Turning eighteen was supposed to feel... big. Like something was supposed to click into place. I was supposed to feel excited. Grown. But instead, it felt like slipping further into the margins—like everyone else got a rulebook and I was still scribbling in the dark.

Ami hadn't spoken to me since prom. Mom had never acknowledged the day. But Christopher—he'd made it matter.

He showed up early that morning, eyes a little nervous, holding a small, unevenly wrapped box in both hands. I chose to ignore the thick bandage on his arm. Inside was a worn paperback—my favorite edition of Jane Eyre—with tiny margin notes scribbled in his handwriting. "Happy birthday, Noa," he said, and it was the way he said it that made something in me soften.

We wandered Annapolis all day. Hit our favorite bookstores, got coffee from a tiny place by the pier. At sunset, we found a hill overlooking the bay. He laid out a blanket, pulled out a cupcake with one crooked candle. "I know it's not much," he said, voice quiet. "But I wanted you to have a happy memory to look back on."

That day stuck with me. Not because it was perfect, but because it was the first time in a long time I felt safe. Like I didn't have to brace for something to go wrong. It felt real. Honest. It reminded me that not everything had to hurt to mean something.

And now—graduation. That word felt like a brick in my stomach. The idea of walking across that stage, hearing my name called, knowing exactly what I was planning to do by the end of today—it felt impossible and inevitable all at once.

I pictured Lucas and Ethan cheering like goofballs from the crowd, their faces bright and oblivious. They didn't know I was leaving, at least they didn't know it was today. And I couldn't tell them—not yet. How was I supposed to explain?

Graduation wasn't only a ceremony. It was the cliff's edge.

I finished my cereal, each bite turning to paste in my mouth, and headed upstairs. As I reached my bedroom, I heard the sound—soft, but unmistakable. Paper.

I pushed the door open.

Mom sat on my bed. My journals were spread out in front of her like a crime scene.

"Noa, what is all this?" Her voice wasn't shocked. It was sharp. Accusatory. She sat stiff-backed, clutching one of the journals like it might slip away if she let go, her fingers pressing into the leather cover hard enough to bend it.

Panic surged so fast it made me dizzy. "Mom, why are you going through my stuff?"

She held up one of the journals. "Are you hiding something from me?"

My throat went dry. I stepped back instinctively, like I could shield the pages with distance alone. Those pages held everything. Late-night talks with Christopher. Our plans. Our fears. Every piece of hope I'd been too afraid to say out loud.

"They're mine," I said, voice low but shaking. "You had no right."

She stood, journal still clutched in her hand like evidence. She stepped forward without meaning to, her body blocking the doorway—as if she could keep me cornered with posture alone. "I won't let you ruin your future over that boy. You're just a child, Noa. You don't know what's best for you."

That word—child—burned like acid.

"I'm not a child," I snapped. "I'm eighteen. I'm graduating. I get to decide who I am."

Her face twisted—less rage, more desperation—she wasn't done. There was fear beneath her words, but she wielded it like a weapon. "You're making a mistake. Christopher is dangerous. You don't know what you're getting into."

The sting of it cut deep. My breath hitched, a blink too slow, as if her words had physically grazed something raw beneath my skin. I didn't back down, not this time.

"No, you're the one who doesn't understand. You haven't cared to understand anything about me my whole life, so I don't see why you would try now." My voice was firm, fueled by years of feeling unseen. "And even if you wanted to, you couldn't. You've never had a Countdown Mark, you've never met your soulmate. You're alone, and as long as you keep treating people the way you do, you always will be."

Her mouth opened, but I cut her off, "I've made my choice. I'm leaving. And you don't get to control me anymore."

The silence that followed was violent. She stormed out, slamming the door so hard it rattled the walls.

I stood in front of the mirror, adjusting my navy-blue graduation gown, smoothing every crease like I could press order into the chaos of everything else. This was the day I'd dreamed of for years—a day of both endings and beginnings. It should've felt like a victory. Instead, it felt like holding my breath.

Excitement and anxiety jostled in my chest. Immediately, I felt the urge to squash it down. Joy didn't feel safe. Not when everything good still came with a cost. My reflection stared back—cap perched perfectly on my curls, gown settled so. But the mirror didn't show how far I'd come—it asked who I'd become.

A girl growing into her bones. A girl who was finally choosing herself—even if part of her still wondered whether she was worth the version she was becoming.

I reached for the locket Christopher gave me. I had added the new key-shaped charm to the chain—the second half of his birthday gift to me. "You hold the key to my heart," he'd said with all the sincerity in the world, his voice too genuine to laugh at even if the words were cheesy. I rolled my eyes then. I smiled now. Fastening it around my neck, I felt something settle. The weight of it grounded me—steadying my heartbeat, anchoring me to something real in the swirl of everything else. Like I wasn't doing this alone.

On my desk sat a photo of my family from when we still felt like one. My brothers were grinning, tangled together with arms flung around each other. My mom and I—softer, less distant. I traced the edge of the frame with my thumb. Leaving them—Lucas and Ethan—was the part I'd tried not to think about. But it was real. And it hurt.

The photo was a snapshot of something already gone. But their smiles still reached me. Still reminded me why I had to go forward, not back. I needed to be someone they could count on—even from afar.

I set the photo down and pulled my speech closer. The paper looked like it had lived a life—creased, rewritten, lines slashed and scribbled, margins filled with thoughts I was still trying to believe. I wanted it to mean something. I needed it to. For them. For me. For the girl who almost didn't make it to this day.

I folded it carefully, like it was sacred, smoothing each crease with my thumb as if the act itself could steady me, and tucked it into my bag.

My phone buzzed. Relief flickered in my chest, a soft counterpoint to everything else unraveling inside me.

> You'll look beautiful no matter what you're wearing.

> So hurry up before we're late!

> Ready when you are.

Christopher. Always knowing how much or little to say.

I attached the tassel to my cap and glanced around my room. Memorizing the uneven stack of books by the bed. The chipped ceramic fox on the windowsill. The sense of familiarity that might never feel the same again. I stepped out, my footsteps quiet but heavy. The silence downstairs was different from the quiet upstairs—thicker, heavier. It had teeth.

At the bottom of the stairs, I saw her. Mom. Sitting like she hadn't moved in hours, her spine straight, hands folded too tightly in her lap—like acknowledging my presence might crack something she wasn't ready to face. Eyes locked on the TV. Rigid. Distant. Unyielding.

I paused, waiting for her to look up. To say something. Anything.

Nothing.

The sting of it burned sharp in my throat; I blinked hard and clenched my jaw, swallowing the ache before it could show. I almost said something. A parting shot, a final plea. But I didn't. Today wasn't about her.

Lucas and Ethan were already at the door. Their eyes lit up when they saw me.

"You look amazing, Noa!" Lucas yelled. "You look like a superhero in a cape," Ethan added, grinning like he'd won a prize, their voices so full of joy. I bent to hug them, arms wrapping tight around their shoulders.

"Thanks, guys," I whispered. "Let's make today unforgettable, okay?"

A black SUV idled in the driveway. As I climbed inside, the chill of the leather seat seeped into my skin—a jolt against the nerves coiled tight in my chest, amplifying how detached I already felt from the day ahead. A sharp contrast to the golden warmth bleeding through the windows. It was one of those mornings that looked too perfect to match how you felt inside.

Two agents occupied the front seats, their eyes fixed ahead, faces unreadable behind dark sunglasses. Their presence was a quiet threat. A shiver of unease crawled up my spine as I fastened the seatbelt, the click too loud in the charged silence.

My brothers scrambled into the back row, their voices tumbling over each other in a rush of excitement about the ceremony. Their chatter filled the SUV, wrapping around the tension like sunlight trying to warm a shadowed room. The sound tugged something loose in my chest—enough to soften the edge of dread, to let me breathe a little deeper. Beside me, Christopher offered a small, reassuring smile.

"You're going to do great," he whispered, leaning in close. "Just remember to breathe."

I nodded, latching onto his voice—without hesitation, without doubt. Trusting him felt as natural now as breathing. Inhale. Exhale. Again. His hand found mine—warm, solid—and with that anchor in my palm, the SUV eased forward, pulling us into motion. Through the tinted windows, Annapolis blurred past—the familiar shops, parks, and sidewalks that had shaped the edges of my childhood. They didn't feel like home anymore. And for the first time, that thought didn't sting.

"Hey, don't forget to wow the crowd with your epic speech," Ethan piped up, grinning like he'd cracked the most important reminder of the day, slicing through my thoughts. I turned enough to meet his eyes and ruffled his hair with a soft grin.

"Of course! It's right here," I teased, tapping my temple. He lit up like he always did when I played along.

As the Showplace Arena came into view, nerves fluttered low in my stomach. This was it. Everything had been building to this moment. My breath hitched. Fingers curled into my palms. The pressure didn't sit in my chest—it pulsed through me, demanding to be felt. The weight of my cap and gown suddenly pressed against me.

The SUV rolled to a stop. Christopher gave my hand one final squeeze, his gaze locking onto mine with a quiet kind of intensity that told me I wasn't alone in this—not for a second.

"You've got this, Noa," he said, his eyes locking on mine, voice low and steady as if he was threading calm into the space between us. "I'm right here with you."

With Christopher and my brothers flanking me, I stepped out of the SUV and into the light. The sun was too bright, the moment too big—but still, somehow, it felt right. The air hit my skin like a breath I hadn't realized I was holding, cool and real. My feet sank into the gravel with each step, grounding me in the weight of now. The end of one life. The beginning of another.

The energy in the Showplace Arena was electric as I walked through the doors, my heart pounding with a mix of excitement and nostalgia. Rows of seats stretched before me, filled with proud families and friends. The air was alive with the vibrant colors of blue and gold caps and gowns—everywhere I looked, it felt like the end of something big and the start of something I hadn't figured out yet.

As I took my place in line with my fellow graduates, I felt the weight of my speech in my slightly trembling hands. But beneath the nerves, there was something steadier too—like the echo of every hard-won moment leading here, reminding me I'd earned this. I adjusted my cap and tassel one last time, trying to calm the nerves bubbling inside me. The grandeur of the event was almost overwhelming—the crowd's chatter blending with music and announcements, echoing through the vast arena.

Mr. Thompson took the podium, his voice resonating through the hall. "Ladies and gentlemen, distinguished guests, faculty, and the graduating class of 2019. It is my great honor to introduce our valedictorian for the Class of 2019. This individual has demonstrated exceptional academic prowess, unwavering dedication, and a commitment to excellence that has truly set them apart. Please join me in welcoming to the podium, the Annapolis High School valedictorian of 2019, Noa Mitchell."

The applause washed over me. It loosened the tightness in my chest and warmed my cheeks with a flush I couldn't stop. I stepped forward, steadier than before. I scanned the crowd, eyes darting through the sea of faces until they landed on my brothers—waving with such wild joy it made my chest ache in the best way. But the warmth of that moment cracked a little when my eyes caught Ami. She rolled hers and looked away. The sting was sharp, but I swallowed it down.

"Good afternoon, everyone," I began, my voice amplified through the arena. "Today, we stand on the brink of a new beginning—a future filled with endless possibilities."

I paused. Let the silence carry the moment.

"We've faced countless challenges. Celebrated unexpected triumphs. Each of us holds a story—a countdown—that shaped who we are today. And now, we turn the page. Armed with what we've learned, with the weight and wonder of where we've been."

The crowd held still. I kept going.

"Change is never easy," I said, grounding my voice. "But change is how we grow. We've learned to adapt. To stand back up.

Let's carry forward the courage that got us here—and the hope that'll carry us wherever we go."

A ripple moved through the crowd.

"There were days I felt lost. Days I doubted everything. And for a long time, I hid that pain—buried it under silence. But standing here now, I own it. Every scar, every question, every step it took to get to this stage. But I've learned that uncertainty isn't weakness—it's the moment right before strength. The space where you choose to keep going. To believe there's more ahead than what's behind."

I looked at my brothers again. Lucas's grin. Ethan's wide eyes. Something about their joy cracked open the weight in my chest, letting the pride slip in through the ache. It helped.

"We're not defined by what breaks us. We're defined by how we rise. Let's take that truth with us. Always."

I closed with gratitude—simple and honest.

"Thank you to the families, the teachers, the friends who stayed. Thank you for believing in us. As we leave here today, may we face the future with clarity, courage, and heart. Congratulations, Class of 2019."

The arena erupted. Applause. Cheers. The sound rushed in like a wave, loud and sudden, rattling through my chest. My body jolted slightly with the force of it, but I stood my ground. It all blurred around me. I stepped down, lungs finally exhaling, chest tight with something that felt like pride. I glanced back at Ami, but she was still turned away. I exhaled slowly and decided I needed to let her go, let the tension ease from my shoulders.

The ceremony continued, a steady rhythm of names echoing

through the warm afternoon air, tassels turning with each step across the stage. When the last name was called and caps soared into the sky—a sea of blue and gold arcing above us—I felt something shift inside me. It wasn't relief, exactly. More like the quiet ache of something ending, something I wasn't sure I was ready to let go of. The noise, the cheering, the flashes of cameras—it all blurred at the edges. And when it ended, when the crowd began to scatter and the stage emptied, Christopher found me without hesitation, like he'd never looked away.

"You were amazing," he said, wrapping me in a fast, warm hug. "I'm proud of you."

"Thanks," I breathed. Relief and something like joy tangled in my voice. "Let's go find my brothers."

The arena was alive with celebration. Families and grads crying, laughing, shouting names across rows of chairs. I moved through the chaos with Christopher beside me, steadying my steps without saying a word. At one point, his hand brushed the back of my gown—enough to keep me tethered, to remind me he was there.

"There they are," he said, pointing.

Lucas and Ethan were bouncing, practically vibrating with excitement. Lucas nearly tripped over Ethan's foot trying to get to me first, which only made Ethan shove him playfully.

"You were awesome, Noa!" Lucas yelled.

"Best speech ever!" Ethan added, grabbing my arm.

"Thanks, guys." I laughed, hugging them both tight. "Let's go find a quiet spot."

We slipped away from the crowd and found a small clearing

outside the arena, tucked far enough from the noise to feel like we'd stepped into a pocket of quiet. The air was warm and sweet with the scent of blooming flowers. Above us, the sky was still streaked with late sunlight, the wind gentle as it brushed over my skin. I let the quiet settle into my limbs. For the first time all day, my body felt still.

Christopher and I sat on a low stone wall, the rough edge grounding me, while the boys raced around in wild, laughing loops. Their joy was loud and free, spilling into the open air without apology. I envied how easily they moved forward.

"How's it feel to be a graduate?" Christopher asked, his voice low and steady beside me.

I exhaled slowly, watching the boys blur past. "Strange. Like I'm stepping off a ledge and hoping there's ground on the other side."

He smiled, soft and knowing. "You did incredible. Your speech... I could tell you meant every word."

I nodded, fiddling with my tassel. "I hope I can live up to them."

"You already are," he said. "You've got something in you most people don't. Resilience. Fire."

He reached over and gently squeezed my hand, like an anchor. Like a promise.

For a while, neither of us spoke. We breathed. Let the moment settle.

I looked out at the fading light, at the boys I loved more than anything, at the boy beside me who had changed everything. I couldn't believe it was real. That high school was truly behind me.

That everything ahead was wide open and terrifying and mine. A vast unknown was stretched in front of me.

Christopher didn't stay long—helped get the boys inside, exchanged a quiet glance with me, and promised to meet at Sandy Point for the grad party. He had a few things to grab. I had more than that.

The second the door shut behind us, Lucas and Ethan were already kicking off their shoes and sprinting down the hallway, shouting something about video games and who got dibs on the controller. Like it was any other afternoon.

But it wasn't.

The weight of the house hit me all at once—thick, stale, and still. The shadows outside stretched long across the lawn, but in here, the quiet didn't feel warm. It felt heavy. Hollow. Like the echo of something that used to matter.

The house smelled like laundry and leftover breakfast, but even that felt distant. Like it belonged to someone else's life. I'd grown up here. Laughed here. Hid here. But now, all I could feel was how much I needed to leave it behind.

I hovered by the edge of the hallway, heart pounding. For a second, I almost didn't call them—almost let the moment pass. But I forced myself to breathe, to speak. I called Lucas and Ethan into the living room. Their footsteps padded down the hall, quick and eager. When they appeared, faces bright and curious, something in my chest clenched. I wasn't ready for this part.

"Come here, guys," I said, lowering myself onto the couch. They rushed in, climbing over each other to sit beside me.

"What's up, sis?" Lucas asked, eyes wide and round.

I took a breath. Then another. "I need to talk to you about something important. You know I love you both more than anything, right?"

They nodded, grins fading, their attention sharpening.

"I might have to go away for a little while," I said carefully, hating how vague it sounded. I wanted to tell them everything—every reason, every danger—but I couldn't. Not yet. Maybe not ever. "It's for something really important. And I can't explain everything yet, but I need you to trust me, okay?"

Ethan's arms wrapped around my middle so fast it knocked the air out of me. "Why do you have to go?" he asked, voice cracking.

"It's complicated," I said gently, running a hand through his hair. "But I promise, I'll come back. And while I'm gone, I need you two to stick together. Be strong for me. Look out for each other."

Tears shimmered in their eyes, and I had to blink hard to keep mine from falling first. I reached into my pocket and pulled out two small necklaces—plain silver chains, one with a tiny moon charm, one with a star.

"These are for you," I said, handing them over. "Keep them close, so you always remember I'm thinking about you."

Their small hands trembled as they clutched the chains, and my throat tightened so suddenly I had to look away. I reached out without thinking, covering their hands with mine.

"We love you, Noa," Lucas said, voice cracking.

"I love you too," I whispered, pulling them close. Their warmth soaked into me, grounding me as everything else felt like it was tilting.

"We don't want you to go," Ethan mumbled into my shoulder.

"I know," I said, pressing a kiss to his head. "I don't want to go either. But I have to. Just for a little while."

We stayed that way for a long time—curled together like we could hold off the world if we stayed still. But eventually, I pulled back and wiped their faces with the edge of my sleeve.

"Be brave for me, alright? I'll be back before you know it."

They nodded, solemn but fierce. "We will," they said together.

One last hug, and then I stood, heart splintering, and turned toward the stairs. I could feel their eyes following me, full of love and worry and silent questions.

In my room, I moved quickly. Clothes. Toiletries. A burner phone Christopher gave me. Everything had to be useful. Light. No space for extras. I stared at my stack of journals, the ones Christopher and I had passed back and forth. Pages and pages filled with thoughts we couldn't say out loud. Fingers twitching, I ripped the pages we wrote to each other out of them—I couldn't take a chance of someone else finding them after we were gone.

I paused by the dresser. My eyes landed on a silver bracelet Ami gave me for my fifteenth birthday. She had meant something to me. She still did, even if we weren't speaking. I wondered if she'd ever know I kept it—if she'd care. Part of me hoped she would.

I slipped the bracelet onto my wrist.

The room started to feel less like mine with each item I packed. The light seemed harsher—like it was exposing everything I was leaving behind. My band posters, my scattered books, a worn hoodie slung over the chair. None of it felt the same.

I touched the desk. The photo frame. Let my fingers skim the edge of everything that mattered. My brothers' faces beamed out of the family photo, and I pressed my thumb gently to their smiles. I quickly popped the frame open and grabbed the photo and stuffed it alongside my things.

With a deep breath, I turned and left my old room behind. I shouldered my bag, walked downstairs, and didn't look back until the very last second. Just long enough to take it all in. My whole life, held in the shape of a house. I opened the door, tightened my grip on the strap of my bag, and took one last breath before stepping out into whatever came next.

CHAPTER FIFTEEN
Rise Up
Christopher

The hallways of Headquarters greeted me with their harsh, unyielding lines. I'd walked these same corridors my whole life, memorized every scuff on the tile and flicker in the lights. Leaving them behind shouldn't have mattered—but it did. Even now, some part of me ached. The architecture wasn't cold—it was suffocating. Everything about this place felt designed to remind you that you belonged to someone else. The air reeked of industrial cleaners and metal, humming with that ever-present drone of machinery—a constant, low-grade threat pulsing through the walls.

Noa's voice echoed in my mind. Just hearing her in my head steadied me a little. Her words from the stage. Her eyes when she found me in the crowd. That look—steady and sure—held me together now. She reminded me what this was all for: not survival, but freedom. Her strength wasn't a comfort. It was a spark.

I stepped into the elevator and hit the button for the third floor. The doors had begun to close when a hand shot in. Dr. Lang. His eyes found mine immediately—sharp and measuring. Two agents followed him in.

"Back so soon, Christopher?" Lang said smoothly. "I assumed you'd be out celebrating with Noa before the relocation."

I forced a smile. "Just tying up some loose ends."

His nod was slow. Too slow. "Always diligent. Good. We'll need diligence for the upcoming projects." His gaze sharpened. "Anything I should be aware of?"

My pulse quickened, but I kept my expression neutral. "Nothing major. Just some last-minute details."

Lang didn't respond, only stared. His lips twitched—barely—but the smugness was there, tucked behind the smooth mask he always wore. The kind of look that made your skin crawl if you caught it too long. The elevator ride stretched on, thick with unspoken tension. When the doors opened, I stepped out, resisting the urge to look back. Only when the doors closed behind me did I let myself breathe.

Back in my room, I barred the door and moved fast—not because I had to, but because lingering too long made it harder. Every drawer I opened felt like cutting ties with a past I hadn't chosen but still carried. The urgency wasn't about time. It was about not giving myself the chance to hesitate. Floorboard, drawer, hollowed-out book—I retrieved the documents I had stashed away over the last few months. The paper felt almost warm in my hands. Each sheet buzzed with risk. With defiance. With everything I wasn't supposed to know. Each piece of potential evidence was a weapon, something real to throw back at them if everything fell apart.

I packed as fast as I could. Clothes. Toiletries. A few things that mattered—mementos I couldn't leave behind. My eyes landed on a dog-eared copy of A Wrinkle in Time. I hesitated, then slipped it in. I knew it wasn't practical. But it was the only thing here I really cared all that much about.

The chessboard outside my room hadn't moved in a while. I stared at the pieces, arranged mid-game, and saw my opportunity. I moved my queen—checkmate. I tipped Foster's king and the piece clicked against the board with a sound that felt final. Not triumphant—just... done. Like I was drawing a line under every lesson he ever taught me. It didn't feel like winning. It felt like walking away from a game I never chose to play.

I let myself smile—only for a second. I finally beat him. He'd once told me, "Every move is a reflection of your strategy and your ability to anticipate the enemy's next step." Back then, I thought he was talking about chess. I knew better now.

I grabbed my bag and moved through the corridors without looking back. The hum of the vents filled the silence. The building never slept, but it never felt more dead. At the elevator, I hit the button for the first floor. The doors started to close—then paused. A hand stopped them.

Harris.

He stepped in without a word, and his eyes met mine.

"Remember, Christopher," he said, voice low, "stay focused. Be careful. This is your only chance."

I nodded. "Thank you. For everything."

He gave me a look that held more than he could say—something that twisted in my gut for half a second. Like I was supposed to notice it. Like it meant something I didn't have time to figure out. "They're watching everyone tonight. Especially you."

His hand touched my shoulder. "Stay safe," he murmured.

The doors opened. I stepped into the lobby, and for a second, I hesitated. This was it—the last time I'd ever stand in this building. I didn't let the weight of that settle, but I felt it, sharp and buried, pressing against the edges of my thoughts. The reflection in the glass doors caught my eye. I barely recognized the person staring back.

I walked out.

The night air slapped my face—cold and electric. It hit harder than I expected, cutting through everything I hadn't let myself feel. Like a reset. The breeze smelled like rain. It cut through the staleness of the Agency like a knife. A black SUV waited at the curb. Two agents in the front. Silent, watching.

The drive was quiet. The city spilled past the window, lights and motion smeared across glass streaked with rain. D.C. faded behind us, and I told myself it didn't matter. That I was ready. But deep down, something hollow settled in my chest. It was more than buildings disappearing—it was the end of everything I'd ever known. And I wasn't exactly sure what came next.

My eyes flicked to the agents. Alert, but not alarmed. I kept still, kept breathing. We reached Annapolis, the houses thinned into woods as we passed through the neighborhoods. Trees thickened around the road, shadows swallowing everything but the headlights. Somewhere in the dark, I could hear waves crashing faintly against the shore. As we pulled closer to Sandy Point, I could see that the beach was glowing.

Fairy lights were strung through trees, soft and golden. After so many years in cold steel and shadows, it didn't feel real and I wasn't sure if I was allowed to stay. There was music rising and falling with the wind. Laughter. The scent of marshmallows, saltwater, and smoke from a bonfire drifted on the air.

I stepped out, my shoes hitting the sand as I exhaled the breath I didn't realize I was holding. I could see various agents moving around the edges of the party like shadows—watching, always watching. I scanned the crowd, and I saw Noa—her silhouette outlined by the bonfire. The fire reflected in her eyes a kind of determination I hope could get us through what was coming.

CHAPTER SIXTEEN

Dog Days Are Over

Noa

T he warm sand beneath my feet was a welcome comfort, grounding me in the middle of everything unraveling. It was soft, forgiving—so different from the cold, jittery edge of adrenaline that had been sitting in my chest all night. I took a deep breath, pulling in the salt-laced air as if it could anchor me to this moment, while the rest of me trembled with the weight of what came next.

Around me, classmates laughed, danced, and said their goodbyes like this was just another party. Some took pictures. Others played games or roasted marshmallows by the bonfire. People I barely knew suddenly knew my name.

"Great speech, Noa!" "Congratulations, valedictorian!"

I smiled. Nodded. Pretended the words didn't sound like they were meant for someone else. Like I hadn't been standing here wondering how someone like me ended up in a spotlight I never asked for. It was easier to float through the praise than to feel like I deserved any of it. Everything felt off, like I was slipping through a version of myself that only existed for tonight. One foot in the past, the other already running.

I drifted through the crowd, scanning faces, half-hoping for something familiar. My eyes landed on Ami. My chest pulled tight. Maybe... maybe we could fix it. One last conversation before I disappeared. I moved toward her, trying not to hope too much. But she saw me. She rolled her eyes, tossed her hair, and walked away. It was like I didn't matter anymore.

The drop of my heart in my chest came fast and sharp. I froze, breath caught somewhere between heartbreak and disbelief. I knew why this had happened, that I had to keep her at a distance. But knowing didn't make it hurt less. The grief of losing her sat heavy on top of everything else I hadn't had time to mourn.

I pulled in a shaky breath. Not tonight. I couldn't fall apart tonight. I swallowed it down—tightened every muscle, let my face go blank. The old reflex. Pretend you're fine until you almost believe it. This night wasn't about endings. It was about the beginning we were about to risk everything to reach. I had to hold on a little longer.

The bonfire crackled nearby, casting flickering light across the sand. I turned toward it, letting the warmth hit my face. It loosened something tight in my chest, soft where everything else had been sharp and bracing. In the shadows beyond the fire, I could almost hear my brothers' laughter from another time—racing through the park, shouting over each other, joy spilling into the sky.

I was leaving them. And I hated that. A part of me felt like I was abandoning them, if I knew deep down this was the only way. The guilt tangled with the grief—thick, unavoidable, and familiar. Hated what it meant. With Mom getting sicker, they'd have to grow up faster. Protect each other harder. And it was my fault. But it was also the only way right now to keep them safe.

The strings of lights above us blinked gently, washing the beach in soft gold. For a second, it almost felt like magic. Like we were outside time. I turned away from the fire and started weaving through the bodies again. Laughter and music swirled around me, both too loud and not loud enough. Then—

Christopher.

He was standing near the edge of the crowd, calm in a sea of noise. His eyes found mine instantly. That look in them—steady, quiet, real—undid something in me.

"Hey," he said when he got close enough for me to hear him.

"Hey," I breathed. Like an exhale I didn't know I'd been holding.

"You okay?"

I shrugged. "Today has been... a lot."

His hand found mine. Warm. Certain.

"We've got this," he said. "One step at a time."

We walked toward the bonfire, found a spot in the sand close to the flames. For a while, we didn't talk. We just sat. Let the warmth settle into our skin. My breathing slowed, and for the first time all night, the chaos in my chest quieted. Like my body finally believed it was safe—for a moment.

"I can't believe this is it," I said quietly. "Everything's changing so fast."

He leaned in, shoulder brushing mine. "It is. But we're ready."

I looked at him. Really looked. In that moment, beside the fire, it didn't feel like we were running. It felt strange, almost unnatural, to let myself believe in something gentle. But I did, for a second. I let myself feel it. It felt like we were finally choosing something, finally free.

Christopher stood, offering his hand. "Want to dance?"

I laughed, surprised by the lightness of it. "Thought you'd never ask."

We found a clear patch near the flames, the sand warm under our feet. Music pulsed in the background. We moved slowly, letting the moment carry us. The sand shifted gently beneath our feet with every step, and the light of the fire caught in Christopher's eyes—soft, golden, like it belonged to a different world entirely. For a little while, it was us—spinning, smiling, daring to believe. Every step was a promise. Every laugh was a refusal to let fear win.

But time wasn't waiting. Eventually, the hum of the party became background static. We shared a look. A silent decision.

It was time to go.

We walked to the edge of the beach, where our bags were tucked beneath a cluster of grass, hidden in shadow. Christopher crouched and pulled out two small devices from his pocket—the decoy tracker and the fake health monitor. He handed me the monitor. It was cool against my skin but felt like it weighed a hundred pounds.

"This is it," he mouthed.

I nodded, throat tight. Our eyes met for one last second, holding all the things we didn't say. Then, together, we turned and threw the devices as far as we could into the sand, toward the sound of crashing waves.

And we ran—into the forest, into the dark, into whatever came next. My pulse roared in my ears, drowning out everything but the sound of our feet hitting the earth, each step louder than the last.

CHAPTER SEVENTEEN

Run

Christopher

The warm night air rushed past us as our feet pounded against the sand, gritty and loose beneath our shoes, kicking up with each step. My breath came hard and uneven, loud in my ears, blending with the roar of the waves—like we were being chased by the ocean itself. Each step yanked us farther from the safety of the party and deeper into the unknown, the distance between what was and what could be growing with every stride. My wild heartbeat echoed the panic in my chest. Noa kept pace beside me, her breath quick, her face set with determination—though fear still flickered in her eyes. I knew it was mirrored in mine.

"Noa, this way!" I called, veering toward the tree line where the underbrush swallowed the moonlight. Our escape car sat hidden beneath a tangle of branches, barely visible in the shadows, exactly where Harris said it would be. As we reached it, the sky cracked open. Rain slammed down in sudden sheets, drenching us in seconds and turning the sand into sludge beneath our shoes. I dropped to one knee, hands fumbling for the key stashed in the wheel well. It took longer than it should have to unlock the car—my fingers were shaking too hard, the way they used to during drills when failure meant pain instead of panic. My hands couldn't forget what my mind was trying to push through.

But finally, the lock clicked. We jumped in, soaked and breathless.

"Go, go, go!" Noa urged, and I didn't need telling twice. The engine roared to life, a sound so loud it felt like it would give us away—but it also meant we were moving. I reversed quickly, bumping over roots and through mud as we tore out of the clearing and onto the narrow dirt road.

I didn't let myself breathe until we hit pavement. My hands were locked on the steering wheel, knuckles white, shoulders tight from holding so much in. Even then, I didn't really exhale—I eased off enough to keep driving straight. I glanced at the glovebox. "Grab the jammer," I told Noa, keeping my eyes on the road. She popped it open and pulled out the device—a slim, slate-gray rectangle with faint ridges along the sides. It looked like nothing. But it could mean everything.

She passed it to me, and I turned it over in my hand, the ridges biting into my skin. For a second, I hesitated. Not because I doubted it would work—but because I felt the weight of everything riding on it. My grip tightened until my knuckles ached. I flipped the switch, and a pulsing green light turned on at the center.

I kept checking the rearview mirror, half-expecting headlights or the wail of sirens to cut through the night. But the road behind us remained empty. The low hum of the engine and the relentless drumming of rain on the roof, blurring the world outside and swallowing everything beyond a few feet.

"Noa, check the map," I said, my voice tighter than I meant it to be. She opened the glovebox again and pulled out a folded map and a small flashlight. Her hands trembled as she scanned the highlighted route, her brow furrowed with focus.

"Left at the next turn," she said. I nodded and followed her lead, steering away from the main road and deeper into forgotten corners.

The streets blurred around us—road signs bleeding across wet pavement, shadows stretching too long. Streetlights flickered like blinking warnings, and my hands stayed tense on the wheel, alert to every motion around us. The hum of the engine vibrated through the seat beneath me. I could feel the edge of every breath I took, shallow and careful, like any noise might shatter our cover. Every time we passed a car, I tensed, waiting for a dark SUV to cut us off. But nothing happened.

I wanted to speak. To say something that would make the moment feel less like a countdown to our inevitable fate—freedom or imprisonment. But the words were stuck in my throat, caught by fear. I hated that I couldn't say anything—hated how small I felt in the face of it all. But there was nothing to say. The knowledge that every second we weren't caught was a second closer to freedom.

"Almost there," Noa murmured, her voice low. I glanced at her. In the dim light, I could see the strain written across her face.

The road narrowed, the city gave way to trees, and with it came a drop in temperature—a crisp bite to the air that pushed through the cracks in the windows. The scent of pine hit strong, earthy and clean, and a few of the branches reached low enough to scrape along the roof and sides of the car in sharp bursts of sound that made me flinch every time. Their limbs arched above us like a tunnel. The only sound was our tires crunching gravel and the wind through the branches.

Then—headlights. A checkpoint loomed ahead, cutting across the road like a wall. My breath caught. Muscle memory kicked in before I could think—years of conditioning wrapped in a single reflex. I killed the headlights and veered hard to the right, down a nearly invisible trail masked by brush. The car jostled and groaned, but held.

We crept through the dark, every second stretched thin and sharp. Neither of us breathed.

"That was too close," Noa whispered. Her hand was clenched around the edge of the seat.

"We'll make it," I said. I didn't know if it was true, but I needed it to be—needed something to hold onto, even if part of me kept whispering that hope was dangerous. That voice had always been there. But this time, I chose not to listen.

At last, we reached a small clearing surrounded by thick trees—our drop-off point. I killed the engine. We stepped out, grabbing our gear and the jammer. My legs ached from the tension of the drive, stiff as I straightened. The ground felt uneven beneath my shoes, and thick with mud. I paused for a beat, letting the lone sound of the rain settle around me—too thick, too still—and felt my shoulders tense against it. The forest pressed in around us, moonlight reaching through rain and the canopy of trees.

"Did we really get away?" Noa whispered.

"Yeah," I said. "I think we did. The decoy must've worked."

She met my gaze. In the dark, her eyes were clear. Fear and hope, tangled together. "Ready?"

I nodded. "Let's go."

We turned toward the woods. The path was narrow, overgrown, almost invisible. But we moved forward—step by step, breath by breath—disappearing into the dark.

The forest enveloped us as we moved deeper into its shadows, the air growing cooler and damper with each step. My grip tightened on Noa's hand as we navigated the uneven terrain, roots and rocks jutting out, threatening to trip us. "Watch your step," I whispered, my voice barely audible over the thick hush of the rain drumming on the canopy above and soaking through the leaves in a steady, relentless rhythm. Every sound felt amplified beneath it—the squelch of mud underfoot, the occasional crack of a twig snapping somewhere too close.

The scent of damp earth and decaying leaves thickened, mingling with the breeze. The darkness felt alive, wrapping around us like a cloak, pressing in with a suffocating weight. Noa's breathing came in shallow bursts, echoing the rapid thrum of my own pulse. "Do you think we're still on the right path?" she asked, her voice strained with a hint of panic.

"I hope so," I replied, trying to inject confidence into my tone, as a knot of uncertainty pulled tight in my gut. I couldn't let her see how unsure I really was—not when she was looking to me to lead. The map Harris had given us, paired with my memory, was all we had to rely on. The thought of veering off course gnawed at me, but I couldn't afford to let her see my doubt.

We pushed forward, the trees closing in around us, turning the path into a labyrinth of shadows and obstacles. It was disorienting and claustrophobic. The farther we went, the more the trail seemed to twist on purpose, each step a gamble in the dark, every twist a threat we couldn't predict. The rain muffled everything, but every now and then, the forest betrayed us with the crackle of a branch or a squish of mud beneath our steps. Each noise was a potential threat.

"Careful," I muttered as Noa tripped over a twisted root. I caught her arm, steadying her before she could fall. Her fingers clamped onto mine, and I felt the tremor of fear in her grip.

"How much further?" she whispered, her breath ragged.

I didn't answer right away. The truth was, I didn't know. Not really. The forest felt endless, the path twisting and shifting beneath our feet like it was trying to lose us. I didn't want to lie, but I couldn't offer certainty either. That silence stretched, heavy with everything I didn't say. Each step dragged us deeper into a night that seemed intent on swallowing us whole. A sudden noise—a sharp rustling ahead—froze us in place. My heartbeat thundered in my ears as I gestured for Noa to stay low. We crouched, every muscle in my body coiled tight as a bowstring.

Voices drifted through the dark—low, clipped, too familiar. That controlled cadence, that cold precision—it could only belong to CCA agents. The sound slid along my spine like a blade of ice. Definitely CCA agents. Their flashlights cut through the gloom, slicing the dark into stark, glaring segments. How had they tracked us here? Panic clawed at my chest, but I forced myself to breathe evenly, to stay calm. We pressed ourselves against a tree, melding into the shadows.

The seconds stretched, each one an eternity steeped in the fear of being found. The agents' footsteps were close enough to feel, their beams bouncing erratically across the underbrush. I squeezed Noa's hand, willing her to stay still, to keep silent as the moment passed. There was a desperate edge to it—an instinct not to hide, but to protect her, to shield her from the fear clawing at my throat. One wrong move and everything we had worked for would be lost.

Finally, the voices faded, swallowed by the wet hush of the forest and the distance between us. The flashlights vanished, leaving only the whisper of rain and the drumbeat of my heart. I exhaled shakily, muscles slowly uncoiling as we waited a moment longer, making sure they were truly gone.

"That was too close," Noa breathed, her voice raw with relief and fear.

"We're okay," I whispered back, masking my own tremors with a steadiness I didn't feel. I'd said that line more times than I could count, in rooms where I wasn't allowed to be scared, where showing anything real meant weakness. It came out too easy now—reflex instead of truth. "The jammer's working. We need to keep moving."

We rose, the forest holding its breath with us as we pressed onward. Mud clung to our shoes with each step, heavy and cold, dragging at our pace. My calves burned, lungs tight from too many shallow breaths, but I kept moving. There wasn't room to slow down—not when every branch felt like a tripwire, and every sound a trap. The trees began to thin—the rain, too—revealing patches of moonlight reflected in puddles. Noa's eyes lit up with a glimmer of hope as she pointed. "Look, the trees are thinning. Do you see that?"

I followed her gaze, squinting until the outline of a clearing emerged from the shadows. Relief surged through me, a wave so powerful I nearly stumbled. "We're almost there," I said, squeezing her hand tighter. We quickened our pace, spurred on by the promise of shelter—by the desperate, fragile hope that we'd made it.

The clearing opened before us, the safe house standing like a beacon. My legs nearly gave out at the sight. Relief hit so hard it made my vision blur, the adrenaline crashing all at once. I tightened my grip on Noa's hand, grounding myself in that moment—one breath, one heartbeat, away from something that finally felt like hope. It was small and unassuming, camouflaged by the wild growth around it. But to us, it was sanctuary. Without another word, we hurried toward it, leaving the fear-soaked path of the night behind us.

The cabin was small and rustic, with weathered wooden walls that blended seamlessly with the surrounding forest. Moss blanketed the roof, and ivy curled up one side like nature was trying to take it back. The clearing barely existed—a patch of moss-covered ground hemmed in by towering trees. Overhead, tangled branches let through only slivers of moonlight, casting fractured beams across the forest floor. The air was cool. Still. The kind of quiet that made every hoot, every rustle, sound like a warning.

We reached the door. I found the key under a smooth, flat rock near the frame. My hands shook as I fit it into the lock, glancing over my shoulder twice before the key turned. I scanned the trees one more time—automatic, ingrained—before pushing the door open. The lock clicked open, and we slipped inside. The wooden floor creaked beneath us.

Inside, the cabin was humble but warm. Worn planks glowed under a flickering oil lamp on the side table, casting golden shadows across the walls. To the left, a tiny kitchen nook: a battered propane stove, a cooler half-buried in ice, and a counter cluttered with mismatched utensils and enough food for a day, maybe two. A round wooden table stood near the window, its surface scarred with dents and scratches.

A modest couch sat near the cold fireplace, its cushions sunken in. Above the mantle, there was a modest bookshelf. The spines of old books were cracked and faded, pages swollen from humidity and time.

Heavy curtains blanketed the windows, shielding us from the outside. The place felt like a fragile kind of safe. Noa's shoulders dropped, her hands unclenching for the first time in hours. "We made it," she exhaled, her voice barely more than a breath as she sank into one of the chairs by the table. Her arms were wrapped loosely around herself, like she wasn't sure yet if she could let go of the tension coiled in her chest. The crease between her brows unfurled, her jaw loosening as if she'd been clenching it all night. Relief moved across her face.

"Yeah," I murmured, locking the door behind us and sliding a chain into place. The deadbolt clicked. That sound alone brought a flood of shaky relief. "Let's get some rest while we wait for Harris."

She nodded and stretched out on the couch, eyes already heavy. I took up position by the window, settling into a chair angled toward the woods. The adrenaline was gone. All that was left was the crash—the weight settling into my limbs like wet cement. The air in the cabin pressed against my skin, thick and unmoving. The chair dug into my spine, and I didn't shift. I let it hurt. My leg bounced, my fingers tapped useless rhythms against the chair. I didn't notice I was doing it until I stopped. That silence made the weight of everything crash harder.

Outside, the forest breathed. The rain had finally stopped. Crickets chirped. Leaves rustled in the breeze. Every sound felt louder than it should, like the trees were whispering warnings. My eyes kept darting to the window, tracking every shift in shadow. I kept imagining a face between the trees, the glint of metal, the flicker of movement that meant we weren't alone.

"Noa, get some sleep," I whispered. She tugged the blanket up to her shoulder.

"Wake me if anything happens," she murmured, her voice softer now. Her eyes fluttered shut, hesitation still clinging to the edges of her expression. Soon, her breathing slowed. The worry in her expression began to ease.

I considered lighting the fireplace, for a little warmth.

But Harris's warnings echoed back—smoke meant visibility. Visibility meant danger. I left it cold.

Time dragged. The cabin creaked, the oil lamp hummed, and I kept watch. My mind kept circling back to the facility—to all the ways they could punish us if they found us. Solitary, sedation, maybe worse. I shook it off, only for it to come back louder. Like my brain didn't know how to be quiet unless it was afraid. My eyelids grew heavier. Shadows outside blurred together, my thoughts tugged backward—then forward—then nowhere at all.

A knock shattered the quiet. Sharp. Insistent. My heart lurched.

Noa sat bolt upright, a sharp gasp escaping her. Her eyes locked on the door, wide and unblinking.

"Is it Harris?" she whispered.

"I don't know," I replied, my voice tight as I pushed myself out of the chair. Each step toward the door sent my heart thudding harder against my ribs. I reached for the lock, slid the deadbolt back, but kept the chain in place. With a deep breath, I cracked the door open, enough to see a figure stood beyond the threshold—still, silent, the edge of a dark coat catching the moonlight. The dim light cast long, distorted shadows across their face, and I realized with a jolt of dread that this was not David Harris.

CHAPTER EIGHTEEN

The Sound of Silence

Noa

The cabin felt like it was shrinking around us, each second weighted with anticipation as Christopher approached the door. Dawn's first light was beginning to filter through the trees, casting long, eerie shadows that slashed across the clearing. The quiet outside was suffocating—every small noise felt amplified.

Christopher's hand hovered over the door handle, trembling, his whole body wound tight with tension. My heart thudded once—hard, deliberate—before settling into a tight, caged rhythm. I didn't move. Didn't breathe. Just listened, like stillness could make me smaller, safer. The door creaked open, and there she was—a woman framed by the dim light of dawn. Her dark brown skin caught the slivers of sun, and her striking green eyes swept the room with unsettling precision.

"Christopher Hawthorne?" she asked, voice steady, threaded with quiet authority.

Christopher stiffened further, his shoulders rigid, eyes narrowing with suspicion—but there was something else under it too. A flicker of fear. "Who are you?" The edge in his voice mirrored the anxiety thrumming between us.

"I'm Elara Kessler," she said, still standing outside the threshold. Her tone softened a notch, eyes flicking between us like she was measuring our reactions. "David Harris sent me."

She paused. Her expression shifted—subtle, but enough to make my breath hitch. "Harris didn't make it."

The words struck like a blow. Color drained from Christopher's face. He staggered back a step, knuckles white where he gripped the doorframe like it might hold him together.

"What do you mean?" His voice cracked, thin and disbelieving.

Elara's gaze shifted—but the steel in her posture didn't waver. If there was softness, it was measured, controlled. A choice, not a slip. "He was captured when you disappeared from the beach. They executed him."

A choked sound tore from Christopher, raw and broken. It filled the cabin like a wound, echoing off the walls. His body trembled, eyes shining as tears slipped free, unchecked.

Watching him unravel made something inside me splinter. I swallowed hard, forcing the ache down before it could take up space I didn't have to spare. I couldn't afford to fall apart too—not now.

"No," he whispered. "That can't be true." He shook his head like denial could undo it, could rewind time and change the outcome. "How do I know you're telling the truth?"

Elara met his gaze steadily, unfazed. She paused, then spoke in a quiet, measured tone. "You don't," she said simply, her eyes flickering between him and me. "But I'm the only chance you've got right now."

I hesitated. But there was something in her eyes, something genuine, that made me believe her. I stepped forward, steeling myself as I reached for the latch. The door opened fully, and Elara stepped inside—her movements careful, contained. She closed the door behind her swiftly. Her eyes scanned us again, assessing, not unkind—but sharp enough to make my stomach tighten.

"I know it's a lot," she said gently, "but we don't have the luxury of time. We need to leave before the CCA finds this place."

I found Christopher's hand with mine, squeezing gently. For a second, I let myself lean into it—let myself believe I was allowed to. The contact grounded us both. "Harris did all of this for us," I said, my voice trembling but firm. "We owe it to him to keep going."

Elara's presence radiated quiet strength—not the kind that demanded attention, but the kind that settled over everything without trying. I couldn't tell if it was something she projected on purpose, or something I needed her to be. She held our gaze—solid, unwavering—the kind of person people followed when everything was falling apart. "Take only what you need," she said. "The journey ahead is long."

The cabin, which had felt like shelter only hours before, now felt brittle. I moved quickly, gathering our belongings with fingers that fumbled from the weight of urgency and grief. I kept telling myself to focus—just pack, just move, don't feel. There wasn't room for that now. Christopher moved slower, haunted. His hands shook as he packed, eyes distant, like he was somewhere else entirely. The loss of Harris was a wound, fresh and gaping. There wasn't time for him to grieve.

When we finished, Elara nodded toward the jammer. I handed it to her, and she clipped it to her belt with practiced ease. Her expression sharpened.

"We need to move silently," she said, voice dropping low. "Sound carries far in the morning. We can't afford to be heard."

I glanced at Christopher. His jaw was clenched, eyes still bright with unshed tears—but there was resolve there too. We exchanged a look, an unspoken promise, then turned to follow Elara into the waking forest. The first rays of sunlight filtered through the canopy, casting long golden streaks over the path ahead. But they didn't warm me. Not enough. Not where it mattered. Behind us, the cabin stood silent.

Elara moved like someone who knew what danger felt like. Every step was intentional. Her eyes were always moving, calculating. It should've been reassuring, but it made something uneasy crawl up my spine. We followed her into the woods, each footstep deliberate. Our breath came shallow. The forest closed in around us—branches reaching, leaves whispering secrets we couldn't afford to hear.

The underbrush crackled beneath our feet, but Elara's signals kept us focused. Silent. Alert. The deeper we went, the less real the cabin felt. It was already a ghost—fading behind us. But the ghost of David Harris stayed close—heavy and unspoken, a weight I didn't know how to set down and wasn't sure I should.

The forest swallowed us in silence, each footstep a cautious push deeper into the unknown. The air was damp and cold, heavy with the scent of moss and something faintly metallic. Every breath tasted like wet earth and tension. Morning light filtered through the trees, golden and dappled, flickering across the dirt path. It was beautiful in the kind of way that made your stomach hurt.

Elara moved ahead with a precision that didn't need explaining—her steps disturbing the underbrush, eyes constantly scanning, never hurried, never uncertain. We followed her, quick and careful. Every breath felt measured. Every snap of a twig beneath our feet sounded like a firework. My heart wouldn't slow down. It pounded against my ribs like it wanted out. Christopher walked beside me, focused, jaw tight. He hadn't said a word since we left the cabin—like speaking might make it all too real. I could see the questions circling behind his eyes, the ones he wouldn't let out, not yet. Not until we were safe.

Elara's hand snapped up. I froze.

She dropped into a crouch, eyes scanning the thicket. We followed her lead—and then I saw them. Two CCA agents, moving like they knew the forest better than we did. Dark uniforms. Sharp, certain steps.

I pressed against the nearest tree, bark biting into my back. My lungs stalled. My pulse crashed in my ears. I hated how quickly my body betrayed me—how easily fear took the wheel. Christopher mirrored me, fear written in the hard lines of his face—though I could tell he was trying to mask it, to stay composed for my sake. They were close. Too close.

Their muffled voices drifted toward us, low and clipped. I

counted the seconds, each one tightening something in my chest. The forest felt like it was holding its breath.

Finally, their footsteps faded. The trees swallowed them. But I still didn't move.

What if it was a trick? What if they doubled back? The silence felt fragile.

Neither did Elara. She was stone. Waiting. Only when everything around us seemed to exhale did she motion for us to keep going.

We moved again, the forest shifting around us. Light filtered through the leaves in ribbons that vanished before they touched the ground. It felt like a warning. We climbed a ridge. The air turned sharp, colder. I had pulled in a shaky breath when I heard it—that low mechanical hum.

A drone.

Elara's eyes locked upward. She dropped low and motioned sharply, fingers flicking in practiced signals—quick, silent, precise. The kind of gesture that said she'd done this before, more times than she could probably count. "Stay down," she mouthed.

We dropped. Into thorns. Mud. Moss. None of it mattered. The drone buzzed overhead, shrill and high-pitched like a mechanical mosquito, slicing through the trees with a sound that made my skin crawl. I pressed into the earth and tried to make myself vanish. The ground was cold and damp, clinging to my skin and seeping through my clothes, grounding me with its bite. Every muscle screamed to run, but I stayed still, willing myself to disappear. Christopher's hand found mine. His fingers were cold. I held on like it might keep both of us grounded. The drone hovered.

Seconds dragged. Then—thankfully—it turned. The sound faded, and Elara lifted her head slowly. When she nodded, we moved.

The trees thinned. The sky opened up a little, and I didn't trust it. Then I saw a sleek black van waiting for us, and Elara directed us toward it.

Hope cracked open inside me—quick and sharp and dangerous. My chest tightened, breath catching before I could fully draw it in. I went still, like acknowledging it might scare it away. The kind that could vanish fast. I didn't know if I was allowed to feel it, or if trusting it would only make the fall worse. We exchanged a look—me, Christopher, Elara. Exhaustion. Relief. And something smaller. Something that almost felt like a win.

The van's engine hummed steadily beneath us, the sound mixing with the occasional thump of branches smacking against the metal sides as Elara took turn after twisty turn down some narrow, tree-packed road. Nobody said anything. It was that heavy kind of quiet where everything felt too loud—the hum of the tires, the tightness in my chest, the rustle of fabric every time I shifted in my seat. I could hear my own heartbeat. Couldn't stop focusing on it. Like if I let my mind go quiet for one second, everything would crash in. Christopher sat next to me, staring out the window. He looked like someone who'd aged five years overnight. His whole face was exhaustion and guilt and some other emotion I couldn't name. He wouldn't look at me. Wouldn't look at anything, really. Just kept his eyes fixed on the trees like maybe if he stared hard enough, the world might rewind.

I hesitated, fingers twitching in my lap. I wasn't sure if I was allowed to need comfort. If reaching for him would make the grief more real. But my chest ached, and I couldn't hold it in anymore. I reached out, weaving my fingers through his. He squeezed back. Not tight, but steady. Enough to say, I feel it too. Enough to keep us both from falling apart.

Harris was gone. And we were just—floating. The van felt like it was packed with ghosts. With everything we didn't say. With everything we'd already lost.

Outside, sunlight spilled across the landscape like nothing had happened. I squinted against the brightness. It made everything feel wrong, like the world had moved on without us. Like it didn't care. The grass looked too green. The sky too blue. I pressed my forehead against the window and tried to breathe through the knot in my throat.

"How much farther?" I asked. My voice didn't sound like mine. It sounded smaller. But it was enough to snap the silence in half.

Elara met my eyes in the rearview mirror. "Not much longer. We're heading toward a secure location."

Her answer was vague and calm and frustrating. But I didn't push. I didn't want to hear something I couldn't un-hear. Better to stay small. Better to pretend I wasn't unraveling.

The road narrowed. The pines closed in. I felt like I was

being swallowed. We rolled into a clearing. Another van—white, windowless, creepy—sat waiting for us like it had crawled out of a crime documentary.

Elara killed the engine and turned around. "We need to switch. They might be looking for this one."

I climbed out, the wind smacking me in the face and making everything feel sharper. I stared at the new van and tried not to imagine every worst-case scenario. "Okay, but... this definitely looks like the kind of van where people disappear and no one ever finds the bodies," I muttered, folding my arms.

Elara didn't flinch. "I get it. I do. But we don't have time. Once we're inside, I'll explain everything."

Christopher's hand found mine again. It steadied me—and him. I could tell. "We don't have any better options," he said. Calm, but not cold. Like he'd already made peace with the danger.

I nodded. Just once. Then followed him in. The next stretch of road felt quieter, but not peaceful. Just... waiting.

"I need to know where we're going," I said after a few minutes. My voice didn't shake this time. That surprised me. It felt weird to sound strong when I didn't feel strong.

Elara didn't look at me. "A bunker," she said. "Hidden. Safe. It's one of our main hubs."

Christopher leaned forward, his whole body tense. "Our?" His voice had an edge. "You keep saying 'our.' Who's we?"

Elara exhaled slowly, like she'd been dreading the question. "Harris was part of something. A resistance. The CCA calls us rebels. But we're a movement. A revolution. We've been working to take down their control."

My brain tried to keep up. I looked at Christopher. His expression was pure chaos. Grief. Anger. Shock. I don't think he knew which one was winning.

"Why didn't he tell me?" Christopher's voice cracked a little.

Elara's voice softened. "Because he wanted to protect you. Both of you. The less you knew, the safer you were. But he trusted you. He believed in you. You wouldn't be here with me if he didn't."

Christopher's hand gripped mine tighter. Elara went on. "We have safe houses across the country. But the bunker in the Quehanna Wilds is our strongest. It's hidden, off-grid. That's where we're going."

Christopher sat back, jaw tight. "How did this all start?"

Elara kept her eyes on the road. "With people who stopped being afraid. People who saw what the CCA was doing—controlling relationships, banning families that didn't fit their mold, turning Countdown Marks into weapons. People like Harris. People like me."

Something flared in my chest. Not only anger this time. Not only grief. Something sharp and dangerous and alive. I wanted to believe her. I wasn't sure I did yet. But I wanted to.

The forest thickened again. Then broke open. My heart thudded hard. My hands were sweaty. My mouth dry. Every part of me buzzed.

As the van came to a stop, Elara turned and glanced back at us. "We're here," she said. "Welcome to the revolution."

CHAPTER NINETEEN
Rebellion (Lies)

Christopher

T he forest seemed to stretch on endlessly, its towering trees casting long shadows that shifted with the light. I kept scanning the trees, half-expecting movement that never came. The longer we walked, the more it felt like we'd stepped into another world—one quieter, older, untouched by the chaos we'd escaped. Elara moved with purpose, like every inch of this place was already mapped in her head.

Elara finally stopped in front of this massive moss-covered boulder. It looked like it had been sitting there since the dawn of time.

"We're here," she said.

I stared at the rock. "Here? It looks like... a rock."

She smirked, crouched down, and pressed something under the moss. A deep rumble shivered through the ground, and the boulder shifted, revealing a hidden door and a staircase plunging into the dark.

"Wow," Noa whispered.

"This way. Stay close," Elara said, already heading down.

We followed. The stairs were steep and cold, the air changing with each step—forest giving way to damp metal and earth. The walls were rusted steel, the kind that made you feel like history was literally closing in on you. It smelled like old water and iron, and every footstep echoed.

At the bottom, a heavy door blocked the way. Elara punched a code into a keypad. The mechanical beeps echoed, and the door slid open.

The bunker was alive. Not in a creepy way, but in a way that buzzed with energy—footsteps pounding with purpose, the low hum of conversation overlapping with the occasional clang of metal or beep of a monitor. It smelled faintly of solder and coffee, the air busy and urgent, nothing like the halls of the CCA Headquarters. People moved everywhere—focused, serious, like they were all part of something that mattered. It couldn't have been more different from the Agency's stiff, pristine halls.

"Welcome to the heart of the rebellion," Elara said, her voice carrying a bit of pride.

A man stood near the entrance, tall and steady, with ginger hair and a kind of presence that immediately commanded attention. His eyes were sharp—an almost grey blue, calculating—but there was something behind them, too. Something steady.

"This is Richard Thompson," Elara said with real respect. "He's our leader."

Richard stepped forward with quiet certainty and offered his hand. His movements were measured, deliberate—the kind that didn't demand authority, but carried it anyway. His grip was firm, but not in a weird, show-off way—just confident. "Welcome, Christopher. I'm glad you're here."

"Thank you," I said. And for once, I meant it. There was

something grounding about him—something steady in the way he stood, the way he looked at me. It reminded me of... but the thought burned too sharp, too close. I couldn't bring myself to think his name.

He turned to Noa. "And you must be Noa. I've heard a lot about you."

She blushed, half smiling. "Thanks, I think."

Richard smiled back and motioned for us to follow. "You're safe here," he said simply, like it was a fact, not a promise. The kind of thing you say when you mean it—and when you expect it to be true. "Come. Let's talk somewhere more private."

The halls twisted like a maze, but they were alive—full of people with quick steps and sharp eyes, maps scribbled over in red ink, and handwritten notes taped to walls beside posters that read WHEN YOU DISOBEY, YOU DISAPPEAR and OUR MARKS, OUR CHOICE. Somewhere down another hall, someone shouted instructions over a radio while another voice cracked a joke that earned a quiet laugh. It didn't feel like a place for surviving. It felt like a place built for fighting.

He brought us to a room that looked straight out of a war movie—maps, papers, stuff everywhere. He gestured for us to sit, then added with quiet clarity, "Let me give you a sense of what you've stepped into. This bunker is our base of operations. Our mission is to take down the CCA. Give people with Marks their freedom back."

He looked at me, then Noa. "You both matter to this fight, a part of this fight. Your experiences, your courage—that's the kind of thing we need around here. Harris thought so, or he wouldn't have gone to so much trouble to get you here."

I flinched at the sound of his name.

Everything in me braced like I'd been punched. "You think because he—because someone risked everything to get us here, we owe you something?" My voice came out tighter than I meant, but I didn't take it back. "I was the face of their machine. The poster boy for their lies. And now I'm supposed to join another group with a cause and a mission? I didn't ask for this. I wanted out. I wanted a life."

Richard didn't flinch. He didn't blink.

"You'll never be free," he said calmly, "not really—not until you fight back. Because they will always find you. They will always own you until you take that power back for yourself. This is your only real shot at that."

I didn't answer. My jaw was locked tight, and I didn't trust my voice. Across from me, Noa shifted.

"We're barely adults," she said quietly. "What could we offer? We don't know how to fight. We don't have any kind of training. We're just—"

"Alive," Elara cut in gently. "And willing to see the truth. That's more than most."

Richard sat back, letting the silence settle before speaking again. "It's okay. We don't have to decide everything right now. For now, I want to understand what you've been through. Start at the beginning—whatever that means to you."

Elara gave me a small nod, as if to say: you're safe. You're allowed to speak now.

So I told him everything.

After our conversation with Richard, Elara introduced us to Thomas, a tall, lean teenager with sandy blond hair and eyes that carried a warmth not often found in places like this. His presence was immediately calming, his easy smile breaking through the tension that had gripped me since we arrived.

"Hey, nice to see you again, Noa," Thomas greeted with a wink, his voice friendly and familiar, but threaded with something quieter beneath it—a kind of heaviness he carried well, but couldn't quite hide.

Noa blinked. "Wait a second... prom?" Her brow furrowed as she pointed at him. "You were there. You were at the punch table. You go to my school?"

Thomas laughed, holding up both hands like he was surrendering. "Yeah. During the year I'm in Annapolis. But I live here in the summers—it's complicated."

Her eyes narrowed slightly. "That's not an answer to what you're doing here."

He smiled with a touch of guilt. "Fair. Let's just say I've been part of this longer than I expected to be."

He turned to me and extended a hand. "You must be Christopher."

I nodded, taking his hand and feeling the sincerity in his grip. There was something grounding about Thomas, something that suggested he was used to holding people together.

Elara gestured with a slight nod. "Thomas here will show you around. He knows this place like the back of his hand."

Thomas's smile widened as he motioned for us to follow. "Come on, I'll give you the grand tour. There's a lot to see."

We walked through corridors that pulsed with life, a maze that combined the echoes of the past with the pulse of a rebellion preparing for its future. The metal walls bore reminders of their Cold War origins, but here they had been given new life.

"This is the living quarters," Thomas explained, nodding toward a row of doors with names and drawings tacked to them. "Everyone has their own space, and we do our best to make it feel like home."

I peeked inside one of the open doors. A faded photograph was taped to the wall beside a bed made with a patchwork quilt, and a worn paperback with a cracked spine lay face-down on the desk. The room was small but cozy.

"It feels more like a home than the Agency ever did," I admitted, the warmth of this place wrapping around the jagged edges of my thoughts.

Thomas nodded knowingly. "That's the idea." Elara, who had lingered quietly behind us, gave a small nod, her gaze scanning the row of doors. "It took us a while to get it this way," she added, voice low but certain. "But comfort matters—especially when many of the people here came from places built to break people."

"Over here, we have the common areas where people eat, talk, unwind," Thomas said lightly, clearly trying to shift the mood after Elara's comment. The common rooms were a whirl of conversation, laughter, and the clinking of plates. The air smelled faintly of something warm and savory—maybe soup—and every now and then, someone's laugh rose above the rest, bright and unfiltered.

As we turned a corner, the low hum of a television caught my attention. The news broadcast on the screen showed a serious-faced anchor delivering a breaking story. I glanced at it disinterestedly until the words hit me like a punch to the chest.

"The victim has been identified as high-ranking CCA Agent David Harris," the anchor announced.

The room blurred. Everyone went silent. My breath caught.

The anchor's voice kept going. "Details suggest Agent Harris was under the influence when he lost control of his vehicle. The CCA has expressed their condolences."

A video clip of Dr. Bennett appeared, her expression carefully composed as she spoke at a podium, Dr. Foster standing like a shadow behind her. "We are deeply saddened by the loss of Agent Harris, a respected member of our organization. Our sincerest sympathies go out to his loved ones."

"Turn it off," I said. My voice was sharp and cracking.

Someone scrambled for the remote, and the screen went black, but the silence it left behind was worse.

"They killed him," I whispered. "And now they're feeding everyone this story, dragging his name through the mud?"

My fists clenched. My chest ached. "He was the only one who—" The words caught, cracking wide open in my throat. My vision stung. For a second, I wanted to yell, throw something, break the whole damn screen. But I didn't. I bit it back hard, swallowing the fury and the ache in one burning gulp. My throat burned with everything I couldn't say.

Noa stepped closer, her hand wrapping around my arm. Her eyes were wet, but steady. "He mattered. You know that, right? No headline changes that."

I nodded, once, too tightly. The room held still, the air dense with a mix of grief and determination. I turned and walked, needing the motion, needing the distance—like if I didn't move, I might shatter. It was instinct by now. Movement made the grief quieter, gave my body something to do while my mind spun out.

Thomas followed silently, matching my pace. He led us deeper into the bunker where large screens lit up walls. I hesitated inside the threshold, my eyes catching on the sea of more maps, graphs, and moving figures. It looked like something out of a movie—too strategic, too overwhelming, too real. A part of me wanted to turn around. But another part—the one Harris helped shape—tightened its grip. I wasn't ready to trust it yet, but something in me stirred anyway.

Groups huddled over blueprints and maps.

"This is the command center," Thomas said. "Where we track everything—operations, missions, intelligence. If the CCA makes a move, it shows up here."

The energy was focused, urgent, but not panicked. Like everyone here believed they could win.

We continued our tour, seeing more and more of the ever sprawling compound. In the training rooms, people moved with precision—sparring, shouting commands, pushing themselves harder. The sounds were sharp and raw, but there was no chaos in it. Just drive.

"I work a lot with LGBTQ youth," Thomas said as we watched. "We've built safe networks, ways to support each other. A lot of these kids have nowhere else to go."

"Why do they need all of that?" I asked, frowning. "The networks, the hiding spots?"

Thomas's face tightened, slightly. "Because for a lot of them, when their Marks hit zero... no one showed up. Their soulmate never came." He paused, jaw clenched. "And then the CCA came knocking. Said they had the right to question them—told them they were mistakes."

Noa looked shaken. "How is that possible? How have I never heard of something like this, seen stories on the news?"

"Because the CCA hides more than most people want to know," Thomas said. "They erase anything that doesn't fit their story. And most of these kids? They're too scared to speak up, even if they could."

A sick heaviness sank into my gut. "How did I not know?" I whispered. "I was their face. Their golden boy. I stood on stages and repeated everything they told me to. And this was happening—this was happening right under my nose."

Noa stepped closer. "Christopher, you didn't have a choice. You didn't know there was another way. That's not on you."

Noa turned to Thomas. "How did they end up here, then? If the CCA has been taking them?"

Thomas looked toward the hallway behind us, like he could still see the kids we'd passed. "Some of them? We break them out. The rebellion has missions for that—to track where the CCA is holding them and get them out. Others... others ran away before their Marks ever hit zero, so sure of their sexuality, and hearing the rumors, they run out of fear."

His voice was steady, but there was a tightness behind it—like he was trying not to let it crack. "We try to find them before the CCA does. Bring them here. Keep them safe."

"That's why you live here in the summers, isn't it? I saw you with your date at the prom. Your mark is still moving, so you haven't met your soulmate yet."

Thomas exhaled through his nose, his face softening. "During the school year, I'm with my dad in Annapolis. Michael. Summers, I come here to stay with my other dad, Richard."

"Wait. Richard's your dad?"

Thomas nodded, rubbing the back of his neck. "Yeah. Richard and Michael adopted me. My birth parents... Well, they kicked me out when I came out to them. I was thirteen. Michael was my guidance counselor. Him and Richard took me in, brought me here. They've been my dads ever since."

Thomas's eyes flicked down to the faint turquoise glow of his Mark. "They've taught me so much." Elara glanced over at him, her expression softening. Noa gave him a small, encouraging smile—quiet, but full of understanding. It landed like a silent kind of reassurance, something steady passed between them without a word.

Continuing our tour, we stopped at the supply rooms last—stacks of crates, bins of gear, shelves of canned food, and first aid kits. Thomas turned to us, his expression clear and steady. "It's a lot, I know," he said, echoing the same calm cadence I'd heard from Richard earlier. "But you're not alone. This place runs on trust, and you've already earned more than most."

I nodded slowly, the truth of it sinking in. "Thank you, Thomas. This place... it's more than I expected."

We walked back in silence, the corridor humming around us—low and steady. It wasn't loud, but I felt it in my chest, a soft thrum that matched the tension still coiled in my spine. Guilt settled in deeper than before, colder now that I knew how much I hadn't seen. I'd been so focused on my own problems, I hadn't noticed the chains they were tightening around the rest of the world. I kept my gaze down, matching Thomas's steps, but my thoughts stayed behind—stuck in everything I didn't fight for all these years.

The tour left me overwhelmed—not by the scale of the rebellion, but by everything I hadn't seen until now. All the things the Agency was doing and somehow I missed it. And yet, all I could think about was Harris. His death clung to me like smoke, heavy and impossible to shake—settling in my chest and thick in my throat.

Noa and I found a quiet corner in the common area, tucked away from the rhythm of the bunker. I dropped onto a worn sofa, dragging a hand through my hair, like that might untangle the chaos in my head.

"I still can't believe it," I said, voice low and raw. "Harris was one of the few good ones. He put everything on the line to help us."

Noa nodded slowly. "I'm so sorry, Christopher. I didn't know he meant so much to you."

"I didn't either, until it was too late."

Anger flared under my skin again, curling tight in my fists—but I didn't let it show. I'd learned too well how to bury things, how to look calm when my insides screamed. Still, it pulsed there, beneath the surface, raw and sharp. "He didn't deserve that. None of them deserve any of this."

Noa's hand found my arm—steady, quiet. "We'll make it count, Christopher. His sacrifice, everything he risked—it wasn't for nothing. We're here because of him. Maybe we can make the most of that."

I met her eyes, the ache in my chest softening slightly beneath her certainty.

That's when Richard approached. Calm and composed, his presence filled the room without needing to say much. "How are you holding up?" he asked, voice low.

I hesitated. "It's... a lot."

He nodded. "I won't pretend it gets easier."

I wanted to believe Harris saw something in me worth fighting for, a reason to bring us here of all places, but doubt settled quickly. He was gone, and I was still here, trying to be something I wasn't sure I could be. I couldn't let myself think about what Harris believed—what I'd lost.

Richard continued. "You should know that Harris wasn't the first, and he probably won't be the last. This fight has taken more than any of us want to give. That's why it matters."

I still couldn't wrap my mind around everything. This fight? What fight? I still didn't understand what exactly all of this was supposed to be. Why didn't Harris tell me? How am I supposed to know what I'm doing here?

Richard gestured for us to follow him. Noa pulled me out of my thoughts, tugging at my hand to come along. We moved through dim corridors into a meeting room where half a dozen people waited. Their expressions were unreadable—not hostile, but guarded.

"This is our leadership council," Richard said. "They've been waiting to meet you."

The room was too quiet. The council sat around the long table, faces unreadable, their eyes like sharp knives that cut through the air as we walked in. I could feel them sizing us up, measuring our worth in a way I wasn't used to. Not the CCA's disinterested gaze, but something much more intimate—personal. It made my skin crawl.

"This is Christopher and Noa," Richard said, his voice steady but with an edge of something I couldn't quite place. "They've been through a lot to get here."

The woman closest to the center leaned forward. Her eyes were cold and calculating, but there was something about them—something sharp—that told me she wasn't here for pleasantries. She was here to decide if we were worth their time. If we were worth anything at all.

"You're here because Harris vouched for you," she said, her voice cutting through the silence. "But making it here doesn't mean you belong. It doesn't mean you're ready to be one of us.

You think you know what we're fighting for. But we've been in this long enough to know that survival isn't about staying alive, or staying off the CCA's radar."

Noa's hand twitched, like she wanted to reach out for me, but I wasn't sure if she should. I felt her hesitation, felt her mind racing, but she stayed silent. I wanted to scream. I wanted to argue, to tell them that they didn't know me, that I wasn't some perfect piece to be slotted into their rebellion. I wasn't some trained soldier. I wasn't sure I wanted to be here. Not after everything that had happened. Not after Harris. But the words stayed in my chest.

A man sitting next to the woman spoke up, his voice rough but controlled. "We need people who can think, who can feel what's at stake. This fight? It's about saving people from a world they don't know they need saving from."

The words hit harder than I expected. A sudden knot in my stomach. He wasn't wrong. We'd been so focused on getting away from the Agency, on what we thought was important, we hadn't begun to understand how deep this ran. My whole life had been a distraction, a carefully crafted lie designed to keep me on track—to make sure I didn't ask too many questions.

I met his eyes, and I felt something shift inside of me. It wasn't relief. It wasn't hope. It was more like a hollow ache, a realization that this wasn't going to be as simple as I'd wanted it to be. I had spent years pushing down everything that mattered, but now? Now, the weight of what I'd done—and what I hadn't done—was pressing down on me, suffocating me.

Noa spoke, her voice tight but steady. "What does that mean?

What do you want from us?"

Before anyone could answer, Richard stepped forward again, his presence a sudden anchor in the heavy air. He gave a quick nod to the council, then turned to look at Noa and me.

"Look," he said, his tone still calm but with a weight behind it. "I'm not going to lie to you. This is bigger than anything you've ever faced. But you're here because you're needed. Right now, you're exactly what we need. But we'll get into that later." He paused, then gestured toward the door. "For now, let's get you settled. You're going to need to rest. We'll talk more after."

Noa glanced at me briefly, her gaze unreadable. We didn't speak as we followed Richard down the narrow hallway. There was so much left unsaid—so many questions I didn't know how to ask.

Richard led us through a door into a small, quiet space. It wasn't much, but it was ours for now. A bed, a desk, a chair. No windows, but there was a sense of privacy. Of something stable, if only for a moment. He didn't stay long, handed us a few supplies and promised someone would check in later.

I stood there for a moment, the silence pressing down on me. Noa sat on the bed, her eyes distant, lost in thought. I had no idea how to process any of this. The weight of the rebellion was heavier than I'd ever imagined. And now that I was here, I had to decide if I was really ready to carry it.

I wanted to be free. I wanted to live, to feel alive without the constant pull of fear and guilt. I didn't know if I was ready for this. I didn't know if I could be the person they needed, whatever that meant. But in that moment, I realized something. I had no choice.

There was nowhere to go but forward. I hated how it felt like I had gone from one impossible situation to another.

CHAPTER TWENTY

Centuries

Noa

A week had passed since Christopher and I arrived at the bunker. The days blurred together—introductions, orientations, and trying to sleep in a room that didn't feel like ours yet. It felt like stepping into another world. One that mingled cautious relief with the heaviness of what still waited for us beyond these walls.

The bunker pulsed with quiet urgency as my eyes instinctively swept the corridor ahead—counting exits, noting who was armed, who was watching. The reflex came uninvited, a habit carved deep by too many nights wondering if safety was another illusion. I tamped it down, tried to breathe through it, but the unease sat heavy in my ribs, coiled and waiting. As Christopher and I made our way to Richard's office, I walked a little closer to the wall, my shoulder nearly brushing it, and dropped my voice without thinking. Despite everything this place promised—safety, purpose, a future—I couldn't shake the feeling that we were still being watched. Still being weighed. Like at any moment, someone might decide we didn't belong after all.

Richard greeted us with a warm, practiced smile when we entered. He paused for half a second before speaking. "Good to see you both. Please, sit."

Christopher and I exchanged a glance before settling across from him. Richard leaned forward, the seriousness in his eyes tempered by something softer. "I wanted to talk to you about your future here with the rebellion. We see great potential in you both and would like to involve you in some of our strategic planning sessions."

He turned his attention to Christopher. "You were the CCA's symbol. I know that comes with more weight than most people can understand—more pain. Their polished, public triumph. If you were to stand with us—visibly, vocally—it could change everything. It could validate the truth we're fighting to expose. People still believe in the image they built around you. If you tore that down yourself, they might finally listen."

Christopher tensed beside me. I saw it in the stiff line of his jaw, the way his hands curled into fists against his knees. The request—no, the implication—felt too familiar. Another costume. Another script.

My gut twisted. "He didn't escape the CCA to become someone else's propaganda," I said before I could stop myself. The words rang louder than I'd meant them to, sharp and sudden in the quiet. Part of me wanted to take them back, to soften the edges—but the other part braced for whatever would come next, refusing to flinch. "He's not a weapon you get to aim."

Richard's expression didn't waver, but his voice gentled. "I understand. And I'm not asking for anything today. Leadership here isn't about obligation. It's about choice. You've both earned time to figure out where you stand."

Christopher drew in a slow breath. "Thank you. We're still

trying to understand everything. It's a lot to process."

I nodded, "We need time to just... exist. Without expectation. We're still learning how to breathe again."

Richard leaned back, nodding once. "That's fair. When you're ready, we'll be here."

The tightness in my chest loosened, a little—but that made me uneasy. Relief felt like a luxury I couldn't afford. I reminded myself it wasn't safety, a pause. A breath. Nothing more. For now, at least, we were being given space to decide for ourselves.

As we left Richard's office, Christopher and I wandered deeper into the bunker. Its halls stretched far wider than I expected—part shelter, part city. The walls buzzed with conversation, and the air carried the scent of old concrete, recycled air, and something faintly herbal. A low hum from overhead lights droned steadily, and the floor beneath my boots held a lingering chill that crept into my ankles. It was utilitarian, but lived-in. Real.

We passed through a common area where people ate together, laughed together. It was strange, seeing joy in a place built around this secret war. But maybe that's how they survived it.

"It's hard to believe how different life could be," Christopher said, pausing to watch a group of children playing nearby. Their laughter echoed off the stone walls, light and bright in a way that made me freeze for half a second. It reminded me of my brothers—of the way they used to run barefoot through the grass behind our old house, chasing each other until they collapsed in a heap of joy and noise. The memory hit like a punch, sharp and sudden. I hadn't let myself think of them in days, maybe longer.

It felt foreign—like something from a different life—and I didn't know whether to smile or turn away. I wanted to reach for it, to let it in, but part of me stayed guarded, uncertain if I was allowed to.

"Yeah," I murmured, my arms folding across my chest—a barrier, instinctive. The laughter made something ache inside me, something I didn't have words for. I wanted to feel it too, that lightness. But all I could do was hold myself together and pretend it didn't sting. "It's strange to feel safe... when nothing is."

Christopher's eyes softened as he looked at me. "It's nice to be around people who actually care."

We kept walking. The bunker had a rhythm—teams managing logistics, medics organizing supplies with the clatter of trays and soft chatter, scouts checking communications while someone shouted updates from the far end of the corridor. No one stood still. Everyone had a role.

We nearly collided with Thomas in a hallway, a teetering stack of papers in his arms.

"Hey!" he grinned, catching one before it slid free. "You two settling in okay?"

"Trying to," I said, my smile crooked. "This place is... a lot."

Thomas nodded, adjusting the stack. His smile stayed bright, but something flickered behind it. He didn't let it show for long, but it was there. "It is. But it works. Everyone pitches in. That's the only way it keeps going."

As we walked with him, he explained more of the day-to-day. His passion was infectious, each word threading pride through the exhaustion in his voice. His eyes sparkled when he spoke, but his shoulders carried a weariness that showed in the way he shifted the papers now and then, like he needed the movement to stay grounded.

"We're tight on security," he added, motioning toward a side room filled with blinking monitors. "The CCA doesn't know where we are. Not exactly. But we never let our guard down. Can't afford to."

That familiar tension curled in my chest again. I told myself it was nothing—that we were safe here, that the sensors and guards and reinforced doors were enough. But my body didn't believe it. It never did. Fear didn't care about logic. So I pushed it down, like I always did, and kept moving. The CCA might not know we were here now, but they always found a way. Still, there was something else in the air—something like resilience. Like defiance.

After parting ways with Thomas, Christopher and I ended up in a quieter wing of the bunker. I leaned against the cool wall, arms crossed, watching him talk with a few other members—laughing, even. His eyes sparkled in a way I hadn't seen since we found out Harris had died.

For the first time in months, maybe longer, I didn't feel like I was waiting for everything to fall apart. We weren't free. Not yet. But we were here.

And that had to count for something.

After dinner and the busy day, Christopher and I retreated to our room. It had become our little sanctuary amidst the chaos, a place where the outside world couldn't reach us. The soft glow of the lamp cast a golden light across the floor, warm and familiar, as we curled into each other on the narrow bed, limbs tangled, breath steadying.

The room thrummed with the low hum of the bunker's machinery, the faint scent of cedar clinging to the blanket wrapped around us, soft and worn like it had held a hundred nights before ours, and the muffled sounds of distant laughter and shuffling footsteps beyond our door. It should've made me feel caged. But it didn't. Not tonight. Not here, wrapped in his arms.

"It's strange, isn't it?" I murmured, breaking the quiet. The words slipped out before I could second-guess them, and for a heartbeat I almost wished I hadn't said anything at all. My voice felt soft, unarmored. "To start to feel safe and at home with everything that's happened."

Christopher kissed the top of my head, lips lingering longer than usual. "Yeah, it is. But I think it's because we're together. As long as we have that... I feel like we can survive anything."

I shifted, enough to meet his eyes. "I'm so grateful for you, Christopher. You've been my anchor through all of this. When everything else felt like it was falling apart, you didn't."

His smile was slow, quiet, but full of something steady. He met my gaze, and I saw the flicker of vulnerability that lived beneath his eyes. "And you've been mine, Noa. You have no idea how much you've held me together. I wouldn't be here without you."

We kissed, soft and slow. The warmth of his mouth steadied me in a way words never could—like I could feel the ground beneath my feet again, even lying down. The kind of kiss that didn't rush or ask anything. It existed. A tether. A truth.

Moments like this made it feel real—the rebellion, the risk, the fear. But part of me still questioned if I deserved to feel this peace, even for a second. Like letting it in might make it vanish. Or worse, prove I was never meant to have it at all.

I pressed my forehead to his chest, listening to the steady rhythm of his heart. "Do you worry about the future? About what'll happen to us? To everyone here?"

Christopher's arms tightened slightly, his breath hitching before he answered. I felt it in the way his hold shifted, the hesitation that flickered through him. "Since the moment we got here. But we can't turn back. We have to fight for a future that means something. One where no one has to live afraid. Where we're not surviving. We're living."

My throat felt tight. "It's so much." I rushed to fill the silence after, like I could smooth the edges with logic. "I mean, maybe it's the exhaustion talking. We've been through a lot lately. Like we're just... small. Too small to fix anything."

"We are small," he said, his voice low but charged with something fierce. "But so is every fire at the start. A spark doesn't seem like much—until it burns everything down."

I looked up at him, startled. That wasn't hope. That was conviction. His eyes held the same spark now.

"For Harris," he whispered.

We kissed again, deeper this time. Not to forget, but to remember what we were holding onto. Each other. This moment. The future we wanted to build.

We stayed like that, whispering promises into the hush between us—soft declarations of forever, of finding each other no matter what came next, of never letting the world take this from us—until the weight of the day finally began to settle over us. My head rested against his chest, his heartbeat a quiet drum beneath my ear.

"Whatever happens," I breathed, "we'll face it together."

His hand found mine under the covers. "Always," he said, and he meant it. His fingers curled tighter around mine, and the warmth of him—real and steady—quieted the noise.

I found myself standing in the hallway of my childhood home, my pulse stuttering with confusion. The sight should've comforted me—but instead, a cold unease rippled through my chest. Something was wrong. Everything was wrong. The walls stretched unnaturally high, casting elongated, sinister shadows. The soft ticking of the old clock echoed ominously, each tick reverberating in my chest like a countdown. My breath caught, and a chill skittered down my spine.

In the dim light, I saw my mother's stern figure in the kitchen, her back to me as she cooked dinner. But when she turned, her face was obscured—blurred as if smeared with shadow, her eyes hollow and accusing. Her voice was a harsh whisper, words of disappointment mixing with the sizzle of the pan in a chilling harmony.

Suddenly, the kitchen dissolved, and I stood in the school gymnasium. The lights above flickered like dying fireflies, casting erratic shadows over the polished floor. The scent of sweat and a cloud of anxiety hung thick in the air as my eyes darted around. A loud buzzer echoed, but this wasn't a game. I turned and saw Christopher standing in the center of the court, his Countdown Mark blazing. He stood rigid in the center of the CCA emblem projected on the ground. His fists were clenched at his sides, as if holding himself together through sheer force of will. His expression was unreadable—too calm, too still—and that quiet tension made my stomach twist.

"Noa." His voice was a whisper, carried by the echoes of the buzzer, barely audible over the pounding of my heart. I ran toward him, but the distance stretched endlessly, each step like wading through molasses. The gym walls twisted and morphed into sterile, cold corridors of what I assumed was the CCA Headquarters. The scent of bleach replaced the musky odor of the gym, and my footsteps echoed, eerily loud against the white walls.

"Noa!" Christopher's voice came again, rougher now—like it scraped its way out of his throat. It cracked at the edges, caught somewhere between control and desperation, the way he always tried to hold everything in until it fractured. I turned a corner and found him strapped to a gurney, the harsh fluorescent blinding me.

"Christopher, no!" I reached for him, but faceless doctors with hollow eyes coldly dragged the gurney away, their movements precise and unfeeling.

The scene shifted. Warm fairy lights bathed the room in a

soft, golden hue. It looked like prom night. The decorations, once elegant and welcoming, twisted like sand slipping through my fingers. A pang of guilt lodged itself in my chest, sharp and sudden, like I'd left something unfinished, or someone behind. The lights above turned into harsh spotlights, and Ami was standing with her back turned to me in the middle of the dance floor. As I tried to walk towards her, she disappeared into the shadows that warped into grotesque shapes. A haunting melody began to play that echoed my fear.

"Help me!" I heard Christopher's voice, distant and muffled. I turned, and the prom scene shattered like a clock splintering into pieces. Shards floated mid-air, red threads weaving through them, binding them together before fraying and snapping, one by one. Each snap came with a brittle, splintering sound—like dry twigs breaking underfoot or bones cracking in the silence—sending sharp vibrations through the air that made my teeth ache.

"Noa, please!" His echoed voice was a desperate plea. I looked up and saw his face reflected in each broken shard, filled with pain and betrayal. Red threads wrapped around my wrists, pulling me toward a black abyss, each heartbeat pounding in my chest. Blood dripped onto the shards, streaking across Christopher's fractured reflection like a crimson veil, blurring his terror into something almost unrecognizable—something haunted.

I landed back in the bunker. The dim light seemed sharp, piercing through the shadows. The walls felt as if they were closing in, the distant murmur of voices blending into an indistinguishable hum. I turned and saw Christopher again, his face pale, eyes pitch black.

"We're running out of time," he blurted, his voice a hollow echo. "We have to go."

A flash of light blinded me, and I was in the park. The swing set swayed in a non-existent breeze, the pond lay still and reflective. I froze, my breath catching as unease curled low in my stomach. Something about the stillness felt staged, like a painting too perfect to trust. My brothers' laughter rang out, distant and eerie. The bridge over the pond stretched forever. I tried to reach them, but the bridge kept lengthening.

"Noa!" Their voices echoed as they faded, dissolving into shadows. Red threads glowed against the darkness, forming a path that twisted before me.

I followed the threads into a dark room with a mirror. Shadows behind me whispered, their voices a sinister chorus. The reflection was not my own; it was Ami, and my chest seized with a sharp spike of guilt. I instinctively flinched, as if seeing her meant I had somehow failed her. Fear curled in my stomach—fear of what I hadn't said, of what I hadn't done. Her eyes were wide with fear and defiance. Her Countdown Mark glowed purple, but it flickered and melted, the light sputtering like a dying flame. Panic surged through me as the whispers grew louder, threats unspoken but clear.

I was suddenly outside again, the night air sharp and cold. The moon hung low, an unnatural blood-red beacon in the sky. I stood on the beach, at the graduation party, the ocean waves crashing with deafening roars. The sand shifted beneath my feet, pulling me down.

Amidst the chaos, Ami stood by the bonfire, flames reflecting in her cold eyes. She turned, a ghostly silhouette, and walked away, leaving me behind, dissolving into the shadows.

The sand swallowed me, and I landed in a forest. I ran down a path that twisted impossibly, branches clawing, snagging my sleeves and scraping my skin. It was as if the forest itself was trying to consume me, refusing to let me escape. Christopher stood ahead, leaning against a tree. His posture was too composed, too still. His arms were crossed, jaw tight, and though his face wore a calm mask, something in his eyes gave him away: fear he wouldn't name, even here. But as I reached him, his features melted away, leaving an empty shell.

Fear gripped me, and I fell forward, back in the bunker. The walls seemed to shiver, the hum of machinery turning almost sentient. Faces of rebellion members twisted, their eyes vacant as they whispered words I couldn't understand. Among them, I thought I saw Elara—her outline flickering at the edge of the group, lips moving without sound. Then Richard's face surfaced in the crowd, his expression stern but unreadable, and I felt a cold rush of doubt. Were they watching me? Judging me? Or were they as lost in this distorted place as I was? The air thickened, pressing down with an unbearable weight.

In the center, a massive clock loomed, glass shattered and cracks spreading like veins. The hands spun wildly, racing toward midnight, each tick reverberating like a heartbeat. Red threads wove through the cracks, binding time and fate in chaotic desperation.

The scene shifted one final time. I stood in a stark white room. Surveillance screens lined the walls, flashing distorted images of my life. The CCA emblem loomed large, casting a long shadow across the floor. A cloaked figure stood in the center, faceless yet commanding. A chill ran down my spine as they raised a hand, pointing directly at me.

The ticking grew louder, frantic. My pulse hammered in my ears, chest tightening like a vice. My knees buckled beneath me, and the world tilted, vision blurring at the edges. I could barely breathe, the panic rising sharp and fast, flooding every corner of me like a dam breaking. My heart raced, panic clawing at my chest as I struggled to break free from the nightmare's grip. Before I could move, the figure's voice rang out, cold and commanding.

"Wake up, Noa!"

Christopher's voice echoed over it, urgent and real—sharp. It jolted something loose inside me, grounding and jarring all at once, before everything went black.

Epilogue

The hum of machinery was the only sound in the fluorescent-lit room as Dr. Foster stood by the wide observation window, hands clasped tightly behind his back. His sharp, calculating gaze cut through the reflections of monitors and data screens that lined the walls. The blue glow from the CCA's emblem loomed large behind him, casting its cold light across the polished floor.

Dr. Bennett entered, her heels clicking softly on the tile, the tension in her movements masked by a serene expression. She held a tablet close to her chest, data streaming across the screen in endless columns. For a moment, neither spoke, the silence between them almost reverent—ritualistic.

"So, it seems our offspring and his companion have slipped through our fingers," Bennett said, her voice even, though a trace of something colder lingered beneath the surface. "Harris was thorough. The trail leads nowhere."

Foster's lips curled slightly, a smile devoid of warmth. The air between them seemed to chill, subtle but sharp, and Bennett's shoulders stiffened as if instinctively bracing against it. "As planned," he said, turning to face her, the harsh light accentuating the sharp lines of his face. "Their escape was inevitable. Necessary. And Harris's death was unfortunate, but all in all it should help us along the way."

Bennett arched an eyebrow, a flicker of surprise in her eyes. "The Agency is already spinning Harris's death as an accident. We've covered our tracks."

Her fingers brushed the edge of her desk, tracing the delicate carvings as if feeling the weight of years past. "Do you think they understand what they're caught in yet?" she asked, the question hanging in the air.

"Doubtful," Foster replied smoothly, a glint of satisfaction in his narrowed eyes. "They've only begun to see the edges of the picture. Their rebellion may be slowly growing, but it's still blind."

"Are the reports from the research team confirmed?" Bennett's tone was clipped.

Foster nodded. "We've gathered everything we need from them. Their interactions, the genetic markers, the psychological profiles—it's all here. The data confirms what we suspected from the beginning—our design holds." His finger traced the screen, pausing over the bold, flashing header: Project Genesis: Phase One Complete.

Bennett let a moment's silence pass before replying, her voice softening into something more reflective. "They think they're free, Ezekiel. That they've outwitted us."

"Let them," he said, amusement threading his words as he leaned back, clasping his hands behind him and staring at the array of screens. "Freedom, after all, is a matter of perspective. And ours is the only one that matters."

A faint ticking echoed in the quiet, as if the room itself was counting down to a revelation only they knew. Bennett stepped closer, her eyes narrowing. "And what about the rebellion? They're more organized than we anticipated."

Foster chuckled. "They're a piece of the puzzle, Alice, not the whole game. Let them believe they've won a small victory. It will make the next step all the more impactful."

Bennett's gaze drifted to the screen, where Christopher's face flickered briefly among a cascade of data. Something unreadable passed behind her eyes before she blinked it away, letting the numbers reclaim the space. "We've come so far since the first experiments," she whispered, half to herself. "Do you think someone will ever uncover the truth?"

Foster's smile widened, cold and unyielding. "Even if they do, it won't matter. By then, we'll be too far ahead. The real game has only just begun."

The monitors flickered, data rearranging into a mosaic of faces, numbers, and DNA strands—a kaleidoscope of the future they planned. Somewhere deep within the Agency, a clock chimed softly, marking the hour. Each chime echoed a silent promise— a shadowed truth waiting for its day.

With that, they turned back to their work, the hum of machines absorbing their low voices. Outside, the world believed in fate, in the romance of destiny. But here, within the heart of the Countdown Control Agency, the architects of that fate watched, planned, and waited.

A Sneak Peek

Book Two Synopsis

Finding your soulmate is supposed to be perfect. For Amelia Collins, it was anything but.

Everything Ami thought she knew about fate is about to unravel. She believed the worst thing to happen would be her prom night—the fight that ended her decade-long friendship with Noa Mitchell. She was wrong. Weeks later, the CCA publicly announced that Noa and her soulmate, Christopher Hawthorne, had been kidnapped by anti-Mark radicals.

As the summer winds down and her Countdown Mark hits zero, Ami collides with Dean Abrams... who doesn't have a Mark at all. Dean was born before the world's first Marked child and trusts only the science he knows: soulmates aren't real, and the CCA's "proof" is political theater at best. But Ami feels the truth in her bones—Dean is hers.

Their clash of conviction turns into uneasy cooperation when Dean's work in biotech leads him to accidentally uncover classified CCA files—evidence suggesting that Noa and Christopher haven't been kidnapped at all, but are on the run from the Agency itself.

Drawn together by danger as much as connection, Ami and Dean find themselves tangled in the CCA's most dangerous secret yet—Project Genesis, a program that could redefine fate itself. Every answer they find raises more questions. Every step closer to the truth makes them a bigger target.

Together, they'll have to navigate suspicion, science, and the undeniable pull between them before the Agency silences them for good.

About the Author

Born and raised in Texas, K.B. Riley has always been fascinated by the power of storytelling to transform and connect. When not writing, Riley enjoys playing the flute, reading, bingeing The Marvel Cinematic Universe, or spending too much time on a video game.

Marked by Fate is K.B. Riley's first novel and the first book in *The Chronicles of Fate* series. Through these books, Riley aims to explore themes of identity, choice, and the consequences of power. She wants to challenge readers to question what they believe about the world around them.

K.B. Riley currently resides in Marion, Ohio with her family and their fur babies, where she continues to work on the next installment of *The Chronicles of Fate* series.

www.ingramcontent.com/pod-product-compliance
Lightning Source LLC
Chambersburg PA
CBHW010734130726
47899CB00015B/3245

9 798999 299983 13